I0596804

DARK DEEDS

A MEGAN SCOTT/MICHAEL ELLIOTT MYSTERY

SANDRA NIKOLAI

DARK DEEDS
Copyright © 2016 by Sandra Nikolai
www.sandranikolai.com

This is a work of fiction. All names, characters, institutions, places, and events portrayed in this novel are either products of the author's imagination or are used fictitiously. Any resemblance to actual persons, living or dead, business establishments, events or locales is entirely coincidental.

All rights reserved, including the right to reproduce this book, or portions thereof, in any form or by any means.

Vemcort Publishing
ISBN: 978-0-9947894-6-4 (eBook)
ISBN: 978-0-9947894–8–8 (Paperback)

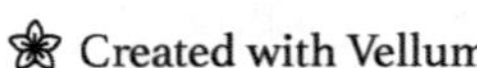 Created with Vellum

To caring friends in small towns.

1

———

Michael hunched over the steering wheel, our car headlights cutting through the darkness. With nothing to guide him but the random reflective post along the narrow country road, he kept a sharp lookout ahead.

Leaning back, I gazed through the sunroof. Towering trees on both sides of the road blended into the starless sky, obscuring defining lines. The night was as soundless as it was black. We might as well have been in the middle of nowhere.

Michael broke the silence. "I can't stop thinking about that cold case file on my desk."

"It's a miracle you managed to get a weekend off," I said, "and now all you talk about is—"

"Hold on, Megan. You had back-to-back meetings with clients the past two months and couldn't take time off either."

I sat up. "At least I'm home every night, not meeting sleazy informants in dark alleys."

He threw me a side-glance. "That's a low blow."

"Not compared to the ones you got chasing the bad guys."

His brow furrowed. "I happen to like my job."

I wished I could say the same about mine. At best, this weekend trip in late May pulled me away from my home office in our Montreal condo. After a week from hell that included lengthy meetings with clients who didn't know what they wanted, to clients who obsessed about every project detail, I was ready to swap my ghostwriting job for Michael's investigative reporting. Damn the risks.

Well...not quite. I wasn't one iota as brave as Michael.

I looked at him. The headlights from the occasional oncoming car swept over his steadfast expression and intense blue eyes. I loved this determined aspect of him the most. "We've been promising Jessica and Ethan for months that we'd book a cabin at their new lodge in Lanark County. This trip is a good break from work. And your cold case files."

"That's asking the impossible," he said. "You already know that."

The sound of sirens crept up on us.

My heart beat faster.

A fire truck raced past—its red light bar flashing, tires spewing dust and stone pellets onto our windshield.

I flinched, raising my hand in a protective gesture.

Michael jerked and hit the brakes, lurching us forward, then back.

My stomach did a flip.

Michael touched my shoulder, his eyes fixed on me. "Are you okay?"

My breath caught in my throat. "For heaven's sake, we're in the middle of nowhere. Who would have expected that?"

"No kidding."

I opened the passenger window and took a gulp of fresh air, then closed it.

A police car sped by, its siren blaring. The OPP insignia identified it as a cruiser belonging to the Ontario Provincial Police.

The sight unnerved me. "I don't have a good feeling about this. Jessica and Ethan just bought their property last fall. It's not far from here. What if there's a fire at their lodge?"

Michael checked his rear view mirror before driving on. "We'll find out soon enough."

A small white feather on the dashboard caught my eye. Did it drift in when I opened the window? I tucked it inside my handbag.

I looked out the window. A shadowy abyss surrounded us,

making me all the more apprehensive about what we'd find when we arrived. "This road gives me the creeps."

Michael drove at a steady pace. "We're almost there." His voice was calm, reassuring, but it did nothing to dispel my uneasiness.

As we neared our destination, billows of white smoke rose above the trees to our left and vaporized in the air. I pointed it out to him. "Isn't that where we're heading?"

"Yes, and it doesn't look good."

We took the turnoff to Jessica's Lodge moments later and drove along a gravel road that separated the resort from a neighboring property on the right. A row of dense trees lined both sides of the road, giving my claustrophobia a boost. The tree-lined road ended abruptly, and Michael veered left onto the asphalt path leading to the resort.

I froze. A fire truck's light bar flashed over a team of firefighters, while thick smoke and flames shot upwards from Jessica and Ethan's two-story clapboard house.

My pulse picked up speed. "Oh, no! Their house is on fire!" I had my hand on the door handle before Michael had turned off the engine.

He peered through the windshield. "No—the flames are further back."

I jumped out and ran toward the scene, my heart thumping. Michael followed close behind.

To the left of the house, flames engulfed a wood shed wide enough to store two mid-sized cars. Firefighters in protective gear battled the blaze with their high-pressure hose, blasting the shed and the lofty trees behind it, sending steam and wet debris flying into the air, the rushing sound from their hoses competing with the crackling and hissing of the blaze.

An OPP officer forced a small crowd of people to move back on the lawn, away from the fiery fringes. Another officer stood next to his cruiser and spoke into his police headset.

I spotted Jessica holding Amy, her eighteen-month-old daughter, and hurried over. The child's tiny arms were wrapped around her mother's neck, her golden curls blending into her mother's shoulder-length blonde hair. Ethan stood on Jessica's left, unmoving, his strong chin jutting out. Shadows from the flames flickered across his troubled features.

"Jessica! Ethan!" I shouted above the noise. "Is everyone okay?"

Jessica focused on me for a long moment, dazed. "Megan... Oh, you made it!" She hugged me with her free arm, then hugged Michael. Her eyes welled with tears and she wiped them away. "So good to see you guys again."

Ethan leaned forward to shake our hands. He stopped short of hugging us, which surprised me. He'd usually been so expressive of his fondness for us. "Believe me, this isn't the welcome we had in mind for you."

"Was anyone hurt?" Michael asked.

Ethan looked at the people huddled on the lawn, their hair blowing in the wind, their attention riveted on the fiery scene. "No. The shed is the problem right now. It's only a hundred feet away from our clapboard house. If a tiny spark hits it, we're in big trouble. There's still a chance the fire could spread to the forest and bordering properties."

A firefighter barked orders over the crackling of wood and gushing of water. His team shifted their efforts to another section of the blaze.

"The debris in the shed could have helped spread the fire," Jessica said. "The previous owner had left old furniture and cardboard boxes in there." Her lips quivered. "We also lost a 1960 Chevrolet Corvette that's worth about fifty thousand dollars."

Michael's eyes went wide. "What?"

"It belongs to our neighbor," Ethan said. "We bought this portion of land from his family next door with the agreement to continue storing the car here."

"I hope it's insured," Michael said.

"Hey, that's not my problem." Ethan smirked. "They can't even fix the broken window at the front of their house."

I exchanged a subtle glance with Michael. Ethan's comments were impulsive and crude, not at all in line with the considerate man we knew.

Ethan went on. "I'm more concerned about the new freezer they delivered here today. I told the delivery people to unload it in the shed. We had no place for it in the house. See that extension over there?" He pointed at a good-sized section jutting out from the side of the house. "That new storage area was supposed to be completed by now." He clenched his jaw in frustration.

Jessica added, "The contractor told us he couldn't finish the floor in the extension because the company had ordered the wrong hardwood. That's why we had the delivery people put the freezer in the shed."

Ethan shook his head. "You can't trust anyone to do anything right these days. It's been one damn thing after the other."

The deafening sound of creaking timbers filled the air. The shed walls collapsed in slow motion, the roof caving in.

The guests shrieked and tripped over one another in their panic to move further back from the blaze.

Ethan gaped at the fiery display, anguish sweeping over his face. "Damn!"

Jessica's eyes moistened, and she tightened her grasp around Amy.

I turned and met Michael's concerned expression.

"What rotten luck," he whispered in my ear.

I jumped as orange sparks burst like fireworks, then drifted and swirled in air drafts above the blaze. A firefighter shouted out orders, and the team repositioned the hose to prevent flames from spreading to the house extension and nearby trees.

"I've had enough of this." Ethan edged toward Michael. "You and Megan are in cabin five. If you want to give me a ride over there, I'll give you a hand with the luggage."

"Sounds good," Michael said.

I watched as both men walked away, then asked Jessica, "Is everything okay with Ethan?"

She juggled Amy in her arms and avoided eye contact. "Why?"

"He seems different. Cynical. Not his usual upbeat self. And especially not like at your wedding a few years ago. Remember the way he danced with you all night, how he sang along with the live band..."

"Wasn't that something? Michael's singing wasn't too bad either. Remember how exhausted we were by the time it was all over?" She giggled.

"Yes." I laughed. "We had a lot of fun."

A cloud passed across Jessica's face. "Getting this place up and running was a lot of work. It still is, but I can't depend on Ethan to help me. His high-tech job in Ottawa puts a lot of pressure on him. Overtime...deadlines... It only adds to his stress level. It might explain the change you noticed in his behavior."

I hoped it was temporary. "You still have a part-time day job, right?"

"Yes. Several weekday afternoons at the public records office in Fernlea. That's after I serve breakfast and lunch to the guests here."

"How did you ever manage to get the resort up and running so fast?"

"I worked like crazy." Jessica rolled her eyes. "I had to oversee the landscaping and home renovations, and furnish the cabins. Lots of running around."

"How are your neighbors?"

"The people here are different."

"What do you mean?"

"Fernlea is a tight-knit community. Residents aren't receptive to strangers moving in, and Ethan and I aren't used to feeling like outsiders. Some of the things they've said to us were downright rude."

"Like what?"

"Oh...silly things." Her attitude brightened as she changed the subject. "We made it, though. We finally realized our dream."

I smiled at her. "I'm impressed. As always."

Amy uttered a few words I couldn't make out.

"Who takes care of Amy?"

At the mention of her name, Amy gurgled with laughter and reached out to touch my hair. She let out a soft "ooh," then pulled back and hugged her mother.

"Mom often babysits her," Jessica said.

"Your mother lives nearby?"

"Only minutes down the road."

"That's convenient."

"For both of us. After Dad died last year, she sold the farmland and didn't have much to keep her occupied. She has lots of friends, but nothing replaces family. She's the main reason we moved to Fernlea. Now her whole life revolves around Amy." She looked around. "There she is, chatting with the guests." She waved her over.

Mrs. Holt waved back. After exchanging a few words with two middle-aged women in pastel tops and pants, she headed our way.

"Jerm'y?" Amy said.

"No, not Jeremy," Jessica said. "He's at home with his dad. Look, Granny's here."

"Granny!" Amy held out her arms and slid into her grandmother's grasp.

"What were you doing there, Mom?" Jessica asked.

"I was trying to calm your guests' nerves." Mrs. Holt's tone was matter-of-fact.

I took in her tall, elegant frame crowned with short, wavy white hair. If anyone could ease the guests' apprehensions with her poised demeanor and comforting voice, it was Jessica's mother.

Mrs. Holt smiled. "Megan, welcome to Jessica's Lodge." She leaned over to hug me. "Jessica told me you and Michael had booked a cabin." She scanned the grounds. "Where is that good-looking man of yours anyway?"

"He went with Ethan to drop off our luggage in the cabin," I said.

"I'll see him later then." She paused. "You can't believe how happy I am that my little family moved to Fernlea. I've been begging them for years to relocate here. Especially after Amy arrived." She balanced the little girl in her arms. "I hope you and Michael enjoy your stay here—despite this unfortunate fire. If you'll excuse me, I'm going to put this child to bed. We've had enough action for today, haven't we, Amy? Say bye to Mama."

"Mama." Amy kissed her mother, then waved to us as Mrs. Holt carried her to the house.

"She's adorable," I said to Jessica. "Is Jeremy Amy's little friend?"

"No, he's our caretaker. A seventeen-year-old who tends to the grounds and does maintenance work in the area. He lives with his father across the lake. Amy likes him. Since seniors make up half the population in Fernlea, there aren't many children nearby. We're sending Amy to daycare this fall. She'll make new friends closer to her age then."

The acrid smell of burnt substances from the charred remains of the shed irritated my nasal passages with each breath I took, but I didn't want to leave Jessica.

Just then, a car pulled up and parked near the house. A slim, dark-haired man got out of the driver's side and headed in our direction, his overcoat flapping in the wind. "Jessica, what happened?" His voice was raspy—a smoker's voice. He spoke with an English accent.

"There was a fire in the shed," Jessica said. "They're trying to stop it from spreading to the trees."

Worry lines formed across his forehead. "Do they know what caused it?"

"Not yet."

He switched his focus to me. "Are you a guest here?"

"Yes," I said.

"Oh...sorry about that." Jessica introduced me to Foster Wade, an historian who had rented one of the cabins this week. "Megan is a very good friend. We go way back to our university days."

"That can't be too long ago." Foster grinned, causing wrinkles to gather around his deep-set eyes. "Pleased to meet you," he said to me, then turned back to Jessica. "Did you have lots of stuff in the shed?"

"Old furniture, a vintage car—"

"A vintage car?"

"We were storing it for a neighbor," Jessica said.

"That's unfortunate," Foster said. "What about the freezer they delivered today?"

"It was probably destroyed too."

"That was a bit of bad timing."

Drops of water hit my hands. Raindrops.

Foster pulled up his coat collar.

"You oversaw the delivery," Jessica said to him. "It went well, didn't it?"

"Yes, it did." He looked down, casting shadows on his face. "Not that it makes any difference now."

Jessica was about to say something but stopped. A firefighter was heading toward us with a determined stride.

Foster placed a hand on Jessica's shoulder. "I'll see you tomorrow. Try to get some rest." He slipped away to join the other guests.

The firefighter came up to Jessica. Dark smudges soiled his face and uniform, while beads of water glistened on his helmet.

"Mrs. Bryant, I'm Captain Everest," he said. "We've got a handle on the fire." His tone was assertive. "We were able to spare some of the trees by the shed and prevent the fire from spreading."

"Thank you, Captain," Jessica said. "I'll let my husband know. Oh…I noticed a broken window on the property next door. As far as I know, no one lives there. Maybe the vandal is the same person who set fire to our shed."

"We'll be investigating." He hesitated. "Are you and your husband new to this town?"

"Yes. We moved in last fall."

He fixed her with a wary look. "We'll need to assess the damage in the shed before we can estimate the dollar value of your losses. You'll receive a report later on." He gave a nod in her direction, causing water to slide off his helmet, then rejoined his team.

"Why would he want to know if you and Ethan are new residents?" I asked Jessica.

"People in small towns are sometimes opposed to outsiders moving in and setting up a business. Like I said, they know how to make us feel like outcasts." She let the topic die on her lips.

I glanced up. "How about that? No more rain."

"It hardly ever rains in Fernlea, and when it does, it's not for long."

Jessica's curls had straightened out from the rain. I put a hand to my curly mane, knowing the rain had the opposite effect on me. Yep, my hair was even frizzier now.

"Come on," she said. "Let's go see what the guys are up to." She led me across the lawn.

A burst of flames behind us lit up the grounds. The light revealed a semi-circle of log cabins not far from the lake's edge ahead of us. Just as quickly, the firefighters overpowered the flames and plunged us into darkness once more.

Unsure of my footing, I hung onto Jessica's arm. "I can't see a thing out here."

"That's because you're a city girl." She laughed. "You'll be able to see this place better in the sunlight tomorrow."

"I can't wait. Do you like living here? Running a resort?"

"Yes to both. I feel safe in Fernlea." She sighed. "I'm eager for the day Ethan and I can quit our day jobs and retire here."

"I hope you get lots of customers."

"Oh...you reminded me. Thank you. Thank you. Thank you." Jessica hugged me, laughing. "That promotional package you put together for the resort was wonderful."

"My pleasure. It was a welcome change from my usual routine."

"We placed the ad in major newspapers right away and had a fantastic start. Our cabins are booked this week and into the next. That is, if word that we burnt down the neighbor's vintage car doesn't get around."

I understood her anxiety. Bad news had a tendency to travel fast, especially in small towns. "The important thing is that the fire didn't cause damage to your home or the cabins."

"That's true." Jessica cheered up. "I'm so glad you're here, Megan. More than ever, I need your advice about something." There was urgency in her voice.

"Go ahead."

She hesitated. "Let's wait until tomorrow when things settle down."

"Okay. Tomorrow."

Jessica had been the go-to friend I'd turned to throughout our university days if I needed to discuss anything from clothes to courses. After my husband Tom died, she came to Montreal to spend a few days with me. That this confident woman needed my feedback now was rather surprising. Then again, maybe I was making too much of it.

The grassy terrain inclined slightly as we approached the log cabins at the far side of the property, the lake glistening beyond them. Intermittent light from the flames behind us revealed five identical log cabins. Each had a sloping, single-gabled timbered roof and flower boxes. It was a pretty sight, but even at this distance from the fire, the dank odor of burnt wood reached me and ruined the ambiance.

Jessica led me to cabin five, the one at the farthest end and closest to the road leading to the property. "The entrance is at the back of the cabin." She guided me around the corner and onto a porch, then opened the door.

Except for a closed room at the back, which probably led to the bedroom, the open area included a kitchenette on one side and a sitting area on the other. The entire space was the size of an expansive bedroom. A table lamp shed a dim glow over a paisley sofa and matching armchair. A ceiling fan hung from the rafters, vibrating noisily, its blades cutting through the air at rapid speed. Two small windows fed my claustrophobia, and I was glad we'd only booked the weekend here.

Michael and Ethan sat at an oak table in the kitchenette. As Jessica closed the door, a draft caused the pendant lamp over their heads to swing slightly and cast macabre shadows over them.

"Management wants to 'retire' employees once they hit forty-five," Ethan was saying to Michael, making quote marks with his fingers. "That's five years away for me. Even if I get lucky and they let me put in ten more years, I can't count on a full pension."

"Which is why we've invested in this lodge," Jessica said, pulling out two chairs for her and me. "We don't want to work for someone else the rest of our lives."

"We might not have a choice," Ethan said. "I was just telling Michael about our plans to expand the resort. We want to build more cabins, but our two-acre lot is stretched to the limit. Purchasing another portion of the lot next door is our only option. The guy owns ten acres."

"Sounds interesting," I said.

"There's a catch." Jessica sighed. "We've made an offer to purchase part of the land next door, but the owner doesn't want to sell. The property is co-owned by Burt Garner and his elderly mother. She used to live there until last fall. Burt told us she suffered from Alzheimer's disease, and he had to place her in a special home. He used to come around every couple of weeks, but we haven't seen him in about a month."

"What does he do?" Michael asked.

"He works for a flooring company full-time and as a handyman part-time," Ethan said. "He's been living in Fernlea for decades and owns another house in town. We don't know why he insists on hanging on to the property next door when he has no intention of moving in. It makes the situation even more frustrating." His lips tightened.

Jessica frowned. "What's more, the house was vandalized lately. I noticed a broken window in front."

"For all we know, Burt probably took a trip and told no one." Ethan tensed up, the veins visible in his neck. "The next time I see him, I'll make sure he takes an extended vacation."

"Don't do anything rash, Ethan." Jessica kept her voice calm.

Anger flashed in his eyes. "Jess, I'm not stupid."

She smiled in an attempt to diffuse the tension. "I know that, Ethan. That's why I married you."

"Ethan, I've never seen you this angry," I said. "You were talking about your job when we walked in. Is everything okay?"

He shrugged. "Like I told Michael, it could be better. There are a lot of frustrated employees vying with me for the same position up the ladder. They'd do anything to discredit the competition."

"Before you decide to punch anyone in the eye," Michael said to him, "talk it over with me. Okay?" He gave him a friendly jab in the arm.

Ethan gave him a shy grin. "Sure."

I changed the subject. "How did you both decide on the name Jessica's Lodge?"

Ethan stuck out a thumb in Jessica's direction. "It was her mother's idea."

"She thought it sounded friendly and homey," Jessica said.

Ethan persisted. "It also sounds like something only your mother would come up with."

"We both agreed it was a good name."

"We had no choice. Your mother had already decided it for us."

There was a knock at the door.

Jessica stared at Ethan. "Who could that be?"

"Only one way to find out." Ethan strolled over and opened the door.

Captain Everest and a police officer stood on the porch.

"Mr. and Mrs. Bryant, we'd like to speak with you," the captain said.

"Sure, come on in," Ethan said, motioning them inside.

Captain Everest spotted Michael and me, then said to Ethan, "It's a private matter. Can we speak outside?"

"Excuse us." Jessica followed Ethan outdoors, leaving the door slightly ajar. Whether she'd done it on purpose or by accident, I wasn't sure, but Michael and I were now privy to their conversation.

"This is Detective Sergeant Lionel Cole from the Ontario Provincial Police," the captain said. "He has something to tell you."

The detective cleared his throat. "There's no easy way to say this. We've discovered a corpse in your freezer."

2

Ethan paced in the living room, fists clenched. "Your mother begged us to move to Fernlea. She lived here all her life and said we'd be safe in a small town. First the fire, now a corpse in our new freezer."

"The police will know the identity of the body soon," Jessica said. "I'm sure there's an explanation for how it got there...and how the fire started."

"An explanation?" Ethan bumped into a side table and knocked over a family photo that included Jessica's mother. He didn't bother to set it upright. "Our guests saw the forensics team transport a body bag out of the shed. Then the detective ordered them to stick around for questioning. Can you imagine what they're thinking?"

Jessica set the family photo upright. "They must be horrified. Just like we are."

"Ethan, I'm sure your guests understand the investigative process," Michael said. "Besides, the detective said he wouldn't take up too much of their time."

Ethan crossed his arms. "He said he'd stop by later tonight. I can't wait to see how that goes."

Mrs. Holt walked in with a tray. She set it on the coffee table next to a stack of trendy home décor magazines. "Michael is right. It's a shocking discovery, but the guests surely won't object to the police questioning them. They obviously had nothing to do with depositing the body in the shed, though someone must have seen something."

Ethan raised his hands in the air. "How could the delivery people not notice there was a body in the freezer? They uncrated the damn thing. They must have looked inside it."

"Unless the body was dropped off later." Michael raised an eyebrow.

Silence hung in the air.

Ethan gawked at him. "Are you saying someone carried a stiff into the—"

A hard stare from his mother-in-law stopped Ethan in mid-sentence. Mrs. Holt gestured toward the tray. "Please, everyone, sit down and help yourself to some decaf coffee."

Jessica and Ethan each took a mug and sat at opposite ends of the steel blue upholstered sofa. Mrs. Holt settled between them.

Michael and I shared the matching loveseat across from them. We preferred caffeinated coffee, but if only to be polite, I reached for a mug and took a sip. The taste was bitter—like coffee that had sat on a burner all day. As I placed the mug back on the tray, I felt Mrs. Holt's eyes on me and pretended to be studying the framed wedding photos of Jessica and Ethan on the adjacent wall.

"We overheard the detective ask you about the delivery company," Michael said to Ethan.

He nodded. "Freeze-it Incorporated. It's a national company. Quite reputable."

"How did you learn about them?"

"I researched a bunch of companies online. Their name popped up under a local supplier." He drank some coffee.

"Detective Cole didn't say as much, but I think he suspects the company transported the body here," Jessica said. "What if it's true?"

Ethan shook his head. "It makes no sense to me. Why would a five-star company risk its reputation like that?"

"It could be a disgruntled employee," Michael said.

"Just our luck he happened to pick our property." Ethan grimaced.

"How well do you know your guests?" I asked them.

Ethan shrugged. "As well as you can possibly get to know anyone who rents a cabin for a few days and then leaves."

Jessica leaned forward. "I met the guests when they checked in and had a chance to chat with them. The young married couple in cabin one arrived here yesterday afternoon for a honeymoon weekend. They've been virtually invisible."

"Who can blame them?" Ethan chuckled.

Jessica went on. "Two middle-aged women in cabin two checked in on Wednesday. They've been shopping and visiting the sites, so we haven't seen much of them either. A middle-aged gentleman checked into cabin three earlier this week. He spent most days fishing in the lake nearby." She glanced at me. "You met Foster Wade. He's a Canadian historian. He booked cabin four for the week and might extend his stay. He's been taking notes and photos of historical buildings in and around town."

"I met many of the guests this week," Mrs. Holt said. "They're a charming group of people."

Ethan gawked at her. "Charming? One of them could be a killer."

She drew in a quick breath. "That's absurd."

"That's not what the detective thinks."

"You mentioned you had a caretaker," I said to Jessica.

"Yes. Jeremy worked here earlier today but left at noon to tend to other customers."

"Is he trustworthy?"

Her voice broke. "Yes."

"Damn it, Jess, stop covering for him." Ethan turned to us. "The boy is a rehab delinquent. Petty theft."

"Jeremy is a hard worker." Mrs. Holt glared at Ethan. "I have no complaints whatsoever about him."

"We have to be fair, Ethan," Jessica said. "Jeremy is trying to re-establish himself in the community."

"You think so?" He smirked. "He stole plywood from us and not only once."

She raised a forefinger. "It was old plywood."

"Does that make it less of a crime?"

"Those pieces of wood were useless to us. Besides, Amy likes

Jeremy. I happen to think that children are innately drawn to good people."

"Where does Jeremy live?" Michael asked.

"Across the lake with his father," Jessica said. "He goes back and forth by canoe."

"A hard worker?"

"He's seventeen years old and a slow learner, but he gets the job done."

"Eventually," Ethan quipped.

"The boy has a good heart," Mrs. Holt said. "He goes the extra mile to satisfy a customer."

"Mom's right," Jessica said. "Even though our neighbor Burt Garner doesn't come around as often, Jeremy still mows his lawn and fills the holes that the groundhogs dig in his backyard. Burt always treats him well, and Jeremy has grown quite fond of the old man."

The front doorbell rang.

"That must be the detective." Ethan rushed to the door.

Jessica followed right behind him and invited Detective Cole inside.

Steps away, Michael and I couldn't avoid witnessing their conversation as they stood with the detective in the hallway.

"I've finished interviewing your guests," the detective said. "They're free to leave whenever they want. We've also made arrangements to transport the victim's body to the coroner."

"Do you know the identity of the person?" Ethan asked.

"We can't establish that fact right now." The detective's tone was composed.

"Nor the cause of death, I suppose," Jessica said.

"Correct," the detective said. "That's for the coroner to determine, as well as whether or not an autopsy is warranted."

Mrs. Holt rose to her feet, her heels clacking as she crossed the floor into the hallway. "Hello, Lionel."

"Fiona," the detective said. "I didn't know you were still here."

"Always the devoted grandmother." Mrs. Holt laughed. "Lionel, I couldn't help overhearing. I hope your investigation won't trigger needless gossip around town. You know how much this resort means to my daughter...to all of us." She placed a hand on Jessica's shoulder.

"We'll do our best, Fiona, but this case is a tricky one. We have an unexplained fire and an unidentified corpse. Residents don't appreciate either, especially when..." He hesitated. "Well, you know what they think of outsiders."

"My daughter isn't an outsider." Mrs. Holt's tone was defensive.

"I appreciate that, Fiona," the detective said, sounding conciliatory. "Look, it's early in the investigation. We have to wait and see where it takes us."

"When do you expect to have some answers?"

"In the following days, though the final report might take more time."

"How much time?" Ethan asked.

"Days," the detective said. "Maybe weeks."

Ethan raised his voice. "Are you kidding me? That long?"

I cringed.

Ethan ranted on. "What if word gets out to the rest of the town? What will people think about us?"

"I have no influence over gossip." The detective kept his voice even. "Truth is, our resources are stretched. Meanwhile, this investigation is ongoing. The fire department will provide an assessment of the damages shortly." He handed Ethan his business card. "Here's where you can reach me. Good night." The door closed behind him with metallic finality.

Ethan and Jessica returned to the living room, their expressions strained. Mrs. Holt reclaimed her seat on the sofa.

"We're finished." Ethan crossed his arms. "If word gets out about the corpse—which it probably will—we can kiss our future goodbye. It's not as if people find a dead body on their property every day."

Jessica looked at him, her eyes widening. "You scare me when you talk like that, Ethan."

"Face the truth, Jess. The detective is just beginning his investigation, and he's obviously not telling us everything. This is not going to end well."

"On the contrary," I said to Ethan. "I thought he was upfront with you and Jessica."

"I agree," Michael said. "You're reading too much into this."

Ethan pointed a finger at him. "You should know better, Michael.

Detectives will follow any path that's short enough, and the shortest path is to Jessica and me."

Jessica snapped at him. "What are you talking about?"

"Look how fast Megan became the prime suspect in her husband's murder. And then Michael."

I gasped.

Jessica glared at him, her cheeks flushing. "That's crude and so inappropriate."

Michael stepped in. "It's unfair to draw comparisons, Ethan. What happened here has its own set of circumstances."

Ethan ignored him and ranted on, waving his arms. "Think of the bad publicity this is going to generate."

"The irony about bad publicity," I said, "is that it fades as soon as someone overturns it with the truth."

"This incident is too big to ignore," Ethan said. "The whole town will turn against us because we're new here."

"Not if I have anything to say about it." Mrs. Holt squared her shoulders. "People know me. They trust me."

"A lot of good that's going to do me," Ethan said. "Jessica might be spared because she's your daughter. But me? I'm a stranger. An outsider."

"Listen to me," Jessica said to him. "This matter is going to blow over soon. In the meantime, I refuse to give in to gossip. I'm going to do everything I can to keep Jessica's Lodge going."

"It's late." Mrs. Holt stood up. "It would be best if we all got a good night's rest and talked about this in the morning. Things always seem better the next day, especially after a breakfast of Jessica's pancakes and sausages." She picked up the tray of mugs and headed for the kitchen.

"I need fresh air." Ethan stomped out without another word.

Jessica flinched at the sound of the front door slamming shut. "You'll have to excuse Ethan. This resort has been a big drain on us, financially and emotionally. Then there's his job. He's been clocking extra hours to prove he's a valuable employee and not an old timer in the high-tech industry."

"It sounds as if you're making excuses for his behavior," I said.

The color rose in her face. "No, I'm not." Her tone hardened. "His job has become more demanding lately. Throw in the discovery of a corpse on our property, and it makes for a lot more stress than most people have to deal with."

"If there's anything Megan and I can do to help," Michael said, "just ask."

Jessica blinked away tears that threatened to spill, then sat on the sofa opposite us. "Okay. I'm asking now."

Something told me that her request was connected to our little talk earlier.

She went on. "You need to know this first. I cleaned up the shed this morning before I left for work. I put the old furniture and tools in a corner and stacked the cardboard boxes in a pile to make room for the freezer. I swept the floor from one end to the other—even under the car. I promise you, there was no corpse in that shed."

"When did they delivery the freezer?" I asked.

She clasped her hands. "Later this afternoon when Ethan and I had gone shopping. We'd left instructions for the delivery people to leave it in the shed."

"The detective said the investigation was ongoing," Michael said. "He'll be talking to anyone who recently stepped foot on your property."

Jessica released a weary sigh. "What I keep asking myself is, why us? Why dump the body here?"

"There could be a connection that you don't know about yet. Who owned the property before you and Ethan purchased it?"

"Burt Garner's mother. It was a rental property, but judging from the poor condition of the house, I'd say it had been decades since anyone lived here. We did major renovations in the house before we moved in. I'm talking replacing the plumbing and installing new floors."

"And the extension to your home is part of that renovation?"

"Yes. Like we told you earlier, we'd arranged to have the freezer delivered today because we thought the extension would be finished by now. Then the flooring company told us they received the wrong hardwood, so they couldn't finish the job in time. We didn't want to cancel the delivery of the freezer. It would have caused more problems, not to mention extra fees. So we asked them to unload it in the shed."

"We had the wood floors done in our condo," I said. "They ran out, but the flooring company had extra hardwood on hand."

"They told us the company only keeps samples in their show-room," Jessica said. "No extra supplies. In any case, our contractor promised that he'd deliver the extra hardwood by the weekend and finish the job. I haven't heard from him."

My view wandered around the room. Decorative moldings bordering nine-foot tall ceilings, matching baseboards, walls in a neutral shade of taupe that contrasted beautifully with the dark oak floors... The color scheme extended to the hallway. "What you and Ethan have accomplished here in such a short time is fantastic."

"Thanks." Jessica beamed with pride. "We were lucky to find such a cool place for our getaway."

"How did you find it?"

"Through Mom. It took a while to get the legalities sorted out, though." She grew pensive. "I hope our little business will create positive vibes. If we can attract tourist dollars, the residents of this town might stop seeing us as outsiders." She hesitated. "What I was getting at earlier... I need your help."

"Name it," Michael said.

"I don't want to interfere with police work, but I know Ethan is impatient with the length of time the investigation might take. Would you mind talking to the guests before they leave? Don't tell anyone you're an investigative reporter, though. It might scare them. Act friendly like. Maybe they saw something before the fire that can help us."

"Megan and I will work it as a couple. We'll be discreet."

To Jessica's questioning look, I said, "I help Michael with the research part of his investigations sometimes." My involvement was often more intricate and dangerous than I let on, but now wasn't the time to discuss it.

"Sounds like a plan," Jessica said. The stress from this evening's events vanished from her face, only to return seconds later. "One more thing. Be careful. Whoever did this can't be too far away."

3

———————

My first glimpse of the resort in the daylight convinced me that Jessica and Ethan had chosen the perfect location for Jessica's Lodge.

Imposing maples and oaks overlooked the spring growth and hugged the resort on three sides. The early morning dew glittered on a thick lawn that sloped from the main house to the log cabins. Gentle waves lapped the pebbled shores of a shimmering lake steps from where we slept and offered a spectacular view, no matter the time of day.

I captured the moment and soaked up the tranquility. Who could ask for more?

As I took a deep breath, the moment shattered. The acrid scent from last night's fire instantly drew my eyes to the shed's charred remnants. Yesterday's sordid discovery of the corpse flashed to mind like an unforgettable clip out of a horror movie.

"I wonder if this place is worth the gamble for our friends," I said to Michael as we headed to Jessica's kitchen for breakfast.

"Are we talking about the time and money they've put into it?"

"More than that. Jessica had to quit her job and leave her friends. You know how it is with friends once you move away. Out of sight, out of mind."

"You're her friend and you're here," Michael said.

"It's not the same. Jessica and I go way back. We have staying power between us."

"Sort of like what we have, right?" He took my hand and squeezed it.

"You could say that," I teased.

"We could make our staying power more official, you know. I can easily picture a small wedding reception here by the lake."

He'd been hinting at tying the knot for a while now, but I'd dismissed the idea as often as he'd raised it. One trip down the aisle had been enough for me. I didn't want to spoil what we had between us. "Nice try, Michael."

He shrugged. "Hey, you can't blame a guy for trying." He stopped and gently pulled me to him. "Maybe I'm wrong, but sometimes I get the feeling you don't trust me."

His gaze was intense. For a brief moment, everything around us seemed to disappear. It was as if time had stood still. "I do trust you."

"Then?"

"It's me. I don't trust myself."

"You've never mentioned this before. Why now?"

"Because of last night. The dead body. It brought back the shocking memories of Tom's death, how he'd deceived me..."

Michael waited for me to go on.

"Marriage seems so...final. Like the end of the road. I just want us to be together. Always."

"I plan to live a long life with you, Megan. Marriage or not." He pulled me closer and kissed me.

Butterflies flew inside me. As long as Michael was by my side, I had all the happiness I needed. I took his hand and we continued our walk.

"What were you saying about this place being a gamble?" he asked me.

"Mainly that Jessica and Ethan's move to Fernlea means a lot of sacrifice and chaos, not to mention caring for Amy all the while. Renovations, construction of the cabins—it went on for months. Throw in a fire and a dead body, and presto! You have monumental stress. It's a miracle they're still holding it all together."

"They're good friends. Despite what the police investigation digs up or not, I'll help them in any way I can."

"So will I."

Michael spread his arms in a wide arc. "Look at this place. The trees, the lake, the vast land, the tranquility... As much as I adore our condo in downtown Montreal, I'd love to live in a place like this when we retire."

His *we* brought a smile to my lips and confirmed that his consideration for me knew no bounds. I couldn't begin to compare him with Tom who had been so deceitful.

Michael placed a hand on his taunt stomach. "Did I mention how famished I was?"

"At least a dozen times since we woke up this morning," I said.

"I keep thinking of Jessica's pancakes and sausages."

His appetite was like a bottomless pit, yet his slim, muscular physique never betrayed the amount of food he ate. I rarely indulged the way he did, and yet I struggled to keep the extra pounds off. Go figure. Of course, if I'd worked out and jogged as often as he had...

"Check out the canoe." He gestured toward the lake where a canoe was tied to a wooden dock. "We can go for a ride in it later."

"I think it belongs to Jeremy."

"Right. The caretaker. We'll ask Jessica where we can find him. Maybe the kid noticed something weird yesterday before the fire."

As we approached the house, two middle-aged women wearing cotton tops and shorts in pastel shades popped out from behind a clump of bushes. I recalled seeing them in the small crowd last night.

"Disgusting," one of the women said. A jade bracelet dangled from her arm.

"Good morning," the other woman said to us. She fingered a blue beaded necklace. "We thought we saw a rabbit running into the forest and we followed it. It turned out to be a large cat."

"A *very* large cat," the bracelet lady said, crinkling her nose.

"There are lots of field mice around here," Michael said. "The cat must have been well fed."

"Disgusting," the bracelet lady repeated.

"Oh, don't pay attention to Patty," the other woman said, waving in her direction. "She finds everything disgusting. I'm Kate, by the way. We're in cabin two."

Michael and I introduced ourselves and followed the women through the back door into the kitchen.

The smell of fresh brewed coffee and sizzling sausages awakened my appetite. Jessica was standing by the stove, flipping pancakes. As she turned, I noticed her puffy eyes. She'd been crying.

"Good morning, everyone." She forced a smile. "Have a seat. Breakfast will be served soon."

From the ceramic-tiled floor to the stainless steel appliances and marble counters, the kitchen reflected cleanliness and efficiency. Pink placemats with matching napkins, two vases of lilacs, and a bowl of fruit adorned a long oak table. White plates and sparkling cutlery completed the setting for eight.

"What a lovely table, Jessica," I said.

"Oh, she changes the table setting every day," Kate said to me. "And it's always lovely."

"Thank you," Jessica said over her shoulder. "I hope everyone slept well."

"Yes," Michael and I echoed.

Jessica glanced at Kate and Patty. "Ladies?"

Kate said, "I did, but Patty tossed and turned all night." She nudged her. "Isn't that right?"

"All I can say is, we've stayed at many resorts but never one that had a fire and a corpse," Patty said, her face pinched. "And we've never been interrogated by a police detective before either." She toyed with the jade bracelet on her left arm. "I suppose we shouldn't be surprised, what with all the horrible things happening in the world these days. It's simply disgusting."

"There you go again, exaggerating." Kate eyed Patty's bracelet and teased, "Isn't that jade bracelet supposed to protect you anyway?"

"Only from illness while on holiday," Patty said. "That's what the psychic in town told me. What I said before is true, Kate. The world isn't a very nice place these days."

"That's why we decided to spend a few days at this wonderful resort," Kate said to her. "And visit those quaint little shops in town."

Jessica set down coffee cups, then returned with a dispenser of maple syrup. "I'm sorry you had to go through this horrible experience, ladies. I'll tell you what. I'll reimburse you for your stay."

"Nonsense," Kate said. "We love this place, and the nearby town is so interesting. Lots of arts and crafts stores to visit. Isn't that so, Patty?"

Patty nodded, then sipped her coffee.

Jessica served Michael and me. The room went silent as we dug into our plates laden with pancakes, sausages, and scrambled eggs.

"Are you expecting anyone else for breakfast?" I asked Jessica.

"Foster came in earlier and had coffee," she said. "The young couple in cabin one and the gentleman in cabin three haven't surfaced yet."

Michael swallowed a forkful of pancakes. "Where's Ethan?"

"He drove into town to get a few things that we forgot to pick up yesterday," she said over her shoulder.

Mrs. Holt waltzed in from the hallway with Amy in her arms. "Good morning!"

We exchanged greetings.

Amy looked adorable in a white playsuit dotted with tiny red roses and a matching hat, her blonde hair falling in soft curls to her shoulders. She waved at us.

"We're all set to spend the day with Granny," Mrs. Holt said.

"Granny," Amy repeated, giggling.

Mrs. Holt turned to Jessica. "Give me a call later, okay? Amy, kiss your mama goodbye."

The child kissed her mother on the cheek and said "mama" in her tiny voice.

After Mrs. Holt and Amy had left, Patty said to Jessica, "Amy is such a beautiful little girl. Best you keep a close eye on her in case someone decides to steal her."

"Oh, Patty, there you go again," Kate said, grimacing. "The perpetual alarmist."

"I'm not worried," Jessica said. "Mom watches her like a hawk." She placed extra plates of pancakes and sausages on the table. "Everyone, please help yourself to more. Enjoy your breakfast." She gave us a nod and left the room.

Michael took the cue and addressed the two women. "That fire last night was something else, wasn't it? Would either of you ladies know how it started?"

Patty shook her head. "It's a mystery to me."

Kate jumped in. "We drove to town yesterday afternoon and had dinner at a delicious Italian restaurant. When we returned, we went straight to our cabin. It's usually quiet at night, but last evening, we heard shouting."

"It was Ethan." Patty's eyes widened.

Kate continued. "We ran out of the cabin and saw the shed on fire. Ethan tried to put out the blaze with a fire extinguisher, but he was too late. It was spreading so quickly. That's when Jessica called the fire department."

"Did you see anyone lingering about that wasn't a guest?" Michael asked.

"Oh, playing detective now, are we?" Kate eyed him.

"Just curious. I like reading books on true crime."

"So do I. To answer your question, we were gone most of the day, so we didn't notice any strangers around here. If you ask me, it's obvious the fire didn't start by itself. And equally obvious that a corpse didn't drop from the sky."

Patty dabbed at her mouth with a napkin. "We saw a delivery truck."

"What delivery truck?" Michael asked.

"Actually, it was a cargo van." Kate cut a sausage into bite-sized pieces. "It raced out of here as we were driving up the path yesterday evening and practically sideswiped us. I assumed it was the same truck that one of the guests was keeping an eye on."

"Foster Wade?" I asked.

"Yes," Kate said. "Cabin four. Ethan and Jessica were expecting a delivery yesterday but couldn't be here. Mr. Wade was the only person available. Everyone else had other plans or had already left for the day."

"You're referring to the delivery of the freezer, right?"

"Yes. Ethan asked Mr. Wade to supervise the delivery people in case they had trouble transporting it to the shed."

I vaguely recalled the conversation about a delivery between Jessica and Foster Wade last evening.

"Foster Wade is a historian, you know," Patty said in a hushed voice, as if she were disclosing a secret. "He's doing research in town."

"Did everything go okay with the delivery?" I asked.

"I believe it did," Kate said. "While we were standing around watching the fire, Mr. Wade came up to us. He said he'd left right after the delivery and everything was fine. He was stunned to see the shed on fire. As we were."

Patty fidgeted with her napkin. "If you ask me," she whispered, "I wouldn't be surprised if the smoker in cabin three started that fire. We saw him smoking near the shed every day."

Kate gave her a stern look. "Be careful, Patty. We don't know what caused the fire yet."

Patty placed her utensils in her empty plate. "I'm just saying."

Kate pursed her lips. "All done?" she asked her.

"Yes," Patty said.

Kate reached for her handbag and stood up. "Come on, then. We'd better go get ready. We have lots more to do and see in town." She said goodbye to us, then ushered Patty out the door.

The sound of the back door closing brought Jessica back into the kitchen. "Did you get the answers you wanted?"

"A few," Michael said. "What do you know about the man in cabin three?"

Jessica sat down at the table. "His name is Sam Norton. He keeps to himself pretty much. I saw him fishing by the lake a few times. I don't know if he was here when the fire started. I do know the police interrogated him. That's about it."

"What about Foster Wade?" I asked her.

"He spent most of the week off the property. I feel bad, but I still have to charge him full price. Aside from what I've told you, he's writing a book on the history of small towns in Canada."

"I'd like to meet him," Michael said.

She looked out the window. "He's still here. His car is parked by cabin four. If you hurry, you might get a chance to speak with him before he drives off."

"One last question. Where can we find Jeremy?"

"He's working on Mom's property today. It's a short drive down the road from here. Look for a white two-story clapboard home on the left. It has a weather vane on the roof. I'll call her to let her know you'll be dropping by."

Michael and I rushed out the back door and past the charred trees and black remnants of what used to be a shed. We darted across the lawn and the gravel path to cabin four.

Out of breath, I tapped on the door.

It swung open.

Foster Wade greeted us. "Come on in. I've been expecting you."

4

———————

Foster pushed aside a pile of books and papers on the table in his kitchenette, then invited Michael and me to sit down.

The pendant light amplified the wrinkles etched across his forehead, making him appear older than the evening before, though round cheeks maintained a degree of youthfulness. Small stains were visible along his hairline, indicating that he'd recently touched up his gray roots. I placed him in his late fifties.

"You were expecting us?" Michael asked Foster.

"Yes. I saw Ethan at breakfast earlier. He mentioned he was frustrated about how long the police investigation into the fire might take. He told me you were an investigative reporter and that Megan assisted you from time to time. He was counting on you to move things along faster."

So much for keeping Michael's occupation a secret.

"We'll get right down to it then," Michael said. "Tell me about the delivery of the freezer here Friday afternoon."

"Ethan asked me to oversee the delivery," Foster said. "He and Jessica had errands to run. It was late afternoon when the truck rolled in. I have a direct view of the shed from my cabin, so I stayed out of the way and supervised the delivery from here. Two men managed to unload the freezer without a hitch. It took them about ten minutes."

Michael went on. "Did any other vehicles drive up?"

"Not that I know of. I left right after the truck drove off. I needed to do some research in town."

"Were any of the other guests around in the afternoon?" I asked him.

Foster ran a hand over his slim, straight nose. "I don't usually keep tabs on what other people around me are doing. I'm more interested in the history of a place. Now, it doesn't mean I didn't see a thing or two."

"Like what?"

"By the time that delivery truck rolled in, everyone had left the premises except the young couple in cabin one."

"How do you know that?"

"Aside from my car, theirs was the only vehicle here."

I raised another question. "Did you happen to see the young couple walk around the resort?"

"No. I'm pretty sure they were indoors." Foster let out a low chuckle. "Those lovebirds are in their own special world."

"Have you met the guest in cabin three?" Michael asked him.

"Oh, you mean Sam. I've seen him around."

"Did you see him smoking near the shed that day?"

"In fact, I did. He's a chain smoker. No doubt about it."

"Did he admit as much?"

"Not in words. Actions. I'm speaking from personal experience. It takes one to know one. I spent years trying to give up smoking. It's a tough one to beat. It left me with a throaty voice."

Foster's remark was questionable. If Sam were a chain smoker, anyone would have noticed his habit—like Patty had.

Michael continued. "Did you notice anything out of the ordinary that day? Other vehicles? Strangers?"

Foster rubbed his chin. "There's the kid they hired to mow the lawn and tend to the garden."

"You mean Jeremy," I said. "What about him?"

Foster briefly glanced down. "He's a peculiar sort of kid."

"How?"

"The way he loiters about, not doing much. I saw him peeping into guest cabins the other day."

I was stunned. "Have you mentioned this to Jessica?"

"No. It's none of my business." Foster checked his watch. "I'm sorry, but you'll have to excuse me. I need to go into town to do some research."

It would only be polite to ask, so I did. "Mr. Wade, I—"

"Please, call me Foster."

"I understand you're working on a book about the history of small Canadian towns."

"Yes, I am. Are you from around here?"

"No, we're from Montreal."

"Is that so? Are you familiar with my work?" Foster gestured to the hardcover books on the table.

"I'm afraid not."

He picked up one of the books. "I'm sure you'll enjoy this one. Before I diverted my research to small towns, I published a book on certain historical settings in Montreal and the famous—or infamous—events linked to them."

I accepted it. "Thank you. This is quite an achievement."

"History plays itself out—sometimes with dire consequences. I merely write about it." He grinned.

I fingered the thick book. "I might not have time to read it before we leave."

"When would that be?"

"In a few days. Maybe longer."

"Don't rush on my account," Foster said. "I'll be staying here the rest of the week. I've got too much material to cover between Fernlea and Ostfield."

"Where's Ostfield?"

"It's about a twenty-minute drive from here. I'm researching an historical event that connects those two small towns." He stood up and grabbed a thick black notebook. "Sorry to cut short our talk. If I don't get to my next appointment on time, I could lose out on important information."

After I'd dropped off Foster's book in our cabin, Michael and I drove down the road to visit Mrs. Holt. We turned onto a narrow path that led to a white farmhouse cottage bordering a vast expanse of agricultural land.

The two-story 1950s-era home looked freshly painted and had metal roofing. Its multi-paned windows with gabled dormers gazed down upon a flower garden infused with color, including yellow Gerbera daisies, white peonies, and red geraniums. High-backed rattan chairs on a wraparound porch added a welcoming touch to the place.

As we climbed the wood steps, wind chimes hanging near the entrance played light, tinkling sounds. An apparent fan of Feng Shui, Mrs. Holt had hung this six-rod piece to attract good luck and suppress bad luck.

Mrs. Holt welcomed us inside, then joined us for coffee at the kitchen table. "I understand you're here to interview Jeremy."

"That's right," Michael said, leaning back in his chair. "There's a chance he might have seen something the day of the fire."

"It's possible," she said. "Though I doubt Jeremy would be forthcoming with any information."

"Why not?"

Her mouth curled up in a Mona Lisa smile. "Because he rarely talks to people—and that includes the people he knows." She took a sip of coffee. "You can imagine how reluctant he'd be to speak with you."

"You can introduce us as Jessica's friends," I said. "It's the truth."

She nodded her head so-so. "That might work."

I drank some coffee and swallowed hard. It had the same bitter taste as the coffee Mrs. Holt had served us the other night. I let this one grow cold as well.

Michael asked, "How long has Jeremy been working for you?"

"Months. From about the time his parole began. Like many of us, his father is a long-time resident here. We believe in supporting the people in our community—especially the young ones who stray. This town helped Jeremy turn his life around through community projects, which he seems to enjoy." Hope permeated her voice.

"We understand that Jeremy lives with his father across the lake," I said.

"That's right," she said. "It amazes me the boy hasn't run away from home yet."

"Oh?"

"His father is a recluse. He only surfaces when he has to go into town to buy groceries. He rarely talks to anyone. It might explain why Jeremy keeps to himself too. The rare time the boy does speak is when he's with Amy. They seem to have a special connection. He's quite protective of her, much like a big brother would be."

"We'd like to talk to him," Michael said. "We promise we'll go easy."

Mrs. Holt gave him a pointed look. "I'll hold you to it." A chuckle softened her expression. "You know, I babysit Amy most days. It's amazing how attached I've become to my granddaughter. Jessica offered to pay me for my time, but I wouldn't hear of it. Amy is the light of my life." Her joy confirmed the deep affection she had for the child.

My guess was that Mrs. Holt's offer to babysit Amy had played an integral role in persuading Jessica and Ethan to finally relocate here. It could well have been the deciding factor.

Mrs. Holt took a sip of coffee. "Call it foresight, but I'll never forget the day I convinced Gabriella Garner to sell me a piece of her land bordering the lake. It was several years ago. She wanted to lease the two-story clapboard house to tenants but didn't want to invest a cent to renovate the place. I offered to take the property off her hands. I explained how she'd save a whole lot of money—and bother—if she sold it to me. I sweetened the pot by promising I'd keep her husband's old Corvette in the shed at no extra charge." She laughed.

"Too bad it was destroyed in the fire," Michael said.

"In her state of mind, she wouldn't give a hoot." Mrs. Holt waved a hand in the air. "Gabriella and I have known each other since we were children, but I'll tell you, that woman wasn't the easiest person to deal with. Nevertheless, I was persistent. It eventually paid off. I knew in my heart of hearts that one day I'd convince Jessica and her family to move here."

I was surprised to hear that she'd purchased the land years ago. I was even more surprised that she knew Gabriella Garner. "Do you know Gabriella's son, Burt?"

"Not really," she said. "He moved out of her place decades earlier."

"I'm glad things worked out with the land," I said, not knowing what else to say.

"Oh, buying the land was the easy part. Financing Jessica's Lodge was something else. When the bank insisted on additional backup to close the deal, I saw no other alternative. I mean, I'd already paid for the land." She pressed her lips together. "I refused to see the project die on the table, so I offered my support and signed as guarantor on the financing end. The deal was sealed." She held her chin up with pride.

Michael said nothing and sipped his coffee.

I shared his discomfort. Being on the receiving end of information that our friends would consider private was awkward. Mrs. Holt talked too much.

I wondered if her financial backing had inadvertently put a damper on her son-in-law's ego. Whatever his reasons, Ethan had openly indicated his dislike of the woman, though I doubted he'd complain about having a reliable babysitter on call whenever the need came up. At least Jessica seemed confident about their investment in the resort.

"This has been a nice break." Mrs. Holt stood up. "Shall we head outside to find Jeremy?"

She led us down a corridor and out the back door of the farmhouse onto a sprawling porch. She motioned toward a backdrop of maple and oak trees interspersed with evergreens. "There he is, sitting under that tall oak tree. I think he finished mowing the lawn and is taking a break."

I spotted a dark-haired boy in shorts and a T-shirt. He'd removed his running shoes and had found a spot in the shade under the leafy tree.

"It would be best if I introduced you," Mrs. Holt said. "Come with me."

We followed her across a stretch of lawn the size of an Olympic swimming pool.

I took in a deep breath. Nothing beat the scent of freshly cut grass.

Bordering the lawn on the left was a vast garden. I spotted rhubarb and the early stages of strawberries and blueberries. Beyond the garden, a lake flowed along the back of the property. Did Jeremy travel here by canoe too?

The teenager jumped to his feet as we neared, straightening to his six-foot-plus height. He lost his balance as he wiggled into his shoes, then leaned against the tree trunk for support.

Jeremy stammered, "Oh...uh...Mrs. Holt. I—I was just taking a short break. I'll go fix the patch of broken fence right now." He started to move away.

"It's quite all right," Mrs. Holt calmly said. "It can wait. I'd like you to meet Megan and Michael. They're Jessica's friends. They want to talk to you about the fire last night."

Panic flashed in the boy's brown eyes as if he were debating whether he should stay or run.

"It's okay, Jeremy. They're only trying to help Jessica and Ethan find out how the fire started."

"I—I don't know nothing about the fire," Jeremy said. "I already told the cops what I know."

"That's cool," Michael said. "By the way, I saw a great-looking canoe by the lake near Jessica's Lodge earlier. It has a blue stripe on the side. Is it yours?"

"Sort of," Jeremy said. "It belongs to my dad, but I help him take care of it."

"You do a lot of canoeing on the lake?"

"Yeah. Mostly in the mornings. It's real quiet early in the day— except when the geese come."

Michael chuckled. "Yeah. They can be noisy, that's for sure."

"Did you travel here by canoe?" I asked Jeremy.

"Yeah. I travel by canoe most everywhere I go. It's a lot cheaper than a car."

"For sure," Michael said. "Jeremy, I was wondering if you saw something—or someone—that seemed out of place at Jessica's the day of the fire."

The boy stiffened. "I—I don't want to get nobody in trouble."

Michael waited.

Jeremy stared at the ground. "I saw one of the guests smoking cigarettes by the shed."

"When?"

"Late that afternoon."

"Would you be able to identify this guest?"

He looked up at Michael. "Not by name."

"Can you describe him?"

"He was old," Jeremy said. "He had some gray hair."

"Did you happen to see this guest put out his cigarette?"

"Yeah. I walked by him to get to my canoe. I saw him flick the cigarette butt in the air. It landed twenty feet away, like it always did."

"Did you see him elsewhere on the property?"

"Fishing by the lake a few times."

I joined the conversation. "Jeremy, you mentioned that you go canoeing in the morning. Do you ever go out at night?"

He shuffled his feet. "Sometimes."

"What about last night? Were you on the water when the fire started?"

Jeremy's eyes narrowed. "I saw the shed burning, but I didn't start the fire."

"I'm not accusing you. I thought maybe you'd seen something that might help Jessica find out how the fire started and how the corpse ended up in the shed."

His voice trembled. "I don't know nothing about the corpse. My dad says sometimes fires start for no reason. People disappear for no reason. Like Burt Garner."

"Jessica's neighbor," I said.

"Yeah," Jeremy said. "Burt is old, but he's a good friend. He taught me how to lay hardwood flooring like the pros do it. I don't know why he didn't say goodbye to me before he left."

The sun shone through the tall trees bordering Jessica's Lodge and cast playful shadows over the grounds. A gentle breeze nudged the row of lilacs bordering the house, its sweet scent reaching Michael and me as we crossed the lawn toward the house.

My feel-good moment was shattered when I noticed ashes floating in the air from the charred remains of the fire. I empathized with Jessica and Ethan. The fire had raised so many questions. Who started it? What was the identity of the corpse? How did a body end up on their property? It was enough to keep anyone awake at night.

Two people stood on the dock by the lake. Both wore baseball caps, T-shirts, and shorts.

"There's the married couple from cabin one," I said to Michael.

"Good timing. Let's go talk to them."

As we neared the dock, I was horrified to see that the man was throwing stones at the seagulls. His wife was hopping from one foot to the other and giggling. She turned and saw us, then nudged her husband.

Michael was discreet as usual. "You guys are bird watchers?"

"Nah." The man lowered his baseball cap, accentuating his toothy smile. "We were just having some fun."

We introduced ourselves.

Cody Vorra scratched his stubby nose. "Jessica mentioned something about you guys talking to the guests."

Brittany stood close to her husband, a silly grin plastered on her chubby face, her brown eyes twinkling.

"Were you here Friday?" Michael asked them.

"We went shopping in town and drove back later," Cody said.

"That same afternoon," Brittany added.

"Did you notice anyone—or anything—out of place on the grounds here that day?"

Cody and Brittany looked at each other. Brittany interlocked her arm in Cody's and whispered something in his ear.

"A delivery truck," Cody said.

"A white truck," Brittany said.

"I don't know if it means anything, but we noticed the guy in cabin four standing by his car," Cody said. "He was staring at the delivery people. Mighty peculiar like."

"It must have been Foster Wade," I said. "The owners asked him to oversee the delivery of the freezer."

Brittany nudged Cody. "That must have been the first delivery," she said to him.

"The first?" I repeated. "How many deliveries were there?"

"Two," Cody said. "When the first truck left, another one pulled in soon after. It was white like the first one, but smaller."

"Like a cargo van?"

"I guess so."

"Did you see what they delivered?"

"Tall boxes. They seemed mighty heavy."

"How do you know that?" Michael asked.

"A guy transported them on a trolley," Cody said.

"Did you see a company name on either of the trucks?"

"No," Cody and Brittany said at the same time.

"License plate number?"

"We couldn't see the plates," Cody said.

"From our cabin," Brittany added.

"Where was Foster Wade?" I asked.

"Still standing by his car, I guess," Cody said.

"What happened afterward?"

"Nothing much. The truck drove off."

"And Foster?"

"I guess he must have left too."

Michael asked, "Are you sure Foster left after the *second* truck had driven off? Could he have left after the *first* truck had driven off?"

The young couple exchanged glances, then broke into giggles.

Cody briefly shifted his attention to the cottages with private docks across the lake, avoiding the question. "Well, we were...umm... a little busy. We don't know for sure when Foster left."

Brittany blushed and looked down.

Michael persisted with his line of questioning. "Did either of you mention the second delivery truck to the detective?"

Cody and Brittany shook their heads in unison. "No."

"Why not?"

"After the fire started in the shed, we sort of forgot about the second truck," Cody said.

"Until now." Brittany giggled and buried her head in Cody's shoulder.

Michael bristled in annoyance, and I shared his concern.

Whatever drugs these two were taking could cast doubt on their eyewitness statements.

5

Jessica stood at the kitchen counter placing sandwiches on serving plates. "Impossible." She glanced over her shoulder at Michael and me. "We only had one delivery that day. The freezer."

Michael stretched his arm over the back of the chair. "Cody and Brittany said a second truck arrived soon after the first one left."

"You think that second truck transported the body?"

"It's possible. Kate and Patty crossed paths with a white cargo van on their way back from town Friday too, though they claim it was later."

Jessica added the last of the sandwiches to the plates. "This truck delivery thing has got to be someone's idea of a sick joke."

"Once the police identify the victim, we'll have more to go on," I said to her. "But right now, they need to know about the second delivery truck."

Jessica didn't answer. She set plates of grilled cheese and bacon sandwiches on the table, then walked back to the counter.

I took a chance. "Would you like Michael to make the call? He can lend his credentials as a reporter and offer them firsthand information."

Jessica returned to the table with side dishes of coleslaw and pickles. "Would you mind doing that for me, Michael? I've got my hands full today."

"No problem," he said.

Relief spread across her face. "Thank you. Ethan usually helps me in the kitchen on weekends, but he had to go to the office to finish a rush project this morning. Other guests will be coming in for lunch soon. Thank goodness Mom came to get Amy earlier." Her eyes flitted around the kitchen.

"I'll give you a hand with the dishes after I finish this yummy sandwich," I said.

"No way," Jessica said. "You're my guest."

"I insist. I need to burn off all these extra calories."

"Okay. Thanks." She paused in thought. "I meant to ask you guys..." She rubbed her hands along the sides of her apron. "I know you planned to spend the weekend here, but would you consider staying on a few more days? As our guests, of course. We haven't even had a chance to talk and I'd like to catch up."

Jessica's voice was taut and changed pitch whenever something was troubling her. I took the cue.

"I'm free." I gave Michael a pleading look.

"I'll ask Steve Burke at the newsroom to extend my leave," he said. "When are your guests checking out?"

"By noon tomorrow, except for Sam Norton," Jessica said. "Why?"

"We've interviewed everyone except him. We'll pay him a visit after lunch." He sipped his coffee.

"Any more guests on the way here?" I asked her.

"Yes, on Monday. A family with two teenage kids. Which reminds me... I need to pick up a few things in town this afternoon. Want to come along, Megan? Ethan should be back soon. He can show Michael his man cave in the basement while we're gone."

"A visit into town sounds good," I said.

Michael smiled like a kid about to enter a toy store. "So does the man cave."

~

Back in our cabin, Michael contacted Detective Cole. He was unavailable, so he left a message.

He slid his phone in his pocket. "Okay, Megan. Let's go interview our last guest."

We found Sam Norton sitting in an Adirondack chair on the deck of cabin three, his legs crossed at the ankles. Short salt-and-pepper hair topped a face with regular features that one might easily forget. A fitted polo shirt emphasized a slender frame.

After Michael introduced us, Sam said, "Jessica mentioned you two were making the rounds."

"Do you have a few minutes?" I asked him.

He took a long puff of his cigarette, then flicked the stub into the air. It landed about fifteen feet away on a patch of sand bordering the lake. "I got all the time you need."

I noticed the tiny green triangles on the soles of his running shoes —probably safety grooves for after-dusk runs. "I like your shoes, by the way."

"Thanks," Sam said. "Got them in Ostfield. They were having a summer sale. What did you want to ask me?"

"Witnesses saw you smoking near the shed Friday afternoon."

"It's the only spot on the property that offers shade. Smoking inside the cabin is taboo, and it can get pretty hot out here." He squinted under the midday sun. "Before you ask me, I left here in the afternoon—long before the shed caught on fire."

"Did you go fishing?" Michael gestured toward the fishing rod that lay horizontally by the cabin wall.

Sam chuckled, crinkling his brown eyes. "No. I haven't done much of that, except for the first two days I got here."

"Why not?"

"The bass aren't biting."

"Right. You said you left here Friday afternoon. How long were you gone?"

"Let's see..." Sam hesitated, recalling. "I drove into town and grabbed a bite to eat. I visited some of the shops till closing time. Then I came back here."

"Did you light one up when you came back?"

"No. I took a nap."

"So you were here when the fire started."

"Yes."

"What did you do after your nap?"

"Nothing. I slept until the siren from the fire truck woke me up that evening."

"Maybe you got careless and dropped a cigarette butt near the shed earlier," Michael said.

Sam stood up and walked to the edge of the porch. "Like I told the detective, that fire was sparked by something inside the shed."

"You seem certain about that."

"I am. In fact, I'm just as certain that it didn't start with a cigarette butt." He grinned. "Funny how the people here jumped to conclusions about me."

"Witnesses called it like they saw it."

"I'm careful about where I ditch my cigarette butts." Sam frowned. "I've tried to quit smoking. You'd think I'd know better by now." He heaved a deep sigh. "My wife died of cancer last month. She was a smoker too. We were married for thirty years."

Remorse flooded through me. Here we were, trying to size him up as an arsonist when he'd recently lost his wife. "I'm sorry for your loss."

"Thank you." Sam squinted at the lake.

I glanced at his hands. No wedding band. Some spouses continued to wear their wedding bands as a sign of loyalty even after their loved ones had passed. Either his wasn't the happiest of marriages or he didn't like wearing a wedding band. I'd removed my wedding band after my husband died. It was the first thing I did after I discovered he'd cheated on me.

Then again, maybe Sam was lying. About everything.

He leaned against the wood railing. "I expected to spend some quiet time here fishing. Instead I turned out to be a suspect in a fire. It's not all bad. I'll have something exciting to tell my three children and six grandchildren when I get back home." He let out a short chuckle.

"The fire department hasn't delivered their report yet," I said. "The results will confirm the cause of the fire."

"I'm a patient man," Sam said. "I won't leave here until they tell me I'm in the clear."

"Did you happen to see a white delivery truck on the premises that day or evening?" Michael asked him.

"No. Are you thinking it transported the corpse to the shed?"

"The cops will find out eventually."

"I sure hope so. I'd hate to have my name added to their murder suspect list." His somber expression told me he wasn't joking.

I sunk into the sofa and leaned back. "We have three different witness statements about the white truck. Two trucks, one truck, no truck. Pick one."

"Crazy, isn't it?" Michael opened the fridge. He reached for two bottles of spring water and handed me one.

"Something else is wonky. Cody said the second truck came in right after the first one that afternoon. But Kate and Patty said they saw a truck—presumably a cargo van—leaving the resort when they were returning from dinner in town."

"It would have been closer to sunset by then. Someone's got their story wrong."

"What's even worse is that we don't know how the fire started. It might not have anything to do with the delivery people."

Michael stared into the distance. A tiny muscle pulsated along his jaw—a sign that something was troubling him. "I doubt Sam Norton is much of a fisherman."

His comment surprised me. "What makes you think that?"

"For starters, he left his fishing rod in the hot sun and in a horizontal position on the porch."

"Fill me in. I never went fishing."

"The first thing my dad taught me about fishing was to store the rod in a vertical position. The second thing was to keep it in a cool place when I wasn't using it—not in the sun."

"It could be a new hobby for Sam."

"A newbie would know those simple rules." He dug out his phone. "I need to check something Sam said about the bass..." After accessing the Internet, he found what he was looking for. "Aha! Fishing for bass in this area begins in June. If Sam had read the by-laws, he'd know it's illegal to fish for bass in May."

I revisited a prior suspicion. "While we're at it, maybe he lied about his wife and everything else too. If so, what's he really doing here? And did he deliberately burn down the shed?"

"If that's true, what was his motive for setting it on fire?"

"He couldn't have known there was a corpse inside the freezer. Or could he?"

He ran a hand through his hair. "Nothing makes sense. We're missing too many pieces of the puzzle. We're going through the motions, trying to make things fit. We need to know the identity of the victim and how the fire started."

"We'll have to wait for the police and fire reports," I said.

Michael's phone rang. It was Detective Cole.

While he spoke with the detective, I sat at the kitchen table and opened up Foster Wade's book. The inside flap displayed a photo of the historian standing on a dock in the Port of Montreal in his younger days, his profile against the city skyline. It must have been a windy day because strands of dark hair partially covered his eyes and cheeks, though the same straight bridge of his nose was evident.

A short bio indicated he was a member of the Canadian Historical Association. It stated that, although Foster had gained recognition in his field, he refused to attend public events and ordered all personal photographs pulled from publication. For obvious reasons, he'd allowed this photo to remain on the inside flap.

The one-hundred-page picture book on Montreal had been published decades earlier and highlighted famous events that had taken place in historical structures I easily recognized today. Photos of downtown Montreal made me homesick, yet I was right in delaying our trip back to the city. I owed Jessica nothing less than my friendship and support during this troubling time.

I fanned the pages and was surprised to find a handwritten note that read: "Follow leads in Fernlea and Ostfield." It had been placed between pages that documented a notorious robbery in Montreal during the 1990s.

Three men had tunneled through steel and concrete to break into the vault of a private investment company. From more than a thousand safety deposit boxes, they stole ten million dollars in gold bars and cash. The ringleader, Rusty Homer, fatally shot a police officer who intercepted his escape. His two accomplices drove off with the bulk of the stolen goods, leaving him to serve a jail term of twenty-five years. None of the stolen goods were ever recovered.

I did the math. Rusty Homer would be out of jail by now. If Foster had written this note, his leads could have something to do with the robbery. Maybe they had prompted his trip here. After all, he did mention that he was doing his research in Fernlea and Ostfield.

Michael hung up. "Guess what? The detective is going to contact the young couple in cabin one about the two delivery trucks. He'll talk to Kate and Patty again too."

"Good. I think you should read this." I showed him the note I found in Foster's book and the write-up on the robbery.

He read both. "Rusty Homer. The name sounds familiar. It could be in the pile of cold cases on my desk. I'll ask Steve." He made the call. "Steve, can you check if one of my cold case files covers a 1990s Montreal robbery? Sure, I'll wait." Moments later. "It does? No kidding. Can you send me the file? Thanks." He placed the phone on a side table.

"Foster's leads might be connected to this Montreal cold case," I said.

"Exactly what I was thinking. We'll touch base with him when he gets back."

"Did Steve say anything else about the case?"

"Only that Rusty Homer is now a free man and no one knows where he is."

6

————————

Michael eagerly accessed the newsroom files Steve had sent him by email. Paraphrasing the article on his laptop screen, he said, "Rusty Homer's two buddies have been the subject of Canada-wide arrest warrants ever since the 1990s Montreal robbery."

Goosebumps rose on my arms. "Are you telling me the police have no idea where they are?"

"Worse. They don't even know their identities. They weren't able to get prints at the crime scene."

"What else is in those files?"

He tapped the keyboard. "The police believe Rusty Homer was responsible for other robberies in the Montreal area, but they were never able to prove it." He raised an eyebrow. "Sounds like a professional thief to me."

"Any trace on the stolen goods from the 1990s?"

"Let's see." Michael scrolled down the screen. "They located the getaway van abandoned on the side of a road west of Ottawa. About an hour east of Fernlea. No stolen loot in the van, though. No fingerprint matches on file for the suspects either."

My curiosity was aroused. "Which could mean that they never did jail time, right?"

"It could also mean that they were clever and wore gloves throughout the entire operation."

"Anything else?"

He read on. "A reporter interviewed an inmate who had spent time in the same jail as Rusty Homer. He confided that Rusty used to get into fights with other inmates. He never complained to prison guards about it, so he gained the respect of other inmates. He turned over a new leaf and began advanced studies about five years before he was released. It doesn't say what. Steve is trying to get more details from his sources."

"We should talk to Foster about the note I found in his book," I said.

"Good idea." Michael looked out the window. "I don't see his car, but Ethan is heading our way." He shut his laptop and went to open the door.

Ethan stood there, beaming like a six-year-old who was eager to share a secret. "Michael, are you ready to visit my man cave?"

"You bet," he said.

"Megan, Jessica asked that you come to the house too," Ethan said. "She'll take her SUV into town."

"I'm ready." I grabbed my handbag and followed Michael out the door.

As we walked to the house, Michael asked Ethan, "How did it go at work this morning?"

"Better than expected. We delivered the project on time and within budget. Management is thrilled."

"Good stuff." Michael gave him a friendly slap on the back.

What a relief it must have been to Jessica to see him happy again!

Ethan moved on to another subject. "Jessica told me there was talk of a second delivery truck on Friday."

"The young couple in cabin one saw another white truck arrive Friday afternoon," I said. "Any idea who it was?"

"I did place an order of frozen food products to be delivered on Friday. They called back and said they couldn't make the delivery until Monday. I mentioned it to the detective when he asked me about any deliveries I was expecting. Maybe they were able to make the delivery after all. I think they use a white cargo van."

"What's the name of the company?" Michael asked.

"Vincent's Meat Shop." Ethan said. "It's located in Ostfield. Did the young couple catch the name on the truck? The meat shop has its name on the side panels."

"They didn't see a name."

"Oh. So it's probably not the truck from the meat shop. Come to think of it, they would have notified us of the delivery—not left it on our doorstep either. They're good that way. Does the detective know about this second truck?"

"We contacted him. He's following up on it."

"Good," Ethan said. "We're making progress. Thanks for your help." He turned to me. "Megan, when you and Jessica are done shopping, Michael and I will meet you in town. We'd like to take you guys out for dinner. We could all use a change of atmosphere."

On the drive to Fernlea, the sun was still shining, though a cluster of ominous clouds was spreading rapidly across the sky from the west.

"Ethan seems happy today," I said to Jessica. "He told us his work project went well this morning."

"Yes, his team met the deadline." Her smile slowly faded. "You know, Ethan has a difficult time accepting failure. His job is the ultimate challenge for him in that respect."

"Are you talking about the workload or the deadlines?"

"Both."

"You mentioned Ethan has a lot of stress on the job. Does this have anything to do with what you wanted to tell me last night?"

"You read me so well." Sadness ran through Jessica's voice. "Ethan had to sign up for anger management courses or else the company would have booted him out weeks ago. You saw how angry he was about the fire. He's worse when he's under pressure. Nothing pushes his buttons more than our next-door neighbor who doesn't reply to our letters."

"About your request to purchase a portion of his land?"

"Exactly." Her shoulders slumped and she concentrated on the road ahead.

"Ethan thought your neighbor might be away on vacation."

"Nobody leaves on vacation for a month without making alternate arrangements for mail delivery."

"How do you know this?" I asked.

"Because Ethan and I went over there a couple of weeks ago," Jessica said, surprising me. "We noticed Burt hadn't emptied his mailbox in a while. We took the mail—which included our letters to him—and fed the stash through the slot in his front door."

"That was thoughtful."

"I'm afraid that's as far as it goes. Ethan has become obsessed with contacting the man. He talks about it every day and how he's going to wring his neck the next time he sees him. I'm so afraid he'll make good on his threat."

"Aren't you exaggerating a little?"

Lines gathered across her forehead. "Last week, he grabbed a co-worker by the neck and almost punched him because he insulted him."

"Oh, no! That would be a probable case of assault and battery. What did the co-worker do? And management?"

"The co-worker didn't press charges. Management gave Ethan another chance."

"That was lucky."

"Tell me about it. Ethan has become so unpredictable. And moody. I pray every day that he keeps going to those anger management classes. He works out at the office gym too. I bought him a new pair of running shoes for his birthday to encourage him. With the problems we've been having lately, he needs all the help he can get."

I flashed back to Ethan's reaction when Detective Cole had told him the investigation might take more time. He sounded like a short fuse ready to explode at any moment—like my late husband. Tom had been unpredictable too, though in a different way. He'd used his business trips as an excuse to sleep with other women right up to the day of his untimely death. Like other wives with disloyal husbands, I hadn't suspected a thing.

I was afraid to ask Jessica, but I needed to know. "Has Ethan ever hurt you?"

She jerked her head in my direction. "Of course not!" She gazed back at the road. "Oh, I get it. You think his problems at work are a reflection of what goes on between us at home."

"I didn't say—"

"Believe me, Megan. I would never stand for it. We're going through a rough patch right now. His job, the new resort—"

"Lots of people go through rough patches. I went to hell and back when Tom was murdered and the police launched their investigation. But I didn't take it out on everyone else around me."

"I remember," Jessica said, softening her tone. "You were so distraught when I went to see you in Montreal that I extended my trip." She came to a stop at a corner, then turned right. "Trust me, Megan. What Ethan said about Tom's murder was spontaneous and callous, but he spoke out of fear. He didn't mean any harm."

"He could have fooled me," I persisted. "He used police suspicions of Michael and me to imply the two of you might be in the same situation regarding the corpse in the shed."

"I'm so sorry, Megan. You know how much Ethan and I love being with you and Michael. Please don't let this investigation put a wedge in our friendship. I need you as a friend right now."

The anguish in her voice resonated with me. I valued our friendship and the strong bond that linked us through good and bad times. "We'll always be friends, Jessica." I gently squeezed her arm.

"Great!" She laughed. "Let's focus on doing fun stuff the rest of the day. Like shopping."

"Good idea."

We entered the town of Fernlea. Its primary street, aptly called Main Street, snaked along six blocks and represented the retail core of this community of eight thousand people. Victorian style, low-rise buildings hugged one another and reminded me of the miniature dollhouses sold in specialty shops. The charming window displays in clothing boutiques, art galleries, jewelry stores, and craft shops immediately drew me in.

Jessica parked in the lot behind a strip mall. Inside, shops bordered both sides of the aisle, many of them displaying items on sale.

"There's an eccentric shop here that sells all kinds of stuff," Jessica said, leading the way. "You'll love it." She made a beeline for the shop.

Within minutes, she chose blue placemats and matching table napkins. She also picked out a set of wooden salad bowls. "These will go perfectly with my steak serving boards on BBQ night."

"Go ahead and choose something for yourself," I said to her. "My treat."

She picked up a large cotton handbag in a floral print. "What do you think?"

I whispered, "My grandmother had one exactly like it."

Jessica laughed. "How about this one?" She held up a small leather pouch.

"It's the same size as my makeup bag."

She giggled. "Oh, Megan." She looked at other handbags and finally chose one we both liked. It was a tan leather shoulder bag and had sections for a phone, sunglasses, and lots more.

While Jessica shopped for fancy dishware and glasses, I added a floppy hat to my selection of colorful notepads and pens, then headed for the checkout counter. I stood in line and was unaware of the conversation between two elderly women behind me until my ears picked up the words *dead body*.

"You have to wonder what kind of people they allow to move to Fernlea these days," one woman said, her voice croaky with age.

"If you ask me, it's a sign of more dreadful things to come," the other woman said, punctuating her sentence with a grunt. "The minute they started to let in those new folks, I knew this town would come to no good. Before you know it, law enforcement will have more crime than they can handle."

"Not to mention more dead bodies," the croaky voice said.

I turned around, prepared to give them my two cents' worth. I'd explain to Jessica later why I told two gossipy women to mind their own damn business—or worse.

But I changed my mind. If anything, I didn't want to make matters worse for Jessica and Ethan.

We continued our shopping spree outdoors. As we passed a bookstore, Foster Wade came to mind. Maybe they'd have a copy of the historical book he'd lent me. Some independent bookstores carried vintage books, and I could ask Foster to autograph a copy for me.

But Jessica edged me onwards, pointing out more interesting

pursuits. After we'd visited an antique shop, an art gallery, a couple of clothing stores, and other vendors on both sides of Main Street, we came across a shop that sold fancy soaps and body oils. Like most stores in town, it was a one-of-a-kind retailer.

Jessica stopped to read a sign in the window. "Look, Megan. We can get our palms read here."

"You can't be serious," I said.

"Oh, come on. It'll be fun." She took hold of my arm and led me inside the shop to set up a meeting with *Madame Ora,* an elderly clairvoyant who read palms.

Jessica took the first appointment. By the time she came out of the back room fifteen minutes later, her complexion had paled.

"Are you okay?" I whispered.

"I'll tell you all about it later," she said. "Go on. It's your turn."

Madame Ora stood five feet tall and wore a red polka dot wrap dress that resembled something I'd once seen in a 1940s movie. Her wispy white hair stood on end, as if it had gone through dozens of perms. She beckoned me into an area at the rear, then pulled a thick curtain along a rod, separating the space from the rest of the shop.

She motioned for me to sit down at a round café table and took a seat opposite me. "Please do not ask me any questions until I have completed my reading." Her voice was thick with a foreign accent—maybe Polish. She closed her eyes and mumbled words I couldn't understand, then opened her eyes. "Please show me your hands."

I extended both hands as requested.

Madame Ora peered at my palms, squinting as if she were trying to decipher coded messages. "My dear, you have suffered a deep loss, but things will change for the better."

It was a pretty general statement.

"Your loss had to do with a man—a man who shared a deep bond with you."

My late husband. Good guess.

"This man died suddenly and tragically."

Okay, this was getting creepy.

"You have since moved on. Another man has entered your life. He is a very brave man."

I swallowed hard.

Madame Ora droned on. "On this particular journey, you are in grave danger, but you are surrounded by protection."

Grave danger? Protection?

She focused at the space above my head. "The white feather will protect you. Keep it with you at all times."

Goosebumps rose along my arms. While she closed her eyes and mumbled the same incoherent words as before, I reached into my handbag and rubbed the tiny white feather between my thumb and forefinger. It seemed beyond coincidental.

Madame Ora opened her eyes. "You may now ask me two questions."

Logic told me the simple white feather in my handbag would never protect me from any kind of danger. Regardless, the fact that she had mentioned it intrigued me. "Can you be more specific about the grave danger you mentioned?"

She closed her eyes. "You are involved in matters concerning death. I see three dead spirits around you—spirits that have met with unexpected death. Take caution. Not everyone is to be trusted." She opened her eyes. "Next question."

Was she kidding? A dozen questions had popped into my head.

I thought of Michael. "Will the man in my life be safe too?"

"He has tempted fate many times and succeeded."

"What you mean?"

Madame Ora pushed back her chair and rose. "I'm sorry, I have already answered your two questions."

"But that's not an answer." I remained seated. "You didn't say he would be safe. Will he be safe?"

She held up her hands, palms outward. "That is all I can say."

Damn!

I paid the woman and left the shop with Jessica.

I hadn't realized I was almost running along the sidewalk until Jessica clasped my arm and said, "Slow down, Megan. What happened in there?"

Not wanting to alarm her, I held back from mentioning what Madame Ora had said about three dead bodies. I improvised instead and took a deep breath to calm a racing pulse. "She told me not to trust everyone and to be careful, that I could be in danger."

"What kind of danger?"

"She didn't say. If you ask me, she was vague. What did she say to you?"

"That I was on the threshold of a new beginning, but that danger surrounded my family."

I laughed.

Jessica nudged me. "What's so funny? That woman terrified me."

"Don't you see? She gave us similar readings. Danger must be the flavor of the day."

Jessica giggled. "You're right. Let's not tell the guys. They'll think we're wacky." She checked her phone. "It's almost time for our dinner date. Let's unload these bags and I'll call Ethan."

Il Tavolino was an Italian restaurant located in downtown Fernlea. Small tables and personal service enhanced a relaxing atmosphere where residents enjoyed fine dining. The place was almost filled to capacity when we arrived.

Thanks to the maternal half of my Irish-Italian heritage, I'd learned a modicum of Italian words as a child. The secret of the establishment's name was revealed when I translated Il Tavolino for the others at our table.

"It means *the small table*," I said.

"I'm impressed," Ethan said. "I didn't know you spoke Italian."

"I don't. It happens to be one of the few words I do know."

Chuckles all around.

"So Michael, did you like Ethan's man cave?" Jessica asked.

"It's amazing," he said, then asked Ethan, "How did you manage to collect all that stuff?"

I edged forward. "What stuff?"

"A pinball machine, a pool table, a popcorn machine, and a vintage turntable," Michael said. "And that's not counting a load of vinyl records from the sixties and seventies." His eyes sparkled. "Oh... and a hockey stick signed by Wayne Gretzky."

Ethan stuck out a thumb in Michael's direction. "Now you know why I had to drag him away from there."

Michael chuckled. "I could spend days in a place like that."

"I inherited almost everything from my parents," Ethan said. "I'd like to add more collectibles one day."

"You can find great bargains at flea markets," I said. "Are there any around here?"

"I don't know about flea markets," Ethan said, "but Fernlea has a lot of antique shops. Unfortunately, I don't get out as much as I'd like to these days." He scowled.

Jessica fidgeted with her cutlery, then looked around as if she were searching for the waiter.

I empathized with her. She was working as hard as Ethan to ensure their future livelihood. Having to deal with his moody disposition made it all the more exasperating.

The waiter saved the moment when he arrived to hand out menus and take our order for beverages. Conversation around the table resumed as we studied the choices on the day's menu.

"So many terrific choices," Michael said. "I can't decide. Do you guys have any suggestions?"

"The Chicken Marsala is delicious," Jessica said. "It comes with mushrooms and veggies."

"For a heartier dish," Ethan said, "try the lasagna Bolognese."

"I'll order the Chicken Marsala," I said.

"It's lasagna for me," Michael said. "I like hearty meals."

I laughed. "You like to eat. Period."

"That makes two bottomless pits." Jessica nodded in Ethan's direction.

Ethan put a hand on his stomach. "I'll admit I've gained a few pounds, but it's hard to resist anything Jessica cooks up in the kitchen."

"Thanks, Ethan." Jessica smiled at him, then turned to us. "I stopped sampling the food I cook. It's the only way to keep the extra pounds off."

"I gave up years ago," I said. "Either Michael accepts me the way I am or—"

"Okay, okay, I accept." Michael held his hands up in jest, causing a ripple of laughter at the table.

The waiter arrived with our beverages. After he'd taken our dinner orders and left, the conversation took another turn.

Jessica leaned slightly forward. "Is it my imagination, or are people staring at us?"

Sure enough, four patrons at a nearby table were speaking in muted tones. One of them glanced our way from time to time.

In keeping with his knack for discretion, Michael said, "Can you blame them? They're staring at two beautiful women who happen to be sitting at this table."

"Thank you, Michael," Jessica said. "You know, Megan, I'd forgotten what a charmer he was."

"He has his moments." I reached over to squeeze his hand.

A woman wearing a white apron approached our table. "Hi Jessica, Ethan. So nice to see you again. And you brought your friends along this time." She smiled at Michael and me.

Jessica introduced us to Teresa, the restaurant owner.

"Nice to meet you," Teresa said. "I hope you enjoy your stay in our town." She switched her focus to Jessica and Ethan and lowered her voice. "I heard about the fire at your place. I'm so sorry. I hope the damage wasn't extensive."

"Minimal at worst," Ethan said, playing it down. "It won't affect business at all."

Teresa lingered, as if she were trying to formulate the next question. She leaned over and whispered to Jessica, "Is it true they found a dead body in your shed?"

Jessica hesitated. "Well...we haven't received preliminary reports on the fire yet."

"Yes, but—I mean—who would spread a story about a corpse on your property if it weren't true?"

"Mean-spirited people, I suppose." Jessica fingered her napkin, avoided her stare.

"I guess so." Teresa cut short an awkward moment. "Well, enjoy your dinner."

Jessica waited until Teresa had moved out of earshot. "Ethan, if she knows what happened at the resort, it's probably the talk of the town by now."

Ethan clenched his jaw. "I expected as much."

"Someone must have shared what they saw at the fire Friday night." She focused on Michael and me. "I'm sure it was neither of you."

I mentally ran through the list of people Michael and I had interviewed at the lodge. Any one of them could have come into town and casually mentioned the fire and the gruesome discovery to a sales-clerk or shop owner. In fact, two women had already talked about it in one of the stores Jessica and I had visited earlier. So much for keeping bad news under wraps.

"Maybe your mother told a friend," Ethan sneered. "You know how she loves to chat."

I drew in a quick breath.

Jessica glared at him. "Mom would never do such a thing. She respects our privacy."

"How do you know? She probably thought it would attract the curiosity-seekers and bring in more business for us."

"Mom has a personal interest in the resort. She wouldn't broad-cast anything that would hurt the business."

"Speaking of broadcasting," Michael cut in. "Did I tell you about the time I was investigating..."

Michael succeeded in changing the conversation, such that the squabble evaporated. I took his lead and expanded the dialogue to the latest books I'd read. Jessica and Ethan commented on world news events. By the end of dinner, we'd managed to keep the discussion on an even keel.

Yet Madame Ora's unsettling predictions about three dead bodies held steadfast at the back of my mind. That she'd mentioned the white feather had especially shaken me. I reached behind me to adjust my handbag on the chair. Although reality impelled me to dismiss Madame Ora's speculations, the presence of the feather reas-sured me.

But what about the three dead bodies she'd mentioned? Would another corpse land on Jessica's doorstep any day now?

7

———————

It wasn't until Sunday afternoon that Michael noticed the reappearance of Foster's car. "Foster's back."

"Good," I said. "Let's go see him about that note I found in his book."

Moments later, we were knocking on the door to the historian's cabin.

Foster seemed surprised but welcomed us inside. "I can only spare a few minutes. I have to go to a meeting soon."

"This won't take long," Michael said.

After we'd settled around the kitchen table, I opened the book Foster had lent me. "I found this note and was wondering if it had anything to do with the Montreal robbery you described in these pages of your book."

Foster snapped his fingers. "Oh. I'd forgotten about that note." He gave me a sheepish grin. "I guess I have no choice but to come clean."

A mischievous glint flickered in his eyes. I braced myself for the juicy tidbit he was about to reveal.

"You see, I've been waiting for a lead in this case for a very long time," Foster said.

"You're referring to the Rusty Homer case," Michael said.

"Yes," Foster said. "I had the opportunity to interview the man while he was serving time in jail. He shared information with me that he claimed he hadn't told anyone else."

"When was this?"

Foster rubbed his chin. "I'd say about five years ago. Anyway, he told me he knew where his two accomplices had been hiding out all these years. He was planning on tracking them down once he got out. It sounded like he had something in store for them, and it wasn't a handshake."

Disbelief flashed in Michael's eyes. "I've interviewed many prison inmates and rarely got that kind of information from them. Maybe Rusty Homer was eager to see his name in print."

"Make no mistake. I had to sign a non-disclosure agreement. Most importantly, he said he'd come looking for me and break every bone in my body if I revealed what he told me. You don't mess with guys like that."

"But you're pursuing leads in the case."

"I'd be a fool if I didn't," Foster said. "The agreement I signed covered information he supplied to me in confidence, not events I might explore in the future based on any leads."

"What kind of events?" I asked him.

"Historical events," Foster said. "From the information I've gathered, I have to assume that his two accomplices are lurking in the vicinity of Fernlea or Ostfield."

"Is that why you came to Fernlea?"

"Not initially. I decided years ago that my next book would cover small town history, so I've been visiting lots of places in Quebec and Ontario. I have the research to back it up." He glanced at a stack of notebooks and a collection of flash drives on the table. "If anything significant were to occur in Fernlea or Ostfield, namely the resolution of the 1990s robbery case, it would make an excellent addition to the book I'm working on." His face lit up with enthusiasm.

"The authorities would expect you to share your information with them," Michael said.

Foster shook his head. "I can't do that."

"Why not?"

His expression darkened. "If word ever got back to Rusty Homer, I'd die an early death."

"Point taken," Michael said. "Can you share your data with Megan and me? We promise it'll never be divulged. Journalistic privilege."

Foster's shrug reflected skepticism.

Michael leaned forward. "I happen to be working on a cold case file covering the same 1990s robbery. As you implied, Rusty Homer is searching for his accomplices and the stolen loot. He needs to find his buddies to get to the stash. That spells trouble."

Foster gaped at him. "What does that have to do with me?"

"Depending on what kind of payback he has in mind for his buddies, you might be considered an accessory to the crime."

Foster blinked. "Oh. I hadn't thought of it that way. What do you suggest?"

"Solving this case means as much to me as it does to the authorities," Michael said. "Problem is, I can't contact them until I have solid evidence. We can work together and share information that might lead to solving the case. The bottom line: I get a scoop on a cold case, you get to write about an historical event, and the police end up finding the accomplices and the loot from the 1990s robbery."

Foster instantly dismissed his suggestion. "I don't think so. I like to work alone. And I don't like publicity."

Michael was persistent. "Please hear me out. To show my good faith, I'll start the ball rolling. Here's what I know. An informant revealed that Rusty Homer built a reputation as a tough guy in jail. He got into fights with the other inmates, but he never tattled on them and eventually won their respect."

Foster chuckled, accentuating his round cheeks. "It doesn't surprise me. Prisoners need survival skills to stay alive in jail."

"There's more. With lots of time to spare, Rusty Homer's interest turned to books and began to read anything he could get his hands on."

"He never told me about that. Anything else?"

Michael sat back. "I'm working on it. I'll let you know if something comes up."

"I appreciate your candor. I'll share this tidbit with you. Rusty Homer was the mastermind behind many burglaries. He admitted that his two accomplices in the 1990s Montreal burglary had served time for minor crimes as juveniles. Petty theft, I think it was."

"Which could mean that law enforcement would have their fingerprints and mug shots on file."

I countered, "If police had found their fingerprints at the scene of the robbery or in the stolen van, they would have been able to identify them. But they didn't find anything, which means the thieves must have worn gloves."

"I agree," Foster said. "It's the only logical conclusion."

Something else came to mind. "What about the surveillance camera at the investment company where the robbery occurred?"

Foster ran a hand over his chin. "Hmm... If I recall, a journalist reported the camera was defective."

I had another question. "Did Rusty Homer happen to mention the names of his accomplices?"

"Now I understand why Michael welcomes your participation in his investigations." Foster grinned. "No, I suppose there were limits to what Rusty Homer was prepared to reveal. If he was planning a revenge of sorts, I'd say he made sure no one knew about it."

"Ten million dollars is a damn good incentive to keep one's mouth shut," Michael said.

"I couldn't have said it better myself." His lips formed a wide grin. "You know, you and I have similar occupations. People make their mark in life, good or bad, and we document their activities. All in the name of history."

"That's one way of looking at it."

Foster checked his watch and stood up. "Well, I have to get going. You can always call me if something comes up."

We exchanged phone numbers and said goodbye to Foster.

After we returned to our cabin, I asked Michael, "What do you think? Will Foster run off to find Rusty Homer on his own and get killed in the process?"

He stared out the window at the lawn. "Who knows? I'll say one thing about him. He got lucky."

"If only he'd share what Rusty Homer told him, it might help you solve the cold case. Wouldn't that be cool?"

"Right." His voice lacked the usual enthusiasm.

"What's wrong?"

"Nothing."

"Come on, Michael. I know when something's bugging you."

"I don't believe in coincidences."

"What are you talking about? Your entire career has been based on lucky coincidences and fluky timing."

"You're right about that, yet something bugs me."

"What?"

Michael ran a hand through his hair. "I don't know."

"I think I know what it is," I said. "Promise you won't get angry if I tell you?"

"Tell me."

"You're feeling a little overwhelmed because Foster managed to get an interview with an infamous criminal. Admit it. I won't think less of you. You'll still be my favorite investigative reporter." I stood on my toes and kissed him on the cheek.

He put his arms around me. "Maybe you're right. I've been reviewing a pile of cold case files for months and never got a lead. We come to this resort and a guy old enough to be my father tells us he has a major break in a case that's been collecting dust on my desk."

"Don't be so hard on yourself. You've proven you're an excellent journalist, time and again. Look at all the awards you've won."

Michael kissed me on the lips. "You're so good to me."

"Mmm...nice." I took his hand and guided him to the sofa. "I've been thinking."

"About us?" He sat next to me, extended his arm behind me along the back of the sofa.

"No, not about us."

"Oh. What then?"

"I don't think we should discuss Rusty Homer or the cold case with Jessica and Ethan. They already have too much on their minds."

"Okay. We'll keep it under wraps."

Loud angry voices close by startled me.

Michael rose to his feet. "They're coming from outside."

We moved to the window. What we witnessed compelled us to race across the lawn to Jessica's house.

Ethan, fists clenched, was confronting Jeremy. Was Ethan going to hit him?

Michael reached them first. "What's going on here, Ethan?"

"I found Jeremy stealing stuff from the shed—or what used to be the shed," Ethan said.

"It's a bunch of old nails." Jeremy opened up his hands to show him. "See?"

Jessica hurried out the back door and joined us. "What on earth is the problem? I can hear you shouting from inside the house." She glared at her husband.

Ethan pointed a finger at Jeremy. "You're a thief. I'm going to report you."

Jeremy held his hands out. "No. Please. I'll give them back to you. Here."

Jessica stood between them. "It's okay, Jeremy. You can keep the nails. They're of no use to us."

The boy's eyes flitted from Jessica to Ethan as fear spread across his face. "I—I don't want to get in trouble. My dad would kill me."

"It's okay," Jessica said. "Your father won't find out about this. Now go home."

Without another word, the teen raced toward his canoe. He didn't look back.

Jessica glowered at Ethan. "What's got into you? That boy means no harm."

"It's the principle of the thing." Ethan stuck his chin out. "Petty theft is what got him in trouble in the first place. I'm doing him a favor."

Jessica put her hands on her hips. "A favor? He told me how his father preaches fire and brimstone to him every minute he gets. He doesn't need two of those in his life."

"Don't compare me to that bible-toting geezer, Jess."

She bit her lip and approached him. In a quiet voice, she said, "Ethan, I know we're going through a rough time, but let's not take our frustrations out on Jeremy. He has his own problems. Let's stay cool." She took his hand. "Okay?"

Ethan drew in a deep breath. "Okay." He hugged her.

Michael and I had been spectators all the while.

In what might have otherwise ensued as an awkward moment, Michael said, "We were wondering if you guys wanted to go into town for ice cream."

Jessica laughed.

Ethan smiled. "Sure beats a cold shower."

Little did we know that the next morning would bring news—the unexpected sort that was guaranteed to stir up emotions to the boiling point once again.

8

Although tranquility permeated the grounds at Jessica's Lodge, the lake surface mirrored the dark, overcast sky and accentuated a sense of foreboding that I hadn't been able to shake since the fire.

Voices reached us from the other end of the property as Michael and I headed to Jessica's kitchen for breakfast. The new guests in cabins one and two had arrived early: parents with their two teenagers.

The boy, about sixteen, was tall and wore his hair clipped close on the sides and long on the top. The girl was inches shorter and several years younger. She wore a T-shirt that was two sizes too large for her—perhaps her brother's. They were leaning against the car and tapping on their phones. A stern reprimand from their father moved them to action, and they each carried a piece of luggage indoors.

"They got here hours before their scheduled check-in time," Jessica said. "Good thing I prepared the cabins late last night." She placed a plate of hash browns on the table.

Ethan poured coffee for everyone. "Two more cabins rented. It's a positive start to the week." His demeanor indicated that he was in one of his better moods. Maybe the fact that he'd taken the day off had something to do with it.

"That's good news," Michael said.

"Has everyone else checked out?" I asked Jessica.

"Not quite. Foster Wade and Sam Norton came to see me earlier. Foster extended his stay to next week for research purposes. Sam booked another week so he could go fishing. Isn't that great?" She had a spring in her step as she returned to the counter to get more plates.

Michael and I knew the real reason behind the two men's prolonged stay at the resort. Foster was waiting for local events to unfold so he could write an extra chapter about an infamous 1990s Montreal robbery. Sam was hanging around in the hope that the fire department's report would exonerate him of blame. His excuse about going fishing provided him with a degree of respect in the meantime.

Along a similar line, Michael and I were sticking around in reply to Jessica's plea for help. That Michael's boss had encouraged him to pursue the 1990s cold case was a secret we would keep from Jessica and Ethan for now.

We'd just finished breakfast when Detective Cole knocked at the back door—an entryway he no doubt preferred. "You folks got a few minutes?" he asked Ethan and Jessica, setting a black portfolio on an empty chair.

Uh-oh. A black portfolio seldom brought good news.

Detective Cole had the detached approach of a law enforcement officer who'd investigated gruesome deaths but learned how to mask his emotions. His stance was solid and stretched to more than six foot something.

"Is this about the fire?" Ethan asked him.

"Yes."

"We'd like our friends to join us, if that's okay." He introduced Michael and me.

"It's an unusual request, but it's your choice," the detective conceded.

Ethan ushered us all into the living room.

The detective sunk his bulky frame into an armchair and retrieved a report from his portfolio. "I have the preliminary autopsy results and assessment from the fire department. We'll begin with the report from the latter. It lists damages to a freezer, old furniture, garden tools, varnished hardwood flooring—"

"Hardwood flooring?" Ethan echoed.

"It accounted for a fair bit of the debris."

Ethan asked Jessica, "Did they deliver extra hardwood here on Friday?"

"Not that I know of," she said.

"What's the name of the flooring company?" the detective asked.

"Build-a-Floor," Ethan said. "It's on the outskirts of Fernlea."

"I know the place." The detective took notes. "Do you mind giving them a call? Tell them you're asking about a shipment of hardwood flooring. Nothing more. Put it on speakerphone."

Ethan pulled out his phone and contacted the company.

After a shuffling of papers at the other end, a desk clerk confirmed that the company had dropped off a shipment of hardwood flooring on Friday. "Our files indicate that no one was home at the time," the clerk said, his voice gravelly. "The guys placed the supplies in the unlocked shed instead of hauling the load back to the store."

"Why weren't we notified?" Ethan shouted into the phone.

"I don't know," the clerk said. "Someone usually calls ahead to confirm delivery. If you'd like, we can schedule the project for completion on—"

"I'll get back to you." Ethan ended the call. "Bunch of morons."

The detective cleared his throat. "That explains the discovery of hardwood debris in the shed."

"Do they know the cause of the fire yet?" Ethan asked him.

The detective scanned the report. "It's assumed to be slow-burning candles, though the presence of other materials in the shed accelerated the fire."

Jessica stared at him. "Slow-burning candles? It doesn't make sense."

Ethan waved his arms. "A stranger could have wandered into the shed and placed the candles there. Do you have any leads?"

The detective responded with a slight shake of his head. "Like I said, this is a preliminary report. A final copy will be sent to you and to your insurance company later."

A scowl accentuated Ethan's rising impatience. "What about the body?"

"I'm getting to that." The detective flipped a few pages. "I have to warn you. The preliminary autopsy report might cause you considerable concern." He eyed Ethan and Jessica.

I braced myself. I could only imagine how much dread that comment had aroused in my two friends.

The detective heaved a sigh. "Here it is. The identity of the victim found in your shed. His name is Burt Garner."

Jessica gasped. "Oh, no! He's our next-door neighbor."

I shivered, despite the warm room.

Ethan looked dazed. "What the hell? Are you sure?"

The detective's expression remained deadpan. "How well did you know this man?"

"We only spoke to him once or twice since we moved in last fall," Ethan said. "We've seen him come and go a few times, but that's about it."

"No other communication between you?"

"We sent him several letters requesting to purchase a piece of his land."

"For what purpose?"

"We wanted to expand our place and build more cabins."

"Did Mr. Garner agree?"

"No. I mean—we don't know. He never answered our letters."

The detective kept his eyes on Ethan. "When was the last time you saw him?"

Ethan glanced nervously at Jessica before replying. "About a month ago. Is that right, Jess?"

"Yes," Jessica said. "We happened to see Burt enter the house next door. We thought we'd have a chance to speak with him, but he was in a hurry and left right away. He doesn't actually live next door. He only comes by to pick up the mail."

Detective Cole perused the report. "We have the property next door registered to him and Mrs. Gabriella Garner."

"She's his mother," Jessica said. "Burt told us she lived next door since the day she was born. He placed her in a retirement home months ago."

The detective slid the papers back into his portfolio. He retrieved a small black notebook and pen from his jacket pocket. "What else do you know about Mr. Garner?"

"He told us he worked at Build-a-Floor," Ethan said. "The same place we got our hardwood flooring."

The detective took notes.

Ethan went on. "He was renovating the house next door in his spare time."

"Renovating it? Did he tell you that?"

"Yes. I bumped into him one day after he'd visited his mother in the retirement home. He told me he wanted to replace some of the wood floors in the house and hoped it wouldn't be too noisy for us. Sometimes we'd hear him hammering away late in the evenings."

The detective scribbled a note. "Have either of you noticed anyone else on the property next door lately?"

"Not really," Jessica said. "The lights are always off. Oh...I did notice a broken window out front."

"Honestly, Detective," Ethan said, "we've been too busy with our own renovations to give a damn about the comings and goings next door."

The detective remained calm. "Have you ever had words with Mr. Garner?"

"I wish."

Jessica hastily intervened. "What Ethan means is that we couldn't understand why Mr. Garner hadn't replied to our letters all this time."

Her interpretation didn't seem to quell the detective's inquisitiveness. He asked Ethan, "When did you say you last saw Mr. Garner again?"

"A month ago," Ethan said. "Why the hell does it matter?"

"Mr. Garner was reported missing a month ago when he didn't show up for work." His gaze held Ethan's. "His corpse was discovered on your property."

I didn't like the direction this conversation was starting to take.

The implication proved too much for Ethan to fathom. He was on his feet in the next moment, fists clenched. "Are you accusing me of murder?"

"I'm not accusing anyone of anything." The detective stood up, his broad frame dwarfing Ethan's. "Is there something you'd like to tell me, Mr. Bryant?"

Jessica rose and put her hand on her husband's arm. "Please, Ethan." To Detective Cole, she said, "You'll have to excuse Ethan. He's been working sixty-hour weeks and tending to the resort in his spare time. The last few months have been tough for both of us."

The detective sat back in the armchair. "There's something else I'd like to share with you." He gestured for them to sit down and they did. "The pathologist has reason to believe that Mr. Garner's body was transported to your shed from another location."

"How do you know this?" Michael asked him.

"I'm not at liberty to discuss that with anyone." His attention strayed to Ethan.

Was he expecting a telltale sign of acknowledgment?

Jessica reached over and gently put her hand over Ethan's, no doubt to thwart another outburst.

Michael drew the detective's focus back to him. "Can you tell us how Burt Garner died?"

"No," he said. "The case is still under investigation."

"Can you tell us when he died?"

"Yes. About a month ago."

This latest revelation cut through the air like a steel sword.

"What the hell?" Ethan's brow puckered. "He's been dead a month? How can that be? The body would have decomposed by now unless—"

"It's assumed Mr. Garner's body had been preserved up until the day of the fire," the detective said.

I had a hard time believing it. "Preserved? How?"

"Sorry, that's privileged information." The detective's tone was firm. "It's assumed the state of the body delayed decomposition."

I was doubly stunned. "The state of the body? Was it frozen?"

The detective's reply was non-committal. "I'm not at liberty to say."

"How did you identify the body?" Michael asked him.

"DNA."

"Have investigators interviewed anyone connected to him— friends, family?"

The detective nodded so-so. "We've launched the investigation, but we don't have the resources available to pursue this case on a full-time basis."

Michael asked, "Wasn't this originally considered a missing person case?"

The detective pursed his lips. "It was."

Michael was relentless. "So if it's not a missing person case, you're looking at a murder investigation. Right?"

"Foul play is suspected, though I can't officially state it's a homicide until our investigation is completed. I can only tell you that we've sectioned off the property next door with yellow police tape. We're treating it as a hypothetical crime scene."

Michael leaned forward. "What about the media?"

"What about it?"

"Will you be releasing details of Burt Garner's death to the press?"

"Not until our investigation is completed," the detective repeated. "Therefore I'm asking all of you to keep a tight lid on this matter. I've cautioned each of the guests here not to discuss what they've witnessed."

"Detective, did you get a chance to speak with the guests about the sighting of a second van?" I asked.

"Yes. We're following up on the information obtained from them." He tucked away his notebook, then stood up. "That's it for now. Thank you for your time."

After the detective left, we gathered in the kitchen where Jessica brewed a pot of coffee. We'd just sat down when a light rap at the back door announced Jeremy's arrival.

"I'm here to work on your garden, Jessica," the teen said, staying by the door. "I brought a bag of fertilizer. It's outside."

"Thanks for letting me know, Jeremy." She stood up and moved to the counter.

"I saw the police officer drive away," Jeremy said to Ethan, his lips quivering. "Did you tell them about the nails?"

"No. I had more important things to discuss."

"Oh." Jeremy blinked. "I—I'm really sorry I took the nails."

Ethan said nothing and took a sip of coffee.

"I'd better go." Jeremy turned to leave.

"Wait," Jessica called out to him over her shoulder. "Take these ginger cookies with you." She handed him a supply wrapped in plastic.

The boy's face lit up. "Thanks, Jessica." He scooted out the door.

"You're too good to him," Ethan said to her.

"Someone has to be." She joined us at the table. "It's bad enough he doesn't have a mother."

The sound of a truck pulling up propelled Jessica back on her feet. She peeked out the window. "It's my delivery from the meat shop." She opened the back door.

A short man bustled in, his stomach protruding beneath an unzipped windbreaker. "Here's your order, Jessica. Sorry for the delay." He greeted the rest of us with a nod. "A computer virus caused a glitch. Friday deliveries had to be postponed to today. The tech doctors were called in, and the system is now healthy and wise." He chuckled.

Jessica smiled and took the parcel from him. "Thank you, Vincent."

"Have a good day, everyone." Vincent waved at us and left.

Jessica stuffed the package in the fridge. "Isn't it inspiring to see someone who enjoys his job so much and has such a good sense of humor?"

"Yeah," Ethan said. "I wish he'd tell me what his secret is."

Jessica sat back down. "Before I forget, thanks for probing the detective with those questions, Michael. I was too stunned to think after he began to treat Ethan and me as suspects."

"At least you know where you stand," Michael said.

"You're damn right," Ethan said. "Is this nightmare ever going to end? I mean, did you hear the detective? The police have limited resources. What a joke! Can you imagine how drawn out this investigation is going to be?"

"I'll help you in any way I can," Michael said.

Lines gathered across Ethan's brow. "Detective Cole hasn't said it in so many words, but he's insinuating I'm a murderer. I'm ready to take you up on that offer right now."

9

———

Michael stretched out on the sofa in our cabin. "Steve gave me the go-ahead to stay in Fernlea for as long as it takes. He expects a follow-up report on the cold case involving Rusty Homer and the robbery in Montreal."

I sat down in the armchair adjacent to the sofa. "That's good news."

"Problem is, now I have to divide my time between the cold case and digging up leads in Burt Garner's death."

"I'm still stunned about what Detective Cole told us earlier."

"One word did it for me. Preserved. The only way Burt's body could have been preserved was if it had been kept in a frozen state."

"I agree. Who on earth would store a body in a freezer and then dump it on an unsuspecting neighbor's property?"

Michael stared at the ceiling. "Speaking of suspects... Ethan isn't making it easy for himself. He has to control his temper. I thought he was going to plant one on the detective back there."

"It's his Achilles heel. Jessica told me Ethan is taking anger management courses at work. You can imagine what he's like when things don't go smoothly at the office."

He sat up. "What happened at the office?"

I told him about Ethan's confrontation with a co-worker.

"I had no idea things had become so volatile at work." His expression turned grim. "The fact that Ethan and Jessica sent a bunch of letters to their next-door neighbor doesn't help either. It borders on harassment."

"Who's going to complain? From what Jessica said, Burt Garner never got to open them. Besides, he's dead now."

"Ethan's attitude bothers me. If he's not careful, he might give the cops a reason to pin a motive for murder on him." He grew quiet. "Do you think he ever hit—"

"Jessica? No, I don't think so."

"Some people are good at hiding secrets."

Michael was right about that. My late husband had a talent for hiding secrets. Painful memories lingered in my mind like endless cobwebs. I had to sweep them away if I wanted to help my friends.

"I suppose everyone has secrets," I said, "but Jessica would never put up with violence. She used to work for a women's shelter years ago."

"She must be one tough cookie."

"When it comes to her family, she has to be even tougher. That's why she can handle Ethan and his outbursts. She realizes they're facing a challenging period right now, and Ethan needs her support most of all."

"She did a good job calming him down in front of Detective Cole, anyway." He joined his hands behind his head and leaned back. "I kept hoping the detective would say something about speeding up his investigation, but he didn't. It sounds as if the OPP don't have the resources they need. In a way, that's lucky for us."

"Lucky?"

Michael's eyes displayed a familiar sparkle. "Time is on our side. It can work in our favor to clear Ethan and Jessica. How about we start digging up what we can on Burt Garner?"

The same mix of apprehension and enthusiasm surged through me whenever he asked me to join him in exploring a lead. It was akin to a traveler venturing into uncharted territory. Part of me wrestled with the innate fear of taking risks in uncertain situations. Another part was eager to do something exciting, if only to get away from the monotony of working behind a desk. But the most important reason I joined Michael in his pursuits was to pull him back from the brink of death he often challenged.

Michael's voice scattered my thoughts. "Well?"

I refused to let my fears win this round. "Sure. Let's do it."

"Good. You said something earlier about a neighbor... About the corpse having been dumped on an unsuspecting neighbor's property."

"That's right. Kill someone and dump the body on a stranger's property. It's the perfect way to cast blame on an innocent party. Don't you think so?"

Michael didn't answer.

"What? Do you believe for one moment that my friends are killers? That they'd be foolish enough to kill someone, freeze him—how, I don't know, since they didn't own a commercial freezer before Friday—then set the shed on fire?"

"When you put it that way, it does sound pretty ludicrous, doesn't it?" He chuckled.

I gave him *the look*.

"Okay, let's get serious." He sat upright. "I was thinking about the unsuspecting neighbor part. I'll bet our killer is familiar with this town and its people. He could even be a long-time resident—someone who didn't want to point the finger at any of the people he knew."

"So he chose strangers. Namely, Jessica and Ethan."

"Right. Add to that what the detective said about Burt Garner."

"What specifically?"

"That he's been missing for a month."

"So?"

He leaned forward and clasped his hands. "It means the killer put Burt's body on ice and waited for the perfect time and place to dump it."

"What better opportunity than to unload it on a property belonging to new residents who also happen to be the victim's neighbor? How convenient is that?"

"Convenient?" Michael asked, doubting my theory. "It depends on where and how Burt was killed."

"The detective cordoned off the property next door," I said. "Maybe he was killed there."

"Could be. Question is, how did he get frozen?"

I shuddered involuntarily. "That's so creepy."

Michael raised a forefinger. "One more thing. If the killer held a grudge against Burt, we need to find a motive."

"Where do we start?"

He stood up. "I have a gut feeling about that mysterious delivery truck. Let's interview the higher-ups of any company that made a delivery—or was supposed to make a delivery—to Jessica's Lodge last week. We'll start with Vincent's Meat Shop."

"Why that shop?"

"We already know the flooring company made their delivery because the hardwood burnt in the shed. Question is, did another truck from Vincent's Meat Shop pass by that same day, even though the driver said they hadn't?"

"Right. He said the delivery was delayed because of a computer glitch. Okay. I'll ask Jessica to contact the shop and let them know we're on our way there."

Ostfield had a population three times the size of Fernlea's and boasted ten times the number of box stores. Resembling gigantic cargo containers, they lined both sides of the main boulevard and were accessible to shoppers every day of the week.

Jessica told me she often made the short trip to Ostfield to purchase items that weren't available in Fernlea from smaller retailers. Monday afternoon's traffic confirmed that it was indeed a shopping mecca for choice-deprived residents of less-populated neighboring areas.

Michael veered off onto a secondary road that housed smaller malls where retail outlets offered specialty goods and services. Our GPS tracking wasn't precise, so we checked the exterior signage at the entrance to a couple of malls until we found the store we were looking for: Vincent's Meat Shop.

The delicious aroma of spicy sausages and fine cheeses hit us as soon as we stepped inside the shop. Glass-covered counters stacked with fresh pasta and sauces, deli meats, and cheeses stretched along two walls of the store, meeting at a corner. Horizontal displays in the center of the floor supported row upon row of fresh fruits and vegetables. Lining another wall was a section devoted to breads and desserts.

"Get a load of all the delicious food," Michael whispered to me. "Croissants, apple pies, bagels... This place is to die for."

"Be careful what you wish for," I whispered back.

We approached the service counter at the front. A young woman in a white cotton coat and hairnet walked up to us. "Can I help you?"

"I'd like to speak with your manager, please," I said.

"That would be Ted Bouchard. I'll get him for you." She headed toward the back of the store.

Ted Bouchard ambled down the aisle toward us moments later, his stride hampered by a plump waistline—perhaps the result of working in such an appetizing setting every day. His blue polo shirt over jeans spelled casual, and he had an easy smile. "Hello. What can I do for you?"

"We're here on behalf of Ethan and Jessica Bryant," I said. "We'd like to speak with you about a fire at their home in Fernlea."

Ted nodded. "Yes, yes. Mrs. Bryant called me earlier. Let's go talk in my office. It's more private."

We followed him through the exit door for employees and down a corridor. An open door on the left led to his office. Several photos of presumably company officials standing next to the shop's white delivery truck hung on a side wall.

"Please, have a seat." He indicated two chairs facing his desk, then sat down opposite us. "What would you like to know?"

I began. "Did your store make a delivery to the Bryants' home last Friday?"

"Like I told the Bryants," Ted replied, "we made no deliveries last Friday. We were backlogged on orders and short on supplies. We had to schedule most of our deliveries for Monday—today—instead."

"Did any of your employees borrow a delivery van for personal reasons last Friday?"

"No. They would need my permission to do that." He paused.

"Funny thing. An OPP detective was in here earlier asking about a delivery truck too. Are you working with them?"

"No," Michael said. "We're friends of the Bryants. We have a personal interest in finding out how the fire started."

Awareness flickered in Ted's eyes. "Are the police saying it wasn't an accident?"

Michael skirted the question. "They haven't issued a media statement yet."

Ted asked us, "What do you guys do for a living?"

"I'm an investigative reporter," Michael said. "Megan is a ghostwriter."

Surprise washed over Ted's face. "How interesting. I've never met anyone in either occupation before. Is there anything else I can do for you?"

"Not at the moment. Thanks for your time."

We'd hit a dead end.

I hid my disappointment and chatted with Ted as he escorted us out of the office and into the store. "Congratulations. You have a wonderful place here."

"Thanks. I manage the store and co-own it with my father, Vincent. He started a butcher business from his home years ago and expanded it into this store. He's semi-retired now but works part-time here making deliveries in and around town."

"We met him at the Bryants' home when he made a delivery there," I said. "Jessica spoke highly of him and his sense of humor."

Ted laughed. "My father loves yakking with customers. He's still a great PR guy. Ever since my mother died a few years back, we've kept him busy. Working here helped to diffuse the depression he felt after he lost her. They were very close."

An employee walked up to him. "Excuse me, Ted. You have a long-distance call on line two."

"Sorry," Ted said to us. "Good luck and drop by any time."

Back in the car, I buckled my seat belt. "What's next on the agenda?"

Michael adjusted his seat belt. "It's time we visit Burt Garner's home."

"Which one? The house next door to Jessica's Lodge or the other one in town?"

"The one next door to Jessica's Lodge."

"The police cordoned it off as a crime scene."

His eyes twinkled with mischief. "Since when has that stopped us?"

10

The single-story cottage where Gabriella Garner had been born and raised was more than a hundred years old. White clapboard siding and a verandah that looked out onto the road added charm to the modest building, though yellow police tape across the front door might deter anyone from ringing the bell.

Late Monday evening, Michael and I crept through a row of fir trees that separated Ethan and Jessica's property from their neighbor's. A starless sky offered protection from prying eyes.

"What if someone sees us in Burt Garner's house?" I whispered to Michael.

"We won't turn on the lights. I brought this." He dug out a large flashlight from his jacket and clicked it on. "Got your vinyl gloves on?"

"Yes." I raised both hands to show him. The thin gloves had become standard wear during our secret escapades. The last thing we wanted was to leave our fingerprints at a potential crime scene.

We stepped across a lawn that had recently been mowed, our thick-soled running shoes a protection against any creepy-crawlies that might happen across our path. As we neared the back porch, the flashlight revealed remnants of yellow crime scene tape on the door. Two of the rear windows had been broken. Positioned only several feet from the ground, they offered easy access to anyone attempting to enter the home.

"Do you think someone broke into the house?" I whispered.

"Let's find out." Michael led the way up the stairs to a small porch. "With all these broken windows, maybe the intruder left this door open." He tried the handle. "Nope. No such luck."

I held the flashlight while he dug out his lock pick kit.

After two attempts, the lock gave way. "Let's go," he said.

I followed him inside.

Despite the broken windows, the house had retained a musty smell, like old books that had been stored in a moldy place for too long. Our shoes crunched over bits of earth and whatever else lay on the kitchen floor.

Michael directed the flashlight horizontally, revealing a sink on the right within an L-shaped counter. A metal container and ceramic knickknacks gave the impression that someone still lived here. A wood chair sat in a corner.

He opened the paint-thirsty green cabinets and aimed his flashlight inside. They were empty, except for a couple of plates and cups. He opened the drawers and went through the same process. "Nothing here but pieces of mismatched cutlery, a pen and pad of paper, and a few utensils," he said. "Ethan mentioned Burt had been renovating the floors here. He probably grabbed a bite to eat while he worked."

The house gave me the creeps. Maybe it was the thought that Burt would no longer be returning here in physical form. If the clairvoyant was right, his ill-fated spirit might be lingering in this house right now.

I imagined him standing near us, watching us, trying to tell us about the dark deed that had befallen him... "I think coming here was a mistake. What did you expect to find anyway?"

"I'm not sure," Michael said. "Something Burt might have left behind. Something that might give us a clue as to how he died."

Cuckoo!

I jumped.

Michael aimed the flashlight at an ornate wood cuckoo clock on the wall facing us. Its occupant lunged forward as each chime pierced the air, producing an earsplitting blend of clangs and clomps.

My heart pounded. "Can it get any noisier in here?"

"I'll say." He chuckled, then aimed the flashlight at the floor. "This doesn't look like new wood flooring to me."

I bent down and examined the dents and scratches in the floor. I ran a hand over the surface. "It's new. I've seen this type of flooring before. It's called distressed engineered hardwood or something similar. It gives the appearance of rustic floors."

"How would you know that?"

I straightened up. "It was one of the floor samples the sales representative showed us for our condo before we moved in."

"I'm impressed."

"Thanks."

He opened the fridge. "Empty. No surprise here."

He advanced toward the archway leading out of the kitchen and aimed the flashlight at the floor. He bent down and ran a hand along it. "There's a different hardwood in the hallway. It's dark too, but it has real cracks in it."

I suddenly felt sorry for a man I'd never met. Aside from his job, Burt Garner had an ailing mother and home renovations to tend to. Unfortunately, time had run out sooner than he'd expected. He'd probably led a quiet life, not one that would have unnecessarily put him in harm's way.

So how did he die? What could possibly have happened to him?

"Let's go check the rest of the house," Michael said.

I followed him down the narrow hallway. The wood floor creaked under a threadbare runner. Both were no doubt as old as the house.

The first door on the right led to a small bedroom. Other than a dark blue bedspread over a double bed, a three-drawer dresser, and a wood chair, the room had little to offer in furnishings.

Michael inspected each drawer in the dresser. "They're empty, except for a few pairs of men's socks and underwear."

We moved on to the next room and found the same sparsely furnished space. Judging from the floral print bedspread and matching curtains, Burt's mother had probably slept here before she was relocated to the retirement home.

Michael opened each drawer in the dresser with a predictable result. "Not much here. Pillowcases. Sheets. That's it."

The hallway opened up into a living room at the front of the house.

I jumped as a sudden howl broke the silence.

Michael reached out to protect me, then aimed the flashlight at the shadows. Sheer curtains flapped wildly in front of a broken window.

"It's only the wind," he said.

I exhaled.

Two faded beige sofas with stains, a glass table topped with a thick layer of dust, and an old TV set hardly left enough space to walk around.

We detoured left to a closet by the front door.

It creaked as Michael slowly opened it. He peeked inside. "Nothing in here. Let's go."

I was only too happy to hear those words.

He directed the beam along the hallway as we retraced our steps. "Wait. We missed one." He opened another creaking door opposite the bedrooms and peeked inside. "It leads to the basement."

"The basement?" I swallowed hard. Venturing into the depths of a century-old house didn't exactly enthuse me. "This house is ancient. What if there are rats down there?"

"I doubt it. There's no food in this place. They have no reason to stick around." He aimed the flashlight at the wood stairway and led the way down.

The stairs groaned under our feet. Would they remain intact and support our weight? For the same reason, I refrained from putting a hand on the cracked banister in case it gave way.

While the flashlight revealed cobwebs in corners, I smelled the same musty odor as upstairs—probably mold. I wished we'd brought along a couple of allergy face masks.

A wave of Michael's flashlight around the rest of the basement left me gaping in shock.

He let out a low whistle. "Now we know where Burt stored his stuff."

Dozens of cardboard boxes had been ransacked. Broken chinaware, Christmas decorations, clothing—everything was strewn across the dusty cement floor.

"I guess someone was in a hurry to find something," Michael said.

I carefully stepped around a pile of clothing. "Maybe they broke into this place before the police got here."

"I bet they broke in afterward—like we did."

He had a point. I added this latest development to the growing list of unanswered questions about Burt Garner. "So what's next?"

I heard a shuffling noise upstairs.

Michael heard it too.

Floorboards creaked along the hallway.

Someone else was in the house!

Michael put a finger to his lips and shut off the flashlight.

We waited.

More creaking, then running.

The back door slammed shut.

Michael clicked on his flashlight and scrambled up the stairs.

A shadowy form zoomed past one of the basement windows.

"He's outside," I shouted.

No answer.

I didn't have a flashlight, but it made no sense to stand in the dark while Michael chased an intruder.

I darted toward the stairs but tripped on clothing and landed on my knees.

The pain was immediate and stung through my cotton pants. "Damn!" I reached down and felt a slit in the fabric over each knee. Just what I needed.

I got my bearings and remembered the stairs were on my right. I slowly maneuvered my way toward them, keeping my right arm outstretched.

Something wispy hit me in the face. A spider's web!

"Ugh!" I pulled it off and, in the process, the basement lit up. I had inadvertently tugged on the thin string of a light bulb!

Good thing Michael wasn't around. He'd have a good laugh.

I hurried upstairs and out the back door, then stopped. It was as dark outside as it was inside. I had no flashlight. It was useless to run after Michael. I had to stay where I was.

The sound of something falling broke the stillness. It was faint and seemed to come from the woods behind the house.

I stared into the darkness but couldn't see a thing.

I listened.

There it was again.

"Michael?" I called out.

Silence.

A flashlight beam danced on the lawn to my left.

I froze.

Had the perpetrator returned?

The beam got closer, larger.

It was Michael.

I relaxed.

"I lost him," he said, trying to catch his breath. "No sign of him anywhere."

"One of the teens staying at the resort could have wandered over here out of curiosity."

"I don't think so. I cut through the trees and didn't see anyone on Jessica's property."

"I heard a noise coming from the woods beyond the backyard."

"I'll go take a look."

"Be careful."

Michael crossed the patch of grass and vanished into the dense shrubbery and trees.

I waited, twitching at every sound that was unfamiliar to me as a city dweller but that local residents probably didn't even notice. Birds fluttering, owls hooting, the rustling of leaves in the wind...

And who knew what wild animals prowled in the darkness of night?

A twig snapped.

I jumped.

The beam from Michael's flashlight announced his return.

"See anything?"

"Only a pile of old plywood that Burt dumped in the woods," he said. "Whoever it was is long gone by now. Let's call it a night."

We closed up the house and made our way back to the cabin.

"What's on the agenda for tomorrow?" I asked Michael.

"We'll visit Burt's other house. If we're lucky, we'll get to talk to his neighbors. I'm not leaving town till I get some answers."

11

———————

Jessica fought back the tears as she placed cutlery on the kitchen table. "The family with the teenage kids checked out an hour ago. They refused to have breakfast here."

Disbelief swept over me. "What? I thought they'd booked two cabins for the week."

"When they found out about the corpse, they packed up and left."

"How did they find out?" Michael asked her.

Jessica sniffed. "One of the other guests told them. It had to be either Foster or Sam."

What would Foster or Sam have to gain by telling the new guests about the corpse?

If anything, Sam understood the effects of malicious gossip. Guests had voiced their suspicions about his implication in the fire, and he hadn't liked it one bit.

As for Foster, he had frowned upon Sam's smoking habit and Jeremy's alleged peeping in cabin windows. Surely he understood the negative repercussions that his comments might generate.

"Detective Cole advised the guests not to talk about it," I said. "The police haven't even informed the media yet."

"Someone's a blabbermouth," Michael said.

"You can say that again," Jessica said. "Wait till Ethan finds out. It's not as if tourists are flocking here to begin with. After Foster and Sam leave, we have no bookings scheduled. Our finances are already stretched, and now this."

I tried to boost Jessica's spirits. "It's early in the season yet. Keep promoting your website."

"I will. Lots of people travel to this area every summer to shop and enjoy local events, so I'm hopeful." She changed the subject. "What are you guys doing today?"

We told Jessica about our plans to speak with Burt Garner's neighbors in town. We felt no need to fill her in on our expedition next door last night. It would only compound the anxiety she and Ethan felt about their neighbor's corpse ending up in their shed and the negative impact the incident was having on their business.

Michael and I searched the municipal property records that afternoon. Burt Garner was registered as sole owner of his other home. We drove there right away.

The 1960s bungalow close to the center of town had a spacious front lawn that appeared to have been mowed recently. We suspected that Burt had hired a contractor to do the work. If so, I wondered if anyone in his family had thought to cancel the service on his behalf after he'd passed away. Like Burt's other house, the front door had yellow police tape across it.

We followed the rustic stone path leading to the front door.

Michael approached the glass panel in the door and peered inside. "All I see is the hallway." He turned and focused on the house across the street. "Maybe his neighbor knows more. Let's go."

As we crossed the street, a man ambled out of the house and leaned on his cane. "Hello there. Are you folks relatives of Burt?"

"Acquaintances." Michael introduced us and explained how we were staying at Jessica's Lodge next door to Burt's other home.

"I'm Larry Caplan, a friend of Burt's." He blinked behind rimless eyeglasses. His stooped shoulders gave the impression he was constantly searching for something on the ground. "The old place used to be his mother's home. It's been in the family for more than a hundred years." He squinted. "What did you folks say your reason was for coming here?"

We had to tread carefully. The police hadn't yet revealed Burt's death to the media, nor the macabre details surrounding their discovery. And yet, because of the police tape across Burt's door, there was a chance that Larry might already know the truth.

"Our friends were concerned about Burt," Michael said, winging it. "They haven't seen him in a while. We drove here and were surprised to see police tape across his door. Is his home part of an investigation?"

Larry nodded toward the ground. "A police investigator came by the other day. He asked me questions about Burt. From the sound of it, I think he's still missing."

He didn't know the truth. The investigator had evidently kept tight-lipped about Burt's death.

I played along. "When did he go missing?"

"About a month ago," Larry said. "It was on the news. I guess you young folks don't watch much TV anymore, do you?" He winked at us.

I prompted him. "Do you know what happened to Burt?"

"Let me give you some background information first." He looked up, his eyes searching the sky as if dredging up a memory. "He kept to himself, Burt did. Except for his job, I think he had little social contact. Oh, we'd chat once in a while when we'd happen to be watering the garden at the same time. Heck, I even convinced him to come over for coffee once."

"Sounds like you two were good friends," Michael said.

"I thought so too at first." He blinked. "One day I suggested we splurge a little and go have a fancy dinner in town. I can't remember the name of the restaurant. Anyway, Burt refused. He said he couldn't afford to eat out too often. I said it was my treat. He still refused. He said he didn't want to owe anyone anything. Besides, he said, he'd eaten there before and didn't like the food. I never invited him again."

"We've been to Il Tavolino," I said. "Do you know it?"

"That's it." Larry laughed. "That's the restaurant I was talking about. It's the only high-priced restaurant in town, but who doesn't love Italian food? I haven't been there in ages, though."

I nudged his memory. "And now Burt has gone missing."

"That's right."

"Any idea what could have happened to him?"

"Maybe." A light glimmered in Larry's eyes. "My kitchen faces Burt's house. One Saturday night about a month ago, I saw a car stop in front of his house. Burt got out. The driver waited until he'd entered the house before he drove away."

"Can you identify the car?"

"No, it was too dark to see much of anything. Anyway, I got up in the middle of the night to get a glass of water. I happened to look out the window and saw Burt going for a walk, all bundled up in his hat and overcoat."

"In the middle of the night?" I asked.

Larry shrugged. "It's not unusual for Burt. He's a nervous type of fellow and often has trouble sleeping. He thinks nothing of taking a walk alone in the wee hours. After all, this is Fernlea. Nothing happens in a town like this where everybody knows everybody else." He smiled widely, revealing partial dentures. "Anyway, I didn't think anything more of it and went back to sleep. I was surprised to see the police parked outside Burt's home days later. I had a feeling in the pit of my stomach that something bad had happened to him. You know what I mean?"

Only too well, I held back from saying.

Larry continued. "Anyway, I went over to find out what the fuss was all about. The police told me Burt hadn't shown up for work that week. His employer had reported him missing."

Michael eased into the conversation. "When the cops returned to Burt's house recently, did you speak with them?"

Larry shook his head. "Not this time. They only stopped by to put yellow tape across the front door. I suppose it doesn't bode well for Burt, does it?"

A tingle of remorse shot through me.

A glance from Michael cautioned me to remain silent about what we knew.

"Did Burt have family or friends?" I asked.

Larry adjusted his eyeglasses. "I believe I'm one of the only friends he has in Fernlea. I'm not aware of any other family members either."

"You mean, aside from his mother."

"Yes. When Burt had to place her in a retirement home, it tore him to pieces. It was the only time he opened up to me about how he felt. If you ask me, he was carrying a load of guilt."

"Guilt?" Michael repeated. "Did he say why?"

"Surprisingly, yes. He told me once how he'd regretted not settling down and having a family. He said he'd chosen to be a loner decades ago, and now he had to live with that choice. Except for his co-workers and me, he probably had little contact with anyone else."

"Did you ever meet any of his co-workers?" Michael asked.

"Not really. Sometimes I see a truck pick him up early in the morning and drop him off at night. It's probably another employee who works at the same flooring business. What's it called now?"

"Build-a-Floor."

"Yes. That's it."

"Could the truck have been a cargo van?"

"Yes, I suppose you could call it that."

"What about the truck driver?"

Larry squinted. "What about him?"

"Can you describe him?" Michael asked.

"No. The driver never got out of the truck. The windows were tinted, so I couldn't see inside."

For no specific reason, I shifted my attention to Burt's house across the street. If it weren't for the police tape, no one would suspect anything was amiss.

Larry's eyes grew watery. "I paid some young chap to mow the lawn on Burt's property. He even filled up the holes the groundhogs had dug in his backyard. Burt will have one less problem to take care of when he comes back."

His generosity touched me, as did his high hopes for Burt's return, which only added to my uneasiness about holding back the truth from him.

"Thanks for your help, Larry," Michael said.

"If you find out anything more about Burt, would you let me know?"

Michael promised he would.

We drove out to Build-a-Floor first. Larry's mention of Il Tavolino restaurant had prompted a second lead that we'd pursue later.

Michael parked in front of a one-story brick building on a secondary road a short drive from Fernlea. Like other commercial structures nearby, it was located in a nonresidential area with ample parking for employees and clients.

We strolled past a dozen pickup trucks, their wagons stocked with hard hats, safety vests, and construction equipment. Several cargo vans displayed the Build-a-Floor logo on the door panels.

"The driver of one of these vans must have driven Burt to and from work every day," I said.

"It's possible." Michael opened the front door to the shop and we stepped inside.

We approached a man at the front desk. *Chuck—Service*, read his name tag. His biceps bulged under the sleeves of his T-shirt, his forearms exposing dark snaking tattoos. When he placed his hands on the edge of the counter, fingers the size of jumbo sausages spread across the surface. "What can I do for you?"

Chuck's voice was gravelly. I recognized it. It was the same clerk Ethan had spoken with on speakerphone when Detective Cole had dropped by.

"We were given Burt Garner's name as a reference for home renovations a while back," Michael said, using one of his sly tactics to obtain information. "We were told he worked here."

"Not lately." Chuck squared his shoulders, amplifying his six-foot-plus height. "You folks from out of town?"

By now, I was convinced that people in Fernlea had an innate talent for recognizing outsiders.

"Yes," Michael said. "Ostfield."

Chuck folded his arms. "You don't say."

"We moved in last week," Michael said, adding another lie to the tally. "Can you give us an employee reference on Burt?"

Chuck raised his chin. "A good employee. Hard working. Reliable."

I joined in. "Do you know how we can reach him?"

Chuck's stare was intrusive, as if he'd scanned my body measurements from head to toe in a nanosecond. "I don't know where he is. He hasn't reported for work in a while. I can recommend someone else."

"It won't be necessary," Michael said. "We're still shopping around for estimates."

"Anything else I can do for you?"

"Not right now."

"In that case, I've got calls to make." Chuck reached for his phone on the counter, fumbled and almost dropped it. He hurried down a corridor leading to the back of the building.

Michael took a business card from a supply on the counter before we returned to the car.

I slid into the passenger seat. "Talk about ambiguity."

"He's hiding something." Michael adjusted his seat belt.

I buckled up. "You can't blame him. Detective Cole probably warned him not to talk to anyone about Burt's disappearance."

"Especially to outsiders like us," he joked.

"I'm sure he saw through our scam. If he believed we were serious about a renovation project, he would have asked more questions and tried to sell us the company's services."

"A gut feeling tells me it's more than that. The guy's body language shows he's scared. Did you see how he almost dropped the phone?" He pulled out the business card he'd collected from the shop. "I'll send Steve a text message and ask him to run a check on Chuck Dorey."

While he sent his request, I looked out at the parking lot. Several trucks loaded with construction gear had left. Business must be good for the flooring company.

Michael put away his phone. "Done."

"Too bad we couldn't ask Chuck if he was Burt's chauffeur to and from work."

"The last thing we want to do is put Larry at risk. What if Chuck is involved in Burt's disappearance somehow?"

"I agree, but don't you think we could have used a more direct approach with Chuck?"

"I doubt it would have worked. Guys like Chuck don't give out information freely. In the meantime, let's hope we don't botch up the next interview."

12

———————

The sky had darkened to a deeper shade of charcoal over downtown Fernlea. Baskets of flowers hanging from storefronts balanced precariously in the wind, sending petals and leaves swirling into the air. People clutched their coats and bags and took refuge indoors to escape the strong winds.

Despite the threatening weather, we headed to Il Tavolino restaurant. Never one to miss an opportunity to eat, Michael suggested we combine business with pleasure and enjoy a light lunch.

His sense of timing was commendable. The restaurant had just opened its doors. We were among the first patrons in line and were promptly ushered to a table.

Teresa came up to us. "How nice to see you again. So you decided to extend your stay at Jessica's Lodge?"

"Yes, a few more days," I said. "We have too much catching up to do. You know how it is between old friends."

"You should see my long-distance bills." Teresa laughed and handed us each a menu. "I'll be back in a bit to take your orders." She left to attend to another table.

I opened the menu. Every description sounded as delicious as the last time we'd eaten here. "Decisions, decisions. Everything looks so good. What are you having, Michael?"

"I think I'll start from the top and work my way down," he said. "How about cannelloni?"

"Sounds like a good idea. Cannelloni for two it is." I placed the menu on the table and whispered, "Something's been on my mind ever since we spoke with Larry. Remember how he told us that Burt didn't like the food here?"

"So?"

"I think Burt only said that because he wanted to get Larry off his back."

"It worked, didn't it?"

Teresa returned with a small carafe of red wine and two glasses. "Compliments of the house." She filled our glasses.

"Thank you," Michael said. "It'll go perfectly with our choice for lunch."

"Excellent." Teresa took our orders, then lingered. "I don't want to be rude, but I meant to ask. Did your friends find out what started the fire at their place?"

I took the cue. "No, but do you have a free moment? We'd like to ask you some questions."

"I'm free now." She hastily pulled up a chair and joined us. "Go ahead."

I lowered my voice. "You know how Jessica's neighbor, Burt Garner, has gone missing."

"Oh!" Teresa said. "Have they found him?"

In keeping with Detective Cole's orders not to disclose the truth, I contrived a feasible reply. "The media hasn't announced anything yet."

"Oh."

"Did you know Burt well?"

"Not really, but I've heard talk that he got Alzheimer's disease like his mother. Some people believe he wandered off somewhere. Poor man."

"Did Burt come here often?"

"Once or twice." She kept her voice low. "But he seemed a little out of the loop the last time he was here."

"The last time?"

"About a month ago—right before he was reported missing. I

didn't even know who he was until I saw a picture of him in the local paper days later. I never forget a face."

"You said Burt seemed out of the loop," Michael prompted her.

"I'll say." Teresa laughed. "He was having dinner here with another man. Both had white hair. At first I thought they were brothers. Most old folks look alike to me." She shrugged. "They ordered wine with their meal. As I was filling their glasses a second time, Burt told me his old friend had come to town for a visit. Customers make small talk with me all the time, so I didn't pay much attention, except that I noticed Burt's speech was slurred. I mean, he'd only had one glass of wine. By the end of the meal, he was unsteady on his feet. "

Michael leaned forward. "Did you get his friend's name?"

"No. We were busy, and it didn't interest me at the time."

"I hope Burt didn't drive back home," I said.

"In his condition?" Teresa laughed. "He needed help to walk out the door. I looked out the window and saw his friend help him get into the passenger side of the car parked out front, then they drove off. Days later, I found out Burt was reported missing. Kind of makes your blood run cold. You know what I mean?"

I encouraged her on. "Yes, it's very strange."

"Everyone is talking about how weird it is that he's gone missing. Of course, word is spreading about the corpse at your friends' place too. Residents aren't used to outsiders—" A lineup at the front of the restaurant caught Teresa's eye and she stood up. "Excuse me. I have to run. Enjoy your meal." She loudly greeted the people in line as if they were old friends.

Michael spoke in a quiet voice. "It appears we have a new mystery man in the area. He might be the last person to have seen Burt Garner alive."

"The description of a white-haired man isn't much to go on. It describes more than half the male population in Fernlea." I sipped my wine. "Then again, Burt told Teresa his friend was from out of town. She even saw Burt get into his friend's car after dinner. Now that's interesting."

"And what about the timing? They were here a month ago."

Our eyes locked as the realization set in.

My heart picked up speed. "It has to be the same car Larry told us about—the one that dropped Burt off at home one night before he went missing."

"His friend must have driven him straight home after dinner," Michael said. "It's only ten minutes away."

My mind replayed Teresa's comments. "Something's off."

"What?"

"Larry told us Burt walked up the path that night. He didn't mention Burt was wobbly or needed his friend's help like Teresa told us."

"Right. I doubt he'd burned off the effects of the wine within minutes."

"Larry saw him go out for a walk in the middle of the night. He seemed okay then too."

Michael paused, thinking. "It might not mean anything, but I wonder why Burt's friend didn't stay over at his place. These bungalows usually have two bedrooms."

"Maybe he didn't want to inconvenience Burt, so he stayed at a nearby hotel," I said.

"It's possible." He drank some wine.

"Larry could be right. Something happened to Burt when he went for that last walk. Now he's dead."

"The question is why. We need to find a motive. I'll touch base with Detective Cole tomorrow. See if he has any news."

I sipped more wine. "Are we still on track for our interview with Gabriella Garner?"

"You bet. We'll pay her a visit in the morning, but with Alzheimer's disease, I doubt she'll be able to help us much."

~

I woke up in the middle of the night, my throat parched. I needed a drink of water.

Michael was droning softly beside me. I rose from the bed, careful not to wake him, and tiptoed to the kitchenette. I reached for a bottle of spring water in the fridge. I took a few gulps, then moved to the window.

The sky was clear. The moon and a vast collection of stars glimmered above. I could make out several constellations, though I couldn't remember their names if my life depended on it.

I focused on the row of fir trees between Jessica's property and Burt's. Jessica and Ethan had reached an impasse in gaining more land to expand their resort. With Burt gone and his mother deemed incapable of handling her affairs, it was anyone's guess who would be managing their legal and financial matters now.

An object glinted near Burt's property. It only lasted a second. Maybe it was the moon reflecting off a stone.

No. There it was again. The glint was more pronounced this time and moving toward Burt's backyard.

My curiosity was aroused. I didn't dare wake Michael. He was sleeping so soundly. Besides, I was a big girl. I could take care of myself. I'd go see what it was all about.

I stopped. It wouldn't do to walk out the door only in my short cotton nightie, so I grabbed my denim jacket and slipped into it, then put on my shoes. It was my good luck that I wouldn't have to pass the other cabins to get to Burt's property.

Michael had left his flashlight on the kitchen table. I was about to take it, then changed my mind. I dug into my handbag, retrieved a smaller flashlight, and tucked it in my pocket.

I closed the cabin door quietly behind me, then ran across the lawn to Burt's property. The moon provided enough light to guide me along, so I didn't need my flashlight. At least, not yet.

I reached the side of Burt's house and stood there, listening. A choir of fluttering wings, chirping crickets, and rustling leaves heightened my alertness.

I stole a glimpse at the woods beyond the backyard. A futile exercise. I couldn't see a thing.

A clattering noise inside Burt's house startled me.

Someone was in the basement!

I stood a safe distance from the broken window so that whoever was in the basement couldn't see me. I slowly bent over and peeked inside. A light was moving back and forth—probably a flashlight.

The idea of returning to the cabin to get Michael popped into my mind. No, it would defeat the purpose. The intruder might be long gone by the time we returned.

What would Michael do if he were confronted with such a situation?

Forge ahead, no doubt.

I crept up the back stairs, keeping my flashlight on low beam. I didn't want to alert the intruder.

I approached the back door and slowly turned the handle. The door was unlocked. I realized too late that I'd forgotten to bring along a pair of vinyl gloves. My fingerprints were now embedded on the handle. I thought about wiping them off with the hem of my nightie but changed my mind. There might be other fingerprints on it by now—including the intruder's.

I walked lightly across the kitchen floor, one step at a time. If I could get to the carpeted hallway without...

A tiny creak emanated from the wood floor. I froze, expecting the intruder to come running up from the basement at any moment.

I waited. Nothing happened. I was safe. For now.

I aimed the flashlight upward at the cuckoo clock, almost daring it to blast forward. Of course, it wouldn't. It was fifteen minutes before the hour. That ridiculous thing only broke the sound barrier on the hour.

As I reached the carpeted area, relief trickled through me. I directed the beam from my flashlight along the wall until I spotted the door leading to the basement. It was closed.

Damn!

I edged closer to the door and listened for any noise.

It swung open and hit me on the head!

Dazed, I lost my balance and fell backward against the wall, dropping my flashlight. The low beam zoomed in on a pair of legs in running shoes tearing down the hallway toward the kitchen. A man's legs!

He suddenly tripped on the carpet and tumbled with a groan.

I lunged forward, latching onto him as he tried to escape, but I only managed to clutch his bare arm.

He tried to pull out of my grasp, but I held firm, digging my nails into his skin. As he tried to pry my fingers off his arm with his free hand, I felt a smooth finish—like plastic. He was wearing vinyl gloves!

I snagged his other arm and dug my nails in.

He kicked me in the shoulder. Hard.

I screamed and jerked back in pain, releasing my hold on him.

He scrambled out the back door.

Retrieving my flashlight, I ran through the kitchen and onto the porch. I aimed the flashlight around the property, hoping to catch another glimpse of the intruder.

Nothing. He couldn't possibly have crossed the backyard into the wooded area by now—I'd have seen him. Maybe he'd run off to the road.

I darted around the corner to the front of Burt's house. I switched the flashlight to high beam and aimed it around the property, then up and down the road.

No movement.

No sound.

I cut through the trees to Jessica's property and repeated the process, aiming the beam in all directions.

Nothing.

He'd vanished.

13

Michael aimed his phone at my shoulder and took several photos. "You should have come back here to get me. That's one nasty bruise."

"Tell me about it." I sat, unmoving, on the sofa.

He placed his phone aside, then reached for the first-aid kit.

As he applied ointment to my shoulder, I cried out, "Ouch! I didn't think he'd kicked me that hard."

"Your survival instincts took over. That's why you didn't feel it right away." He examined the bruise. "His kick was hard enough to leave a partial shoe imprint in the shape of an inverted V."

"I wasn't defenseless, you know. I fought back. I managed to scratch his arms."

"You should have come to get me when you first saw the light next door," Michael repeated for the third time since I'd returned to our cabin.

"Like I said, he would have been long gone by then."

"You could have been killed, Megan. You realize that, don't you?"

That much was true. I'd crossed the boundary from curious to daring and ended up with an ugly injured shoulder to prove it.

Yet the words spilled out of my mouth before I could contain the sarcasm. "Sorry. I promise I'll wake you up the next time."

He clenched his jaw, then stormed off to the bathroom to deposit the first-aid kit, mumbling something under his breath that sounded like "no next time."

He had a right to be angry. I'd shared similar feelings when two thugs had tried to thwart his investigations into organized crime. They had roughed him up—enough to send him to the hospital to get stitches on his face and treat a broken rib. His injuries had disturbed me so much that I'd voiced my angst about his safety for days. Compared to his experience, the intruder in Burt's house had let me off easy.

Michael resurfaced.

"We should tell the police what happened," I said. "It could lead to a break in the case."

"No way that's going to happen. Trespassing onto a crime scene can result in penalties."

"But we've done it before."

"We were lucky to get away with it." He briefly glanced down. "You said the back door to Burt's house hadn't been broken into."

"It was unlocked. Why?"

"It means whoever broke into the house can easily pick a lock. He's probably a pro."

"He also wore vinyl gloves." Fear rose inside me. "Oh, no! I didn't wear gloves. What if the police check for prints and find mine on the door handle? Like you said, they could accuse me of interfering with their investigation. Even press charges."

Michael sat next to me. "They probably finished collecting fingerprint evidence over there."

"So why did the police leave their yellow tape on the front and back doors?"

"They usually give it a few days in case they have to go back to further investigate the evidence."

I recalled the mess in Burt's basement. "What do you think the intruder was looking for? The boxes only held clothes, dishware, and other personal items."

"Maybe he thought there was something of value down there. It could be the same guy I chased the other night."

My mind took off on a tangent. "About the shoe imprint... Sam owns a pair of running shoes with tiny triangles on the soles. I'm not accusing him, but it sure is a coincidence."

"Most people around here wear running shoes with all kinds of grooves on their soles. I'd bet many of them would provide a partial match to your bruise."

"How are we going to find out who the intruder was? We can't start looking under everyone's shoes."

"Right." Michael checked the time on his phone. "It's three o'clock. Come on. Let's go back to bed. We need to sleep before we head out tomorrow."

"Out where?"

"We're visiting Burt's mother at the retirement home."

"Oh. I forgot about that."

My nerves tingled. I felt as if mixed emotions were about to explode after the unexpected assault I'd experienced.

My ego was drowning in self-pity, but I couldn't cry.

I was angry, but I couldn't file a complaint with the police.

I felt guilty. About what, I hadn't a clue.

That I could have fared much worse during the confrontation with my attacker hit me with full force. I started to shake. "I—I'm sorry, Michael. I don't know what came over me."

He wrapped his arms around me and held me close. "You're safe now. Everything's going to be okay. I promise."

Several hours' more sleep had done little to restore my mental and emotional functions to normal levels. It didn't help that my subconscious mind kept replaying scenes from my skirmish with the mysterious intruder next door.

Michael seemed like his old self—cool and collected. That he was able to sleep through the worst of circumstances continued to baffle me.

As we stepped outdoors and headed to Jessica's for breakfast, Foster Wade exited his cabin, a briefcase in hand. He saw us and waved us over.

"Good morning," he said. "Would you do me a favor and tell

Jessica I won't be having breakfast this morning? I'll be out for the rest of the day. Business meetings."

I took in his sports jacket, jeans, and running shoes. "Sure. By the way, we discovered that a second white truck left supplies in the shed Friday afternoon before the fire."

Foster gawked at us. "Really? What was the delivery?"

"A shipment of hardwood flooring for the extension to Jessica's house."

"Oh. Were they expecting it?"

"Yes and no. The company forgot to notify them about the delivery date. Are you sure you didn't pass their truck on your drive out from here Friday?"

"I'm sure. It must have arrived after I left."

"There are conflicting witness reports about the timeframe," Michael said. "The cops are investigating, so it shouldn't be long before they track down the vehicle that transported the corpse."

"Precisely what I was thinking," Foster said. "Any news on the identity of the victim?"

"From what we've heard, the investigation is still ongoing," Michael said, notching up another lie.

"These matters can take time." Foster fingered his car keys. "I'd better hurry. See you later." He got into his car and drove off.

We were crossing the lawn when my eye was drawn to the spot where the shed had once stood. A contractor had removed the charred mass of debris produced by the fire. The vacant area now offered a clear view of the dock and lake from this angle of the property.

Jeremy's canoe was tied to a post and rocked gently on the rippling water. Its presence confirmed that he was working on the grounds here.

A car honked behind us. Sam waved as he whizzed by, a few fishing rods visible in the back seat.

Michael chuckled. "I guess Sam found a new fishing spot."

As we neared Jessica's house, Jeremy came into view. In his usual work clothes and running shoes, he stood beside Amy, talking to her while she played in a red sandbox. We sauntered up to say hello.

I surveyed the straight wood borders of the sandbox. "Is this sandbox new?" I asked Jeremy.

His face radiated pride. "Yeah, I built it myself."

"Good job," Michael said to him.

"Cake." Amy giggled, then dug her hands into the sand and dumped bits of it into a blue pail.

Jeremy reached into the sandbox for a blue plastic shovel. "Here, Amy. Use this."

I noticed scratches on Jeremy's arms and nudged Michael.

"Been working hard, Jeremy?" he asked.

The boy shrugged. "Keeping busy."

"What are you working on today?"

"Gotta mow the lawn here. Gotta head out later down the road to fix a fence."

"It can be rough work sometimes."

"Yeah."

"Is that how you got those scratches on your arms?"

Jeremy quickly folded his arms. "Uh...sort of. Got those pruning shrubs at Burt's house."

"Jerm'y, wook." Amy tapped the full pale with her shovel and squealed with delight.

Jeremy laughed. "That's a great big cake, Amy."

Michael and I said goodbye, then made our way to the house.

"What do you think about those scratches?" I whispered to Michael. "Could he have been the intruder next door?"

"Let's not jump to conclusions," he said. "I don't think the boy makes a habit of telling lies."

"How can you be so sure?"

"Just a gut feeling."

His instincts were usually reliable. I let it go at that—for now.

Inside, we conveyed Foster's message to Jessica.

"I'm not surprised," she said, filling our cups with more coffee. "Our resident historian spends more time traveling from town to town than he does sleeping here."

Michael's phone rang. He answered. "Hi, Steve. Hang on a sec." He excused himself and stepped into the hallway.

"We saw Jeremy with Amy," I said to Jessica. "She loves her new sandbox."

"Isn't it pretty? Jeremy built it on his own time." She poured herself a cup of coffee, then sat at the table. "I don't know how we'd manage without him. He always does more than what we ask him to do. He tends to the flower boxes at each cabin. I used to do it, but then he told me how much he loves to pull out the weeds." She laughed.

I lowered my voice. "He doesn't suspect anything. About Burt, I mean."

"No. He still mows Burt's lawn because the man always paid him well. I think Burt tried to help him in any way he could. I help Jeremy too. I give him snacks when he's working here. He's so thin, I don't where he gets the energy to keep going all day."

"He loves what he does. It counts for a lot."

"For sure." Jessica sipped her coffee. "I've heard people say his father is a grouch. It's probably why Jeremy enjoys coming over here. If only Ethan would give the boy a chance."

Michael stepped into the kitchen and casually said, "It was the news desk in Montreal. They wanted to confirm details on a case I was following."

We'd been playing this "news desk" game for so long that I could interpret the meaning behind his choice of words. He had news to share with me later.

"Help yourself to an orange or some grapes." Jessica pointed to the fruit bowl on the table. "I'll fix us some scrambled eggs and toast in the meantime." She moved to the stove.

Michael put a bunch of grapes in his plate. "Have you heard from the detective?" he asked Jessica.

"Oh, thanks for reminding me," she said over her shoulder. "He dropped in last night. He told us the forensics team couldn't match any of the tire tracks here to the tires on the trucks from Build-a-Floor and Freeze-it Incorporated."

"Why not?"

"He said too many vehicles had traveled to and from the resort. And it rained the night of the fire. It was impossible to get a clear tire imprint off the road. He said the evidence was inconclusive. Ethan is so frustrated with the lack of progress in the investigation. He wants answers."

"Tell Ethan we're working on digging up other leads." Michael gave me a subtle wink.

~

Michael drove away from Jessica's Lodge with a smile on his face.

"Okay, spill the beans," I said to him. "What did you find out?"

"Steve confirmed that Chuck Dorey spent time in jail three years ago."

"What were the charges?"

"Manslaughter. The case was eventually thrown out of court."

"Why?"

"Too much time had passed from charge to trial," Michael said. "The Canadian justice system expects court proceedings to move in a timely manner."

Something nagged at me. "Why would Build-a-Floor hire Chuck if they knew he had a criminal record?"

"That's the hitch. There's no way they would know about it. Since the case didn't result in a conviction, his jail records were sealed."

"How did Steve find out?"

"He weaseled the information from one of his numerous Montreal sources."

"Are you saying Chuck is from Montreal?"

"Originally," Michael said. "He must have had a contact here. Someone who got him a job and made it easy for him to be accepted in the small community."

Something else bothered me. "Burt Garner and Chuck knew each other from work. Aside from having the same employer, I find it hard to believe they had anything else in common. Least of all, jail time."

"Steve already checked. There are no criminal records on Burt. Nothing about his life before Fernlea either. The guy's a mystery." He veered onto the highway.

"So is it even possible these two men were friends?"

Lines formed along Michael's brow. "All I know is that Chuck's attitude rubs me the wrong way."

I had an idea. "Why don't we follow him one night to find out if he's involved in anything shady?"

"Megan, sometimes you surprise me."

"Only sometimes?"

He laughed. "Okay. How about tailing Chuck tonight?"

"Count me in."

"I knew you'd jump at the opportunity."

"I might be down, but I'm not out."

14

—————

Nestled within a forest of tall evergreens and maple trees, the elegant brick and stone building stood on a sprawling plot of land. The modern four-story institution had a vaulted entrance supported by four white columns. Rows of colorful pansies bordering the front of the premises—their violet and pink faces brilliant with yellow centers—waved at us as we drove in.

Michael took a right toward the visitors' parking lot at the side of the retirement home. He slipped into an empty space and we stepped out.

"I hope Burt's mother can provide us with a clue to his disappearance," I said.

"It's a long shot," Michael said. "It depends to what extent her memory loss has progressed."

We entered the building and approached the front desk.

The hefty concierge, who looked more like a prison guard in his dark uniform, handed us a pen and motioned us toward a registry book. "Please sign here."

An aide wearing a light blue uniform and a cheery attitude strolled up to us. "Hello. Who are you visiting today?"

"Gabriella Garner," I said. "We called beforehand to arrange a visit."

"Please follow me."

She led us down a wide corridor. Framed prints of colorful landscapes decorated light beige walls. Signage boards listed various services supported by directional arrows to help residents find their way to the locations. I understood how important the simplicity of the signage was to residents suffering from memory loss.

The aide ushered us into a common room where a handful of residents were seated in armchairs, waiting for visitors to arrive. Windows were slightly open and blinds were raised, but an overcast sky barred any sunshine from filtering in.

"I'll go get Mrs. Garner," the aide said. "Please make yourselves comfortable."

As Michael and I settled on a sofa, all eyes in the room zoomed in on us. One white-haired woman smiled. A man sitting across from us waved. Their attention soon swung to the arrival of a family accompanied by another female aide. Three children broke away from their parents and scampered toward an older woman who I assumed was their grandmother.

The female aide who'd greeted us at the entrance wheeled Burt's mother into the room. "Look, Mrs. Garner. You have visitors today."

Mrs. Garner squinted at us from a face weathered by more than nine decades of living. "I don't know these people. Who are they?"

"They came here to visit with you." The aide positioned the wheelchair close to us. "Their names are Megan and Michael."

"Nice to meet you, Mrs. Garner." I held out my hand.

Michael did the same.

"Well, I'll leave you three to chat," the aide said. "I'll be nearby if you need me." She moved a short distance away to speak with another patient.

"Mrs. Garner, we'd like to talk to you about the old house," I said. "The one that you shared with your son, Burt."

At the mention of his name, Mrs. Garner perked up. "You know my son Burt?"

Evidently, the police hadn't told her that her son was dead.

"We're friends," I said.

"Friends?" She hesitated. "Oh, yes. I remember you now. You're his friend from school." Her face crinkled up in a smile.

"Mrs. Garner, do you remember the last time Burt came to see you?"

She pressed her lips. "Hmm...I think it was in the spring. He brought me a bouquet of flowers. Yellow daisies. He picked them from the field behind the high school. They last a long time, you know."

Michael leaned forward. "Did Burt ever mention any problems he might have had?"

"Oh, I don't know. Burt isn't much of a talker." She fingered the blanket on her lap. "Is my son in trouble?"

"No, it's nothing like that."

Her brow creased. "I warned him about staying out late with those nasty friends of his."

Nasty friends?

I questioned how much of what she said was reliable in today's context. "Did Burt have any problems with co-workers? His boss?"

Her manner lightened. "Burt gets along with everyone. His boss said he was a fine employee."

"So they haven't had any problems with him on the flooring installation sites either?"

Mrs. Garner blinked. "Flooring? You must be mistaken. My boy works evenings and weekends flipping burgers at the drive-through in town. He's going to college in September, you know."

My stomach sank. One of the symptoms of dementia was the ability of the patient to draw on memories from the past and believe they were actually occurring in the present. As of now, Mrs. Garner believed her son was still a teenager.

Michael diverted the topic. "Mrs. Garner, do you remember the house where you and Burt lived?"

"Of course I do," she said. "The only reason they brought me here was because they needed help with the gardening."

"The gardening?"

She smoothed the blanket covering her lap. "Burt is much too busy to take care of the garden. He has a lot of responsibilities. I only hope he stays away from those nasty boys."

"Have you met these boys?"

"No, but when Burt told me he had gambled and won a lot of

money, I knew something was wrong." She sighed. "Burt is no gambler."

My heart beat wildly.

Anticipation radiated from Michael. He asked Mrs. Garner, "What did Burt do with the money?"

Her eyes darted across the room as if she were trying to dredge up a forgotten memory. "I don't remember."

"Did he spend it?"

"Not at all." She laughed. "My boy isn't a spendthrift. He saves his money. He put it away." Her lips tightened. "In a place so far away that his horrid friends can't find it."

Burt's mother had redirected the conversation to a place we hadn't anticipated. An understanding passed between Michael and me, and he nodded for me to go on.

"Do you know where Burt hid the money?" I asked.

Mrs. Garner grew agitated. "Mustn't tell. Mustn't tell." She leaned forward and stared at the floor. "Dig. We have to dig." She gestured as if she were holding a shovel with both hands and made digging movements. "Dig. Mustn't tell."

I stretched out my hands, willing her to stop. "Mrs. Garner. Please, Mrs. Garner."

She didn't respond.

Michael shifted in his chair and looked around.

"Just one more shovelful." Mrs. Garner dug again, her breathing increasing. "Just one more." She kept repeating the words and the movements until the female aide rushed over.

"Mrs. Garner, it's okay." The aide placed her hands on the old woman's arms. "You can stop now. You're safe. It's okay."

As Mrs. Garner began to relax, her breathing eased. She stared into the distance, eyes glazed, her mind held captive by a memory that allowed no one else to access it.

The aide said to Michael and me, "That's all the time Mrs. Garner has for visitors today."

"I'm sorry if we disturbed her," I said.

"It's nothing you said or did. She goes into these repetitive sessions sometimes and thinks she's digging. We don't know what triggers them. Thanks for coming to visit her." She wheeled Mrs. Garner out of the room.

As we returned to the car, I asked Michael, "What do you make of the story about Burt gambling and hiding—or burying—his money? It's hard to believe it's only in Mrs. Garner's mind."

"Right," he said. "There are too many coincidences. My gut tells me Burt isn't who everyone thinks he is."

~

"This is a good spot." Michael parked the car down the road from Build-a-Floor. "The closing time on the store's business card says six o'clock." He checked the time. "One more hour to go before they close up shop."

"Three company vans are parked out front," I said. "Chuck has to be driving one of them."

Michael reached for a pair of binoculars from his satchel in the back seat. "Here. These should help."

We took turns surveying the parking lot. One by one, the vehicles pulled out, until only one company van and a red pick-up truck remained.

It was almost closing time. Michael sat back, eyes closed and ears plugged in to the music on his phone while I kept watch through the binoculars.

The front doors of Build-a-Floor swung open, and a man wearing a white baseball cap walked out. He slid behind the wheel of the pick-up truck and drove off. I focused on the front door and waited for a sign of Chuck.

Our car windows were down and the air hung heavy with humidity. Dark clouds had gathered overhead. Rain would only impede our surveillance.

Ten more minutes passed before Chuck emerged.

"There he is." I poked Michael in the arm.

He jolted upright.

Chuck locked the front door of Build-a-Floor, then hopped into the white cargo van and drove out of the parking lot. We waited a few seconds, then followed him up the road.

We were surprised when he took the highway and exited at Ostfield.

"Maybe he's stopping for a drink or a bite to eat with friends," Michael said.

But Chuck drove right through the town.

We almost lost sight of him at a main intersection when we hit a red light. Luckily, the traffic was light, and we glimpsed Chuck's van as he left the city core and hit the highway again.

Rain began to fall. Scattered drops immediately turned into heavy beads of hail. The bombarding sound inside the car was deafening.

"Keep track of him with the binoculars," Michael shouted above the noise. He peered through the windshield as the wipers struggled against the barrage. "This freak weather is only going to make things harder. Damn!"

Hail pelted the car, making it almost impossible to see Chuck's van. We nearly missed his right-hand signal when he took the exit onto Briar's Road.

"There won't be much traffic on this road," Michael said.

Anxiety swelled inside me. "What if he notices we're following him?"

"Don't worry. I'll stay back."

Our journey ended minutes later when Chuck turned left onto a private path bordered by a thick forest. Michael drove past his turn-off point and made a U-turn, then parked on the side of the road.

"Stay here," he said, making a move to step out of the car.

"Fat chance. I'm going with you." I grabbed our waterproof rain jackets from the back seat and handed him his.

It was a short, muddy walk along the side of the road to the path where Chuck had turned off. My running shoes would need a good cleaning after this little venture—if they survived.

We'd covered about fifty feet along the path when we spotted Chuck's van. It was parked in front of a two-story white pine cottage. A light over the front steps cast a glow on a blue-and-white striped cushion and a wicker chair on the adjoining porch. No other vehicles were visible, but that didn't mean anything. The two-car garage at the side of the house might be sheltering them.

Michael found a spot behind a clump of thick bushes where we could hide unseen and survey the premises. He pulled out his phone and took a photo of the van in front of the house. "Let's give Chuck some time. If he doesn't come out in a few minutes, we'll call it a night."

We waited.

Five minutes passed.

Then ten.

The rain slid down the hoods of our jackets and formed tiny pools at our feet. The temperature had cooled.

I shivered involuntarily. "What's taking him so long?"

"He's probably visiting family or a friend." Michael studied me with concern. "You're cold. Let's go. We're done here."

We were about to move when the front door clicked open. We ducked behind the shrubbery.

Chuck stepped out of the cottage and ran toward the van. A shorter man wearing mud boots and a short raincoat with a hood followed close behind. He turned to lock the front door before dashing into the passenger side of the van.

Michael and I huddled low until Chuck's van raced by.

I straightened up. "What if he sees our car at the side of the road and decides to go take a look?"

"I doubt it," Michael said. "They were in a big rush to get somewhere. Besides, neither of those guys would recognize our car. Let's go."

We hurried back to the car.

Michael sped up until we caught sight of Chuck's van. With no other vehicles on the road, it proved an easy target to track.

The rain continued to fall hard as we reached Ostfield. To top it off, a multi-car accident had taken place at a major intersection in town, and traffic was backed up. Police were merging vehicles into one lane and waving them through the intersection as if it were a four-way stop.

In addition to the rain blurring my vision, two more vehicles slipped into the lane ahead of us. "Uh-oh. I can't see Chuck's van anymore."

Michael squinted. "I can't see it either."

The slow-moving lane finally opened up into two lanes, and we picked up speed.

It didn't matter.

Chuck's van was nowhere to be seen.

Michael hit the steering wheel. "Damn! We lost him."

"It's not a complete write-off," I said. "Now we know where his friend lives."

"Right. We might be able to verify the address at the records office and get a name. Who knows where it might lead?"

15

———

Rainclouds lingered into the next morning. Although the gloomy atmosphere cast a somber mood over the resort, it hadn't diminished Foster's desire to further his research activities.

Since his car wasn't parked in front of his cabin, Michael and I assumed that the historian traveled to Ostfield yesterday and decided against driving back in the storm last night.

Sam's car wasn't there either, though we doubted his absence was due to an early morning fishing expedition. His behavior continued to be oddly suspicious in our books.

On our way to Jessica's house, we crossed paths with Mrs. Holt. She hurried out of the house carrying Amy in her arms, an overnight bag slung over her shoulder.

"Play wif Jerm'y," Amy said as tears ran down her cheeks.

"You can play with Jeremy tomorrow," Mrs. Holt said. She greeted us with a quick hello before whispering, "No decent woman should have to put up with the likes of that man." She rushed off to her SUV parked nearby.

Uh-oh. What had Ethan done now?

As we entered the kitchen, Jessica turned from the stove with a tear-stained face. "Oh... Good morning."

I put a hand on her arm. "Jessica, what's the matter?"

"Come. I'll show you." She led us into the living room and pointed at a hole in the wall. "Ethan did this."

"What happened?" Michael asked her.

She wiped her eyes. "Ethan had another temper tantrum at work yesterday. He said his co-workers were spreading rumors to prevent him from getting a promotion. He got into a shouting match with one of them. His boss sent him home yesterday with a final warning. He told Ethan to take time off and think seriously about the future of his job."

I gestured toward the wall. "When did this happen?"

"Last night, before we went to bed," Jessica said. "Detective Cole dropped by. He said the police hadn't made any progress in investigating the fire. They planned to do a media release about it and give out Burt Garner's name to gather any possible leads. Ethan was furious. He claimed it would hurt our business even more."

"So he punched the wall."

"Yes, but there's more. The detective hinted that we were potential suspects when he said we might have to answer more questions sooner or later. That pushed Ethan over the edge. After the detective left, he punched the wall. He'll be coming downstairs soon. I don't want him to see us here. Let's go back to the kitchen."

After we gathered at the table, I said, "Jessica, we're here to help you and Ethan. It might be best if we all discuss what's happening."

"No amount of talking has helped so far. Even Ethan's anger management sessions can't solve his problem. He's never behaved this way until we moved to Fernlea. I'm convinced that Ethan can't begin to get over the frustration he feels until the police solve this case. I'm frustrated too, but I have to be strong for him."

Ethan walked in, his right hand bandaged. He pulled up a chair next to Jessica. "Sorry, guys, I couldn't help overhearing." He turned to Jessica and took her hand in his, his eyes misty. "Jess, I apologize for my behavior. What I did was inexcusable. I know I frightened you, and I'm very, very sorry. I'd never hurt you, you know that. I want things to be good between us, the way they were before. I'm glad that you confided in Megan and Michael." He glanced at us. "I'm sure they're wondering what the hell is wrong with me too." He sniffed. "Maybe they can help me make things right again."

Jessica leaned over and gave him a hug. "You're a good man, Ethan. We're facing a lot of stressful challenges right now, but we'll work things out."

Ethan said to Michael and me, "Jess is right. The discovery of Burt's body on our property was bad enough, but now we have the police breathing down our necks. Not to mention the humiliation we suffer every time someone in town looks at us sideways—like we're from another planet and don't belong here. On top of that, I have to endure insults from jealous co-workers who step all over one another to climb the corporate ladder."

"We hear you," I said to Ethan. "Michael and I have always been there for you. Whatever problems you have, let's sit down and talk them over."

Ethan's phone rang and he answered. His demeanor turned serious. "Yes, I was calling about the delivery of hardwood you made here last Friday. You guys left it in our shed and we had a fire. The hardwood was destroyed. I'd like to place another order, but I'm not paying for it." A brief pause. "Why? Because no one called to say there would be a delivery Friday. You guys left the hardwood in our shed without our permission. I'm not paying extra for your mistakes." Ethan scowled. "You go ahead and do that." He slammed the phone on the table.

Jessica kept her voice calm. "What did they say, Ethan?"

"They'll have to check with their boss. Bunch of crooks."

Ethan's behavior baffled me. Was it even possible to exhibit such a range of mood swings in such a short time? Something was bothering him—that much was certain. Bullying and taunting at his workplace, getting the cold shoulder from neighbors, veiled accusations from the police...

These were legitimate reasons that might reasonably upset anyone, but were they enough to cause such erratic mood swings? Temper tantrums? Punching a wall?

Ethan was clearly out of control.

The image of Mrs. Holt whisking Amy away from the house flashed through my mind. It was unusual for her to babysit Amy if Ethan was home. Was she afraid to leave Amy with him?

Observing Ethan now, I squirmed in my seat. Mrs. Holt's earlier comment implied that she disapproved of Ethan. Had she always felt that way? Was Jessica telling us the truth about Ethan?

At the same time, it was possible that Mrs. Holt played a role—knowingly or not—in contributing to Ethan's mounting frustration. Despite Jessica's claim that it all started when they relocated here, his anger might have derived from something deeper than current events.

Jessica stood up. "I'll get breakfast ready. We have the kitchen to ourselves this morning."

"I'll help." Ethan reached for a container of eggs in the fridge.

It was a relief to see them function as a team in the kitchen. Gone was the stress of moments earlier when we'd been staring at a hole in the wall and listening to Ethan reprimand a clerk at Build-a-Floor. In its place was a quiet communication between husband and wife about the scrambled eggs, toasted bagels, and perked coffee they were preparing with synchronized timing.

Watching this latest display of Ethan's mood transitions reminded me of *Jekyll and Hyde.* Had Jessica lied to us about his mood swings being recent?

Soon our hosts served the plates and joined us at the table.

"By the way," Ethan said between bites. "The detective told us they examined the trucks from Freeze-it Incorporated and Build-a-Floor. The same ones that dropped off deliveries here on Friday. They're both clean. No blood splatter and no DNA that would link them to Burt Garner. Nothing. Next thing they're going to say is that the body fell from the sky."

"I'm sure the detective doesn't buy that silly theory, Ethan." Jessica sipped her coffee.

"You're right. They think we killed him, which is even more ridiculous." He grimaced.

"When was the detective planning on feeding the news to the media?" Michael asked.

"This morning," Ethan said. "The hourly news will probably run it. We can watch it in the living room."

Tires on gravel alerted us to vehicles outside. Doors opened and closed, and a clatter of noise ensued.

Ethan stood up and looked out the window. "Media vans. Do you believe it?" He raised his arms in frustration, anxiety flowing through him.

Crews unloaded and assembled video equipment. TV reporters, with their perfect hair and polished appearance, jostled one another to get the best spot for their interview.

"They're acting on the news report the police gave them," Michael said.

Ethan smirked. "Exactly what we need. Curiosity seekers."

"They're just doing their jobs," Michael said in defense of his fellow reporters.

"It won't be for long." Ethan pushed open the back door.

Jessica followed on his heels. "Remember to be polite, Ethan. Keep your answers short. And don't say more than what the police told us." She left the door ajar.

Reporters closed in as Jessica and Ethan made their appearance and bombarded the couple with questions.

Ethan held up a hand. "One at a time, please."

A male voice rose above the others. "We understand Burt Garner was your neighbor. How well did you know him?"

"We barely talked to the guy," Ethan said.

"Burt Garner's body was discovered in your shed after it caught fire. Was the fire the cause of his death?"

"Ask the cops."

"How did the corpse end up on your property?"

"We don't know," Ethan said.

Another reporter probed, "Do the police have any suspects?"

Frustration mounted in Ethan's voice. "Why don't you do your job and ask the cops instead of hassling us?"

Jessica gently touched Ethan's arm and said to reporters, "We know as much as you do. I'm sure the police will have updates as they discover more details."

Another female reporter asked, "Are you concerned about your family's safety?"

"Wouldn't you be?" Ethan barked.

Another question reached them. "Has the discovery of a corpse on your property hurt your lakeside business?"

Ethan put his arm around Jessica. "This interview is over. Get off my property." He abruptly steered her inside, then slammed the door behind him. "Damn reporters!" He clenched his fists.

Jessica gave Michael an apologetic shrug.

A glimpse outside confirmed the media crews were starting to pack up their gear.

"What a fiasco," Jessica said to no one in particular.

"What did you expect?" Ethan shouted. "They ask whatever the hell they want. Anything to get it on the evening broadcast." He checked the time. "It's on. Let's go watch it on TV."

Michael threw me a dubious look. What would the morning news broadcast do to Ethan's mood?

On our way to the living room, Ethan pointed a thumb toward the hole in the wall. "Ignore the décor. Someone is coming to fix the drywall later."

Michael gave him a friendly pat on the shoulder. "I thought your man cave had everything you needed for stress release."

Ethan responded with a sheepish grin. "I know. I lost my cool. I'm trying, though."

His reply annoyed me. If the press conference was an indicator of his latest attempt at controlling his anger, he wasn't trying hard enough.

We settled on the sofas and watched intently as the local news broadcast began. After a major national story, the topic moved closer to home.

The banner at the bottom of the screen read: "Scorched body found at Jessica's Lodge." The video was clearly taken with a cell phone and showed firefighters dousing the fire. A subsequent clip lingered on the burnt shed.

Jessica gasped. "That's horrible!"

Ethan watched in horror too. "Who the hell took a video of the fire and gave it to the media?" He looked at Michael.

"Not me." Michael raised his hands in the air. "I was with you all evening."

"It must have been one of the guests," Jessica said.

The announcer ended his report with a plea to the public to come forward with any information about the victim. Then a commercial aired.

Michael calmly said to Ethan and Jessica, "It was no accident that they used your shed as a dumping site for Burt's body. It was a deliberate attempt to hurt you as outsiders. Someone wants to set you up as murder suspects."

Ethan nodded. "That's exactly what I've been saying all along. Someone is out to get us."

My pulse raced as I recalled my attack in Burt's house. "I agree. This is definitely serious—and personal."

Jessica paled. "What on earth are we supposed to do?"

"Maybe you should give your mother a call to make sure she's aware." I gave her a knowing look.

"Yes, I have to warn Mom." Jessica reached for her phone. "Mom? Did you watch the latest newscast?" Anxiety flashed in her eyes, then relief. "Good idea. So Amy's okay? Good. I'll talk to you later." She ended the call. "Mom is terrified. She bolted all the doors right after the news aired."

"I've heard enough." Ethan grabbed the remote and was about to shut off the TV when a familiar face appeared on screen.

"Wait," I said. "I know that man."

"So do I," Jessica said. "That's Ted, the owner of Vincent's Meat Shop."

Ted stood in front of a cluster of microphones. His wife and two young children stood by his side. Two OPP officers stood behind him, including Detective Cole. In a live news conference, a distraught Ted appealed to the public for help in finding his father, Vincent, who hadn't arrived at work this morning in Ostfield.

"It's not like my father to disappear and not tell anyone," Ted said. "He loves his family too much." His lips quivered. "Dad, if you hear this, please call us. We're here, in front of your home, waiting for you. Whatever the problem is, we can work it out. We love you."

The photo of a heavyset man with thick bushy eyebrows appeared on the screen. A brief description of Vincent Bouchard accompanied it.

"How sad," Jessica said. "Vincent is such a cheerful man. He loves people and his job and enjoys sharing jokes."

As the next clip panned to the landscape behind Ted, it sent a shiver down my spine. The scene was eerily familiar—a two-story white pine cottage bordered by a dense forest. A wicker chair with a striped blue-and-white cushion sat on the porch.

What were the chances that two identical cottages had been built along the same highway, not to mention each having the same chair and cushion on a porch? It had to be the same cottage we'd seen when we followed Chuck last night.

Astounded, I grabbed Michael's hand. He returned a troubled glance.

The detective stepped up to the microphones and encouraged the public to contact the OPP tip line with any leads they might have. He refused to answer questions from reporters and quickly wrapped up the conference.

Ethan turned off the TV. "What the hell is happening around here these days?"

"Poor Ted." Jessica wrapped her arms around herself. "His family must be going crazy." To Michael and me, she said, "You were here Monday morning when Vincent dropped off a delivery, right?"

"Yes," I said. "I hope they find him soon."

Michael rose to his feet. "Yeah, I hope so too."

I followed his cue and stood up.

"You're leaving already?" Ethan asked. "I thought we'd play a game of pool or something, Michael."

"Maybe later. Megan and I have some errands to run."

"Okay. Drop in any time. I'll be home all day."

I didn't have to ask Michael where we were going when he dug out his car keys. It was all about doing the right thing.

16

—————

Michael concentrated on the road ahead. "About the cottage we saw on the news, the detective might still be on site. It would save us a trip to the police station."

"Exactly what I was thinking," I said.

Michael slowed down along Briar's Road and veered onto the path to Vincent's property. His hunch proved correct.

Two OPP vehicles were parked in front of the cottage. Yellow police tape cordoned off the property.

As we stepped out of the car, a uniformed officer approached us, waving his hands. "You can't park here. It's private property."

"We need to talk to Detective Cole." Michael gave him our names. "We have a lead in this case."

Stepping away briskly, the officer spoke into his two-way radio, then walked back to us. "Detective Sergeant Cole will meet with you. Please wait here."

The detective promptly opened the front door. He stepped out and hurried up to us. "You're the last two people I expected to see here. What's up?"

Michael began. "We saw Ted Bouchard's press conference. We might have a lead about his father."

"Go on."

"Megan and I were here last night. We saw Vincent Bouchard leave the house with a guy driving a white van."

The detective reached into his jacket for a notebook and pen. "Any idea who the other guy was?"

"An employee named Chuck Dorey. He works at Build-a-Floor. I took a photo of the van when it was parked here." Michael retrieved the photo on his phone and showed it to him.

"Send me a copy." The detective wrote in his notebook. "How do you know Chuck?"

"Megan and I met him once when we visited Build-a-Floor."

"My friends, the Bryants, bought their wood flooring there," I said.

Awareness flickered in the detective's eyes. "Yes, I remember. They had a problem with the hardwood delivery."

He hadn't admitted as much, but I had no doubt he'd spoken with Chuck during the course of his investigation into Burt Garner's disappearance.

The detective asked, "What were you doing here in the first place?"

"We followed the white van last evening after it left Build-a-Floor," Michael said.

"Why?"

"I had a gut feeling about Chuck. My sources revealed he spent time in jail for manslaughter but wasn't convicted."

The detective grimaced. "That's hardly solid evidence." He tapped his notebook. "Did Chuck drive straight here from Build-a-Floor?"

"Yes."

"Did you follow the van when he and Vincent left here too?"

"Yes."

"Where did they go?"

"Toward Ostfield. We lost sight of the van at an intersection. There was an accident and cops were redirecting traffic."

The detective scribbled in his notebook. "Can you tell me what Vincent was wearing when you saw him?"

"A short raincoat with a hood and mud boots," I said.

"Did he willingly get into the van?"

"Yes. He opened the door on the passenger side and got in."

"Anything else you can tell me?"

"No," I said.

"Detective, on another topic," Michael said, "the Bryants told us you made a clean sweep of the two delivery trucks that accessed their property last Friday. They said you found no evidence to link either truck to Burt Garner."

"Nothing incriminating." Detective Cole tucked away his notebook and pen. "If you remember anything else that can help us locate Vincent Bouchard, you know how to reach me." He approached the officer who'd greeted us when we arrived and said, "We're done here. Keep the place cordoned off for the next day or two. It keeps trespassers away."

As we drove by a landscape lush with tall evergreens and leafy trees, I mulled over recent events. For all we knew, Vincent Bouchard might be dead by now, his body dumped deep inside this almost impenetrable forest.

Though Michael kept his attention on the road, I could tell the wheels were turning in his mind. He was probably forming a theory based on what Detective Cole had told us.

And so was I. "What do you think the detective meant when he said they found 'nothing incriminating' in the delivery trucks?"

"Maybe forensics found evidence of some sort, but the cops couldn't label it as incriminating," Michael said. "If Chuck picked Burt up every morning and dropped him off after work, maybe they found Burt's DNA in the Build-a-Floor van. It would be inconclusive at best."

"Since we saw them together, it would be easy to assume that Chuck is linked to Vincent's disappearance too."

"Could be. The detective will probably run a second test on Chuck's van. Standard procedure. This time it'll be for Vincent's DNA. I wouldn't be surprised if they don't find any substantive evidence there either."

"The connection between Chuck and Vincent is baffling."

"At first glance, it looks as if Vincent wanted to install new wood flooring and contacted the only company around here that does it. Both men work during the day, so they met after hours."

"You're not buying that flooring theory, are you?"

"No way." Michael chuckled. "Vincent's disappearance is too coincidental. Chuck is involved. I'd bet my life on it."

"Something else bothers me," I said.

"What?"

"I heard Detective Cole say the yellow police tape would stay up for a while, which could mean—"

"They have probable cause for suspecting foul play."

Fulfilling our promise to Burt Garner's neighbor in town, we paid him a visit.

Larry Caplan opened the front door, then grinned. "Oh, it's you young folks again. Friends of Burt's. What brings you to this neighborhood?" He stepped outside and left the door behind him ajar.

"We promised we'd come back to give you news about Burt," I said.

Larry's expression was hopeful. "Have they found him?"

A lump formed in my throat.

Michael caught my hesitation and asked Larry, "You didn't catch the news on TV?"

"No, I haven't been feeling too good lately," he said. "The rain makes my arthritis act up."

"I'm sorry to have to tell you this, but Burt is dead."

Larry gaped at him. "Are you sure?"

"Yes," Michael said. "The police issued a statement to the media this morning."

"Oh, that's too bad. How did he die?"

"They didn't state the cause of death."

"Oh." Larry's head drooped more than usual. "You know, Burt told me once how he wanted to travel one day, maybe sell his property and head down south." His eyes misted up. "It was a funny comment coming from someone who never bought a car and didn't like spending money on restaurant food." His gaze drifted to the house across the street. "I guess this means Burt won't be coming back. I'll have to cancel the lawn maintenance for his property."

I found my voice. "We're sorry for your loss, Larry."

He blinked. "I should go now. Thanks for dropping by, folks." He pushed open the door and slowly stepped inside.

Back at Jessica's Lodge, we found Jeremy pulling weeds from the flower box outside our cabin. As we neared, he wiped his forehead with the back of his gloved hand. His eyes were bloodshot, as if he'd been crying.

The first words out of his mouth were, "I heard that Burt died."

I empathized with the boy. It must have come as a shock to him. I swallowed hard. "I'm so sorry, Jeremy. I know you and Burt were friends."

"Burt was a nice man. I'm going to miss him." He looked down with sadness, then up at us again. "My dad says it's not safe in Fernlea like it used to be. He says it's because too many new people moved here. But I think Jessica is nice. Amy is nice too. And they're new people."

"Some people are like weeds. Others are like flowers. If you get rid of the weeds, there will always be more flowers than weeds."

Jeremy examined the flower box, then turned to me with a smile. "I have to tell my dad about that. Michael, bad guys are like weeds, aren't they?"

"That's right," Michael said.

"Jessica said you were a reporter and that you catch bad guys."

"Yes, I'm a reporter. And yes, sometimes reporters help to catch the bad guys."

Jeremy pulled off his garden gloves. "A bad guy killed my friend Burt. Do you think you can catch him?"

"What bad guy?"

"I don't know. He digs holes in Burt's backyard next door when he thinks no one is watching. I thought a groundhog had done it, but my dad says groundhogs dig tunnels—not holes all over the place."

Michael asked, "Did you see this person digging?"

"No, but I heard noises one night," Jeremy said. "Shovel noises. I was too chicken to go see." He kicked a stone with his foot.

My adrenaline surged. "You did good to stay back. He could have hurt you."

"Yeah, I know," Jeremy said. "My dad would have been mad at me too."

Michael pressed for more details. "What were you doing out here late at night?"

"I wanted to set a trap for the groundhog," Jeremy said. "I got fed up with filling the holes on everyone's properties. That was before my dad put me straight about the groundhog."

"Whose properties?"

A door clicked open and Foster walked out of his cabin. He waved at us. "Michael, are you free to come over? You too, Megan."

"Sure," Michael said. "Give us a minute."

"Okay." Foster went back inside.

So Foster had returned from his trip. So had Sam, judging from the car parked next to his cabin. Was it an odd coincidence that both men had returned to the lodge at the same time?

Silly me. I was probably making too much of it.

Jeremy picked up his garden tools. "I gotta go. Got work down the road." He turned to leave.

"Wait," I said. "You mentioned there were holes on people's properties. Whose properties are they?"

Jeremy kept on walking and said over his shoulder, "Burt's old house next door. Jessica's too. Oh... Burt's other house in town." He scurried across the lawn.

Foster handed each of us a cold bottle of water, then took one for himself. "Sam Norton is following me. Every time I drive out of here, he's on my tail. I'd like you to check him out, Michael."

Michael did a double take. "Me? Why not ask the police?"

"In this small town?" Foster scoffed. "They'd be hard-pressed to find the guidebook on the subject."

Michael twisted the cap off his bottle and took a sip. "The cops have already spoken with Sam. He's been cleared."

"As far as the fire is concerned, perhaps. But shadowing me around town is a different matter."

"Have you confronted Sam?"

"No. I invited you here to talk about it." He drank some water. "I think he's trying to find out about my research."

"You think he's a journalist?"

"Not at all," Foster said. "More like a gold bullion thief."

Michael leaned forward. "One of the trio involved in the famous Montreal robbery?"

Foster nodded. "One of Rusty Homer's two accomplices, to be precise. I hadn't considered it before, but Sam would be about the same age as them."

"You never did describe Rusty Homer," I said.

"I'll try, but those baggy uniforms the inmates wear don't help. Let's see..." Foster rubbed his chin. "I'd say he was of average height with a slim build. Gray hair. Brown eyes. Oh...he had a scar along his left cheek—probably from one of his brawls in jail."

"Would you happen to have a recent photo of him?"

His attention briefly wandered to his notebook and the pile of papers on the table. "No, I was too busy shaking in my boots during that interview to remember to ask for one. Anyway, it's not important right now." Annoyance laced his raspy voice. "Look, I'm trying to tell you that Sam could be one of Rusty Homer's two accomplices."

"There's no way we can prove Sam is who you claim he might be." Michael sliced the air with his hand to get the point across. "To begin with, we don't even know the names of those two accomplices or what they look like."

"What you do have is the detective's ear." Foster raised an eyebrow.

If anything, Foster was presumptuous. I reached for my water bottle and took a few sips, eager to see Michael's reaction.

Michael sat back, his response increasingly guarded. "We can't assume Sam is guilty of anything without proof. I'm sorry, Foster, but I can't help you. You should talk to Sam directly."

My shoulder still ached from the swift kick I'd received from the intruder in Burt's house. An image of the running shoes I'd seen on Sam's feet the other day flashed through my mind. Could Sam have been the intruder in Burt's home?

"Michael, I don't know if approaching Sam is a good idea. What if Foster is right about him? He could put his life in danger. He should talk to Detective Cole first."

Michael was insistent. "Like I said, Foster, you need proof. The cops won't do anything without substantial evidence."

Foster's eyes darkened. "Then I'll go find it."

17

———

We found no updates online for Vincent Bouchard, other than Ted's renewed appeal to the public for tips leading to his father's whereabouts.

"I feel so sorry for Ted and his family," I said. "I wish we could help him find his father somehow."

The intense look on Michael's face told me he was devising a strategy to that effect. "I have an idea," he said. "Let's go back to Vincent's cottage tonight. We might find something that ties in with his disappearance."

"But the police must have already swept through his home for clues."

"There's aways the chance they could have missed something."

~

We waited until dark, then took the highway out of Fernlea. Michael had to swerve to avoid a raccoon that scurried across our path and road kill that had met an untimely fate—namely a skunk.

Even though he suspected that Detective Cole didn't have the budget to post an officer full-time at Vincent's cottage, he switched to low beams when he turned onto the path leading up to it. He parked the car a safe distance from the house in case someone might unexpectedly be there.

Unlike the evening before, the air was cool and the sky was clear. The rain had stopped earlier, though the heavy downpour last night had most likely washed away any trace of tire tracks—specifically, those of the Build-a-Floor van. Other then our photo and testimony, Detective Cole had no proof that Chuck might be implicated in Vincent's disappearance.

Yellow police tape still bordered the front of the property. The cottage was in darkness. The outdoor fixtures weren't lit.

As often happened at quasi break-ins Michael and I initiated, my moral compass flashed a warning sign.

I ignored it. It wasn't as if we were planning to steal anything. Logic maintained that we were breaking into someone's home for a good reason. The end justified the means, so to speak.

We crept along the side of the house, using our flashlights to guide us around. We peeked through the windows for any sign that someone might be inside.

"We're clear to go." Michael tucked his flashlight under his arm. He dug out a pair of plastic gloves and pulled them on.

I turned off my flashlight and dropped it in my pocket. I pulled on my plastic gloves. I wouldn't make the same mistake twice.

A stone walkway led us to the backyard and opened up into an expansive patio. Michael's flashlight revealed a gazebo over a wrought-iron table and four lounging chairs. To our right was a small tool shed. To our left was a rectangular in-ground pool. A thick layer of leafy debris from last night's downpour had fallen onto the plastic sheet covering the pool.

"Let's go." Michael climbed the stone steps stretching to the back door of the cottage.

I hesitated. My apprehension barometer had kicked up a notch. "Are you sure you want to go through with this, Michael? What if someone pops up?"

"Look at it this way. How else are we going to find clues that might explain Vincent's disappearance? We agreed we'd try to help his son Ted, right?"

That much was true. We didn't expect Detective Cole to share any leads he'd discovered. We were definitely on our own.

Michael handed me his flashlight.

I aimed the beam at the door while he fiddled with the lock pick.

"We're in." Michael opened the door a crack.

We stepped inside, our senses alert to anything that might suggest someone else was here. We removed our wet shoes and left them on a mat by the door.

The ceramic flooring was cold, and I was glad I'd worn socks.

Michael aimed the flashlight around the room. Polished white marble countertops. Dark mahogany cabinets. Gleaming copper pots hanging over an island. No cuckoo clock, thank goodness.

He whispered, "Let's move on."

I spoke in a normal tone. "Why are you whispering?"

"It's a habit, I guess."

"Only when you break into someone's home, you mean." I laughed.

"You got it."

We moved from the kitchen into a spacious foyer, the same ceramic tiles underfoot. To the left was the living room, furnished with a mounted TV above a fireplace and comfy fabric sofas and armchairs. Wood flooring replaced ceramic tile here and felt less cold under my feet. On the coffee table, a wine decanter and four glasses sat on a tray next to a selection of hardcover books. One title read: *The Wines of France*.

To the right of the foyer was the dining room housing a polished wood table and eight chairs. A matching hutch containing elegant chinaware formed the backdrop along one wall and was bordered by framed photos—probably family members. A crystal chandelier hung from the ceiling and reflected the moonlight filtering in through soft woven curtains. The same wood flooring enhanced the room here as in the living room.

The decorating scheme so far was fancy—and expensive. Not something I'd expected to see in the home of an unpretentious, hard-working man who enjoyed making deliveries and chatting with customers.

Burt's house next door to Jessica's Lodge came to mind. Unlike the modest furnishings in that home, the décor in Vincent's cottage hinted of a professional touch. His lifetime investment in the meat shop meant he could afford upscale services that catered to his expensive taste—or those of his decorator.

I retrieved my flashlight and aimed it at the wall by the front door. "Vincent has an alarm system."

Michael examined the panel. "It isn't activated. His family wouldn't have had access to the house otherwise. Nor the cops."

I inadvertently swung the beam toward the floor and gasped. "Aren't those Vincent's mud boots?"

Michael lifted the boots and shone his flashlight on them. "They're still wet." He put them down.

"Oh, good. It means he's okay. He must have dropped them off before he left the house again." On a whim, I opened the closet in the foyer and aimed my flashlight inside. "Vincent's raincoat is here too. It's damp." I lowered my voice to a whisper. "Oh, my God! What if he's in the house? He could be asleep upstairs."

"Let's go see," Michael said.

"What? Are you crazy?" My whisper was hoarse with fear.

"If he is here, he has a lot of questions to answer."

My heart thumped faster.

What if Vincent was in the house and woke up? Did Michael have a Plan B?

We cautiously mounted the wood stairs leading to the upper floor. The tiny nightlight on the landing glowed softly, revealing two bedrooms and a bathroom. Their doors were wide open

I stood beside Michael at the entrance to one of the bedrooms. The beam from his flashlight revealed a queen bed topped with decorative pillows. A dresser, a short bookcase, and a small TV on a stand completed the room. The bed hadn't been slept in recently. I assumed it was a guest bedroom.

The bottom drawer in the dresser was open. I crossed the wood floor and looked inside. Empty. The bathroom was next. I directed my flashlight inside and tiptoed across the tiled floor. I slowly pulled back the shower curtains.

Nothing.

I exhaled.

We moved on to the master bedroom. I felt like Goldilocks about to check out the next bed.

A wave of my flashlight around the room disclosed an old-fashioned four-poster king bed. The sheets had been pulled down.

I let out a sigh of relief to find no one here too.

Michael directed the beam from his flashlight around the room. To the far right, two armchairs sat by a corner fireplace. The only thing amiss was the armoire in the opposite corner. The drawers had been open, their contents strewn over the floor.

"Someone came looking for something," I whispered.

"This doesn't sit right with me. Let's go visit the en-suite bathroom."

My pulse sped up. Ted had mentioned that his mother had passed away last year and that his father had been somewhat depressed.

Had Vincent taken his own life? Would we find him dead in the shower or the bathtub?

A quick peek inside the bathroom revealed that the counter drawers were open. I aimed my flashlight inside them. Men's toiletries. Nothing more.

Michael examined the shower stall. "Drops of water. It's been used recently."

I inspected the roman tub. "The tub is dry."

"I guess we're done here." He headed back into the bedroom.

I trailed close behind. "Wait."

"What is it?"

"Something you said about wood flooring and Vincent... Ah, yes. Here's proof that Vincent wouldn't have met with Chuck to arrange for wood flooring to be installed here." I aimed my flashlight at the bedroom floor. "These wood floors are in good shape. So is the wood flooring on the main floor."

"Right. So there's more to their connection than we know. I hope the detective took us seriously and is investigating Chuck." He turned and headed for the stairs.

I'd taken a step forward when something on the floor caught my eye. A tiny white feather.

My pulse quickened. Madame Ora's words echoed in my mind. It meant the imminent discovery of another corpse.

No. She was wrong this time. There was no dead body in Vincent's cottage. The feather probably came from a pillow. I stepped over it and followed Michael downstairs to the foyer.

"Too bad we didn't find anything." I walked past him and toward the kitchen.

"Not so fast," Michael said. "We forgot the basement and the garage." He opened the door to the garage and flicked on the switch. "Now this is interesting."

I peeked over his shoulder to see a white cargo van. It had no inscription on the side panel. "It must be the van Vincent uses to make deliveries for the meat shop."

"Yeah. The cement floor is dry, so the van hasn't been driven recently. Let's see." He opened the passenger door and got in. He leaned over to the side, then stepped out. "There's nothing in the glove compartment except the vehicle license and documents. Nothing in the cab section either. Let's go down to the basement."

We went down a flight of carpeted stairs. To my surprise, we found a finished basement akin to a bachelor pad with a wet bar and a small kitchenette.

"This is so cool," Michael said. "Hey, there's another door at the back." He swung it open and aimed his flashlight inside.

My jaw dropped at the sight of a butcher table and an assortment of knives. Then I remembered. "Ted told us his father had once worked from home as a butcher."

"I'll bet he has more fun these days making deliveries for the store and chatting with customers."

"He even has a huge freezer." I pointed my flashlight at it.

Michael pulled open the lid. "It's empty, except for a few drops of water at the bottom." He shut the lid. "Okay, let's go."

Upstairs, we put on our shoes and left. Michael made sure the back door was firmly closed and locked.

As we stepped onto the patio in the backyard, he stopped. "Wait. We forgot the pool."

"The pool?" My voice sounded small.

He didn't answer but headed directly for it.

I aimed the beam from my flashlight at the plastic cover as he pulled it back.

He bent over the edge, pointing his flashlight at the water. "There's something dark at the bottom. I need more light."

We aimed our flashlights at the water.

I screamed and recoiled in horror, the flashlight flying out of my hand.

Michael swore and bounded backward. "Looks like we just found Vincent."

18

———————

The discovery of Vincent Bouchard's body at the bottom of the pool left a lasting imprint on my mind. I would never forget the look of confusion and terror on his face, the way his eyes stared wide open, as if he were asking why fate had been so cruel to him.

Michael wrapped his jacket around me and held me close while we waited for the police. Despite his soothing words, I couldn't stop shivering. The cool night air only emphasized the emotional shock I'd experienced from finding another dead body—yet another testament to Madame Ora's prediction.

Upon their arrival, Detective Cole and his officers secured the scene with yellow tape, ignoring us beyond a suspicious glance. Another half hour passed before the coroner and the forensics team appeared. After they took crime scene photos and collected evidence, they wheeled away Vincent's draped body.

Detective Cole finally strode up to us. His bulky figure loomed against the backdrop of portable spotlights the forensics team had set up in the backyard.

"Michael, your name came up in discussions with my police colleagues in Montreal," he said. "They had nothing but praise for your investigative work."

Relief flooded through me. We wouldn't be treated as suspects.

The detective switched his attention to me. "I guess you're in it for the ride."

Michael tightened his arm around me. "Megan is my research associate. We sometimes work as a team."

"Oh." The detective threw a wry smile my way. "Well, I can't wait to hear how you both happened to be in the vicinity of yet another dead body, namely Vincent Bouchard." He retrieved a notebook and pen from his pocket. "Care to tell me what brought you here this time?"

Since Michael and I had agreed earlier that we wouldn't mention our illegal entry into Vincent's cottage, we winged it.

"A gut feeling," Michael said. "Vincent's son, Ted, told us how his mother's death last year had affected his father. He implied that Vincent had a tendency to become depressed."

"You know the family?"

"Only Ted."

The detective raised an eyebrow. "So you came here because you had a 'gut feeling' his father was dead in the swimming pool?"

Michael ignored the sarcasm. "Our coming here was a fluke."

"A fluke?"

To his credit, Michael improvised. "We saw the news broadcast earlier and thought Ted might still be here. We wanted to help him find his father."

"I guess you just did." The detective looked at me. "What's your story, Megan?"

"I came along for the ride," I said, tongue-in-cheek.

The detective raised a pen in the air. "Gotcha." He studied us. "I've been wondering if I should add both of you to our payroll. On second thought, maybe I should add your names to our list of persons of interest."

His expression showed no emotion. I couldn't tell if he was joking or annoyed.

"We wouldn't be here if we weren't concerned," Michael said.

A uniformed officer approached Detective Cole. "A word, sir?"

The detective stepped aside and conferred with him for a few moments. "Keep me posted," he said, dismissing the officer.

My heart beat wildly. Michael and I had been careful not to

disturb anything. Whatever the police had found, I hoped it wouldn't lead back to us.

The detective approached us. "We found mud boots and a raincoat presumably belonging to the victim. They're still wet." He stared hard at me, more for strategic effect than anything else, I'd gathered by now. "You told me Vincent was wearing these items when you saw him leave his home last night."

"That's right," I said. "I guess he was still wearing them when he came back here."

"Which would be…"

I stated the obvious. "Some time between last night and now."

A knowing smile played on the detective's lips. "Forensics will narrow the timeframe. And the coroner will eventually release a statement regarding the cause of death."

"Any idea when you'll get the preliminary results?" Michael asked.

The detective's forehead furrowed. "Hard to say. The coroner covers a large area and has a lot on his plate these days."

∼

Michael answered a call from Ted Bouchard the next morning. He wanted to meet with us. Since he expected reporters to descend on Vincent's Meat Shop once the media announced his father's death, he suggested we meet at his home in Ostfield instead.

We'd barely had five hours of sleep the night before, but it didn't diminish our curiosity. Since Ted had taken the extra step of contacting Jessica to get Michael's phone number, we figured he had critical information to share.

Ted's two-story stone house and three-car garage bordered a crescent-shaped driveway. His comfortable lifestyle was most likely derived from the business his father had established years ago. He was no doubt reminded of it every time he walked through the doors of Vincent's Meat Shop.

Ted invited us into his sprawling living room. Rich earthy tones in furniture and accessories created an inviting setting. I imagined informal get-togethers with family and friends in front of the widescreen TV that spanned the width of a wall. The topic of our discussion this morning would certainly feel out of place.

"After the police came here last night to give me the news," Ted said, "I sent my wife and two kids to her sister's place. I wanted to spare them the anxiety of having to deal with... You know."

"We're sorry for your loss," I said.

"Thank you." Ted gathered his thoughts. "The police told me how you'd gone to my father's place and made the discovery. How did you know to go there?"

"We saw the TV broadcast earlier." Michael used the same reason he'd given Detective Cole but then added an extra bit. "We located your father's address and wanted to meet with you to offer our help."

"My father's passing is still fresh in my mind. I'm having a hard time believing it. I half-expect him to ring me at any moment and ask if there are any deliveries." He blinked. "Can I get you some coffee? Tea?"

I didn't want to cause him any trouble. "No, thanks. We're fine."

Ted grew quiet. "The way my father died is baffling. Things don't make sense."

"The police are investigating his death," Michael said. "Have you mentioned your concerns to them?"

"Yes, but I doubt anything will come of it. It sounds as if they're understaffed." He gave Michael a perceptive look. "You said you're an investigative reporter, right?"

"Right. Would you like Megan and me to do a little digging?"

Ted hesitated, as if he were weighing the possibility. "I might have something for you." He reached for a flash drive on a corner table. "My father gave me this in an envelope about a month ago. He'd written a note on the envelope, something to the effect that I was to open it only if something happened to him." He fought to maintain control of his emotions.

I felt his pain. I'd lost my father to cancer years ago and, although it hadn't happened as suddenly as in Ted's case, the grief was intense and enduring.

Ted went on. "I sensed that something had been bothering my father lately. He seemed distant at times. My first thought was that he was dying from a fatal disease, but he denied it. He told me he'd done

some bad things in his life and deeply regretted it. He'd covered up
the guilt all his life and hoped that his family would forgive him."

"Bad things?" I repeated.

Michael leaned forward. "How bad?"

"If you'd known my father, you'd have thought it was the most
unbelievable thing he'd ever said. The man was practically a saint.
Every Christmas, he delivered food baskets anonymously to twenty-
four families. Every first weekend of the month, he held a raffle for a
free grocery order at the store. I could go on and on. There were so
many instances where he showed his generosity. I can't begin to name
them all." His shoulders sagged. "And now he's dead."

"How can we help?" Michael asked.

"This is for you." He handed him the flash drive.

"What's on it?"

"A letter from my father. A personal confession of sorts. I made
copies, so you can keep this flash drive."

Michael slipped it in his pocket. "Did you give a copy to the
police?"

"Yes. Since my father was well known in the community, they'll be
issuing a press release about his passing. They might have preliminary results from the autopsy by then, but I'm not holding my
breath."

"What do you mean?" I asked Ted.

"I'm a successful businessman. I believe in getting things done
swiftly and efficiently. I can't afford to waste time. I want answers
now."

"We'll explore all avenues," Michael said.

"Let me start you off on the right track. My father had too much to
live for. He'd never kill himself. I think he was murdered."

19

———

The first thing Michael did when we returned to our cabin was insert the flash drive in his laptop. We sat at the kitchen table and read Vincent's letter off the screen:

"Dear Ted,

Your mother and I had a happy marriage and were doubly blessed the day you were born. It's no secret that I miss her terribly, and I know you do too.

If you're reading this, it's because my spirit has left to join your mother's. I pray I'll be rewarded for the good deeds I've done and that God will have mercy on me for the bad ones.

A man I knew decades ago has recently passed away under mysterious circumstances. As reckless juveniles, we spent the same period of time in jail for petty theft. That's right, your old man isn't as perfect as you thought. I won't tell you my friend's name because I wouldn't want to give more grief to those who might know him. Let's call him Dizzy.

Dizzy and I remained buddies for years. We stole, gambled, and managed to avoid getting caught through sheer luck.

A professional thief approached us one day. He needed our help in carrying out a major robbery in Montreal involving ten million dollars in gold bullion and cash. This guy was the real deal.

Dizzy and I were impressed, so we agreed. If you've never heard of this armed robbery, you can look it up on the Internet. It took place in the 1990s and was one of the largest heists in Canadian history."

Goosebumps rose along my arms. "Vincent was one of Rusty Homer's two accomplices!"

Michael kept his attention on the screen. "This solves a huge piece of the puzzle. Let's read on."

"Looking back, I realize how gullible Dizzy and I were. We thought it was cool that a pro would choose us to help load the loot from the robbery and drive the getaway van.

The sad part of the heist was that a police officer was shot and killed as we were trying to get away. No, son, I did not kill him, but I know who did. He was the mastermind who recruited us for the robbery, the genius who taught us how to use disguises and wear plastic gloves so we didn't leave prints at crime scenes.

Dizzy and I panicked when the police arrived at the site of the robbery. We drove off with most of the loot, leaving our mentor behind. Dizzy drove the getaway van into Ontario where I asked him to drop me off, and we went our separate ways. He took off with the stolen goods, but it didn't matter to me. I was so scared. I hoped we'd never run into each other again. I got my wish.

After I arrived in Ostfield, I made a new life for myself. The town was booming with new business, and I was lucky to land a job at a new butcher shop. I was even luckier that the police never caught up with me.

What happened to my mentor, you might ask.

He spent the last twenty-five years behind bars. Now he's out and it's payback time. He's looking to get even and to recoup the loot from the robbery. His name is Rusty Homer. And I just found out he's coming after me.

This evil man works in the shadows and hires minions to do his dirty work, like he did with Dizzy and me. He tracked me down in

Ostfield not too long ago and threatened to tell the police about my involvement in the Montreal robbery if I didn't hand over the loot. I told him I didn't know where it was, that Dizzy had taken it all, and that I hadn't a clue where he was. I think he believed me or else he would have killed me on the spot. I'd seen him fatally shoot that police officer with no hesitation.

The scary thing about Rusty is that you never know what he's really thinking. What he wanted from me was one last favor. I wrote this letter because I had a feeling that, after I did him the favor, my time would soon be up.

I've done some awful things in my life, but I'll never share them with anyone—especially not with you. I'll take those memories to the grave with me. It's better that way. I don't want to burden you with my guilt. It's not what this letter is about anyway. I only want to give you a heads-up about the devil on my tail. I doubt he'll come after you. It's me he wants. If anything happens to me unexpectedly, give the police a copy of this letter. It will explain a lot of things.

Be happy, Ted. Enjoy your family and friends. Life is too short for regrets. Your mother and I will be waiting for you on the other side.

Love forever,

—Dad"

Excitement ran through my veins, and I couldn't get the words out fast enough. "Foster told us that Rusty's two accomplices in the gold bullion heist might be living in the area. That part in the letter about Vincent's teenage friend... I think Dizzy and Burt Garner are one and the same."

"Yes. Yes." Michael pumped a fist in the air. "It all makes sense now."

I jumped out of my chair and paced the floor, my anticipation mounting. "Then Burt and Vincent would be the two partners involved in the 1990s Montreal robbery with Rusty Homer."

My mind flashed back to Mrs. Garner. Her timing was off, but her long-term recollection of Burt's "nasty" friends was right on the money—literally.

Michael mulled things over. "Burt and Vincent were about the same age. Their deaths are suspicious and occurred in quick succession. If Vincent was right about a threat, Rusty Homer went after them. It's all falling into place."

A tiny doubt trickled in. "Are we jumping to conclusions? What if their deaths are a coincidence?"

His eyes sparkled. "Absolutely not. The pieces fit. We just have to prove it."

A frightening realization sunk in. "Rusty Homer tracked down his partners, but he's still out there. Jessica and Ethan are not out of danger yet."

"From Rusty or one of his minions."

"Chuck could be one of his minions. If he's working for Rusty, he might be responsible for both deaths."

Michael leaned back and put his hands behind his head. "Hard not to suspect as much. That guy keeps popping up everywhere. Rusty Homer has been virtually invisible, but Chuck hasn't."

"Are you saying Chuck is Rusty Homer?"

"No way. Chuck is a thickset guy. He doesn't fit the physical description Foster gave us."

"We've been through this before, but what about Sam Norton? Maybe he works for Rusty Homer."

Michael sat upright. "I'm not buying any of Foster's suspicions about him. We have no solid evidence that Sam is involved in any of this."

"I could give you the same argument about our elusive Rusty Homer." I folded my arms. "Zero on the evidence scale."

"Then we'll keep going until we find it."

I tried another approach. "The police can't prove Burt and Vincent were accomplices in the Montreal robbery. All we have as evidence is the letter Vincent wrote to his son. He talks about doing a favor for Rusty Homer. Do you think the police might consider Vincent's letter as sufficient proof of their connection?"

"It's a start." He paused for a moment. "About the freezer in Vincent's basement... It would have been so convenient to store—"

"I was thinking the same thing. It might be the favor Vincent was referring to." I shuddered at the notion of Vincent storing his friend's body in his freezer. "We have to find Rusty Homer."

"That's a pretty tall order. We don't even know what the scumbag looks like today or where he is."

"We should talk to Foster Wade. He might have stumbled on more information. You'll have to wheedle it out of him, though. During our last meeting, he seemed more interested in getting *your* help than offering his own."

Michael reached for his phone. "I'll check with Steve first. See if he has an update on our notorious ex-con."

While he called the newsroom, I evaluated our assumptions. What if we were right? What if two teens who had been partners in crime decades ago had unwittingly ended up living minutes away from each other? It was feasible. That they'd avoided contact with each other afterward was understandable. Vincent had wanted to distance himself from anything to do with the Montreal robbery—especially the stolen money.

As for Burt Garner—also known as Dizzy—he would have had a difficult time trading in gold bars for cash. If each bar carried the mintmark of a producer and a serial number, it would have been traceable to the robbery. He had no doubt stored them in a safe place until he figured out what to do with them.

Michael ended his call. "Steve's source couldn't find a recent photo of Rusty Homer. He did confide that Rusty got into so many fights in jail, he needed reconstructive surgery to fix his face."

"Never mind surgery," I said. "Twenty-five years behind bars would change anyone's appearance. If I had to eat the food they served, I'd look like a hag in no time."

Michael walked up to me. "You'd never look like a hag. Not in a million years." He kissed me on the lips.

Butterflies stirred inside me and my knees went weak, the way his kisses always affected me.

He slowly pulled away. "Okay. We'd better get going before I forget what we're supposed to be doing next."

"Which is...?"

"Visit our resident historian."

I lingered by the door before stepping outside. "Michael, let's not share too much information with Foster. We don't know what gossip gets around these days."

"Right. The last thing we want to do is interfere with Detective Cole's investigation into these latest deaths."

"Do the names Burt Garner and Vincent Bouchard mean anything to you?" Michael asked Foster.

Foster pushed aside several envelopes on his kitchen table, snagging one on his long-sleeved cardigan. He gently tugged at it and placed it aside. "No. Who are they?"

"Local residents in their mid-fifties who recently passed away under suspicious circumstances," Michael said, holding back details as we'd agreed. "We thought they might be linked to the Montreal robbery you told us about."

Foster chuckled while he arranged a pile of papers. "Wouldn't that be convenient? Why do you think they might be connected?"

"Burt Garner was the co-owner of the house next door to this property," I said. "The police are investigating his death."

"Burt Garner... Oh, the guy they found in the fire?" Foster pointed with his chin toward the area where the shed had once stood.

"Yes. There was a recent news report about it."

Recognition registered in his eyes. "Yes, I remember now. I saw the coverage on TV at a local pub one night." He pressed his lips together. "Ethan didn't get along with him at all."

"Did Ethan tell you that?"

"Not directly. He ranted about his neighbor at breakfast a few times. You know, contempt breeds anger, and anger leads to violence if we don't curb it. In retrospect, I wonder if Ethan—" He waved the rest away.

I wasn't about to let his comment pass without reacting to it. "Are you insinuating that Ethan could have killed Burt Garner?"

"Not at all. I was going to say that Ethan must feel bad about having bad-mouthed his neighbor. We all feel regret for one reason or another when someone we know has died." He gave me a shrewd look. "Anyway, getting back to Burt Garner... Did I miss something? What is it that makes you think he was linked to the Montreal robbery?"

"Call it a hunch," Michael said.

Foster tipped his head from side to side. "That's not much to go on. What was the other name you mentioned?"

"Vincent Bouchard," I said. "He was found dead in his swimming pool."

"I didn't hear anything about it on the news."

"He worked at a meat shop in Ostfield and was well known locally. The police suspect foul play, but they're waiting for preliminary autopsy results. They should be holding a press conference soon."

Foster grinned. "It's gratifying to see that the police in small towns are informing the public about these incidents."

"Gratifying?" I echoed.

Foster blinked. "Sorry. I get my words confused sometimes. Reassuring. That's what I meant."

"From your recent trips, have you found out anything more about Rusty Homer's accomplices?" Michael asked him.

"No, I've been too busy with my research on local history."

"What about Sam Norton? Is he still tailing you?"

"Well... I might have exaggerated somewhat." He bowed his head. "I paid him a visit one night. He told me he spent a lot of time sightseeing in and around town this week, like I did. You should see the stuff he picked up for his grandkids." He chuckled.

"It might be a ploy," I said. "A cover-up to conceal his real identity."

"I thought so too at first," Foster said. "But then, the way Sam talked about his family was so convincing, I didn't know what to think anymore." He shrugged. "I have better things to do anyway." He made a move to get up. "Well, if that's all the questions you—"

"Hold on," Michael said. "You told us you didn't have a recent photo of Rusty Homer. Is there a slight chance you'd be able to identify him if you saw him on the street?"

"Maybe. If I were looking for him, that is."

"Aren't you?"

Foster shook his head. "Not really. Since I already have Rusty Homer's side of events, why would I go chasing a ghost? I mean, I might pass him on the street and not even know it. And since you believe he's seeking retribution, I'll leave that hunting trip up to you."

Annoyance filtered through Michael's voice. "Why the sudden change in plans? You led us to believe that finding Rusty Homer was your goal."

"From what you've told me, I think you're more interested in tracking down his accomplices. Getting your breaking story into the historical book I'm writing would be a feather in my cap as well as yours." He winked at him.

"What if they're already dead?"

"That would be unfortunate. But history is always about the past, isn't it?" He grinned, then checked his watch. "I have to beg off here. I have a meeting with a heritage group."

I stood up, prompting Michael to do the same. "We've taken too much of your time already."

"Nonsense. I love talking to young people. It makes me feel alive." Foster smiled. He grabbed his notebook and followed us out the door. "Have a good day." He slid behind the wheel of his car and drove off.

"Talk about throwing us a curveball," Michael said.

"Yet he still expects you to help him solve the cold case," I said. "It takes some nerve."

"Forget Foster. We'll help Ted Bouchard figure out if his father's past caught up to him."

Jessica called out at us from across the lawn. "Can you come over?"

As we neared, I noticed she was crying. In her hand was a clear plastic sleeve containing a letter and an envelope. "Jessica, what's wrong?"

She held up the bag. "I got another anonymous letter today. They're threatening to kill Ethan and me if we don't leave town."

20

———————

This morning's leftover breakfast sausages and scrambled eggs infused the air with a stench that made me queasy. A stack of dishes filled the kitchen sink. Pots and pans lingered on the stovetop. Something had definitely disturbed Jessica's routine.

Michael and I examined the letter and envelope that Jessica had slipped into a plastic sleeve. Letters cut out from newspapers were pasted on a white sheet of paper. The message read: "Get out of town now, you murderers, before it's too late!"

Sitting at the table across from us, Jessica dabbed at silent tears that rolled down her face. "It's exactly like the other one."

Had I misunderstood her? "You received another letter?"

"Yes. A few days ago. We thought it was a prank, that some crazy person was blaming us for Burt Garner's death."

"Do you still have it?"

"Yes." She walked over to the counter and retrieved another plastic sleeve from a drawer. "Ethan wanted me to throw it out, but I kept it. The women's shelter where I worked used to receive threatening letters on a regular basis. I know a real one when I see it." She placed the sleeve containing the first letter and envelope on the table, then sat back down.

The first letter displayed the same message as the second one.

The only difference was that the cutouts from the newspaper were more skewed in the first one. It was as if the sender had experimented with the first letter and managed to place the cutouts straighter the second time around.

"Clever of you to have put those letters in sleeves," Michael said to Jessica. "Have you told the police yet?"

"Yes, they're on their way here. As for fingerprints, only Ethan and I handled the letters, and our prints are already on file with the police. They have been since the day Burt's body was found here."

"Where's Ethan?"

"Battling his demons in the man cave. Feel free to join him before he wrecks the place."

"I will." Michael squeezed my shoulder, then strode out of the room.

"It's almost time for lunch." Jessica frowned at the load of dishes in the sink. "I haven't had time to clean up after breakfast. All Ethan and I did was argue this morning after I showed him the second letter." She dug a fresh tissue out of her pocket and blew her nose.

"You stay put." I stood up. "I'll take care of the dishes. What did Ethan say about the second letter?"

"He had the same knee-jerk reaction as the first time. He thinks we should sell the property and move out. You should have seen him, Megan. He reacted like a raging lunatic. I told him to calm down, so he headed for the man cave. Then I phoned the police to tell them about the letter. I was coming over to see you and Michael. That's when I lost it."

I stacked the dishes in the dishwasher. "Where's Amy?"

"Mom came to pick her up earlier. That poor woman. At least she didn't have to witness this second outburst. The first one was bad enough."

"Oh?"

"She was here when we received the first letter." Jessica rose from her chair and moved toward me. "Ethan said it was her fault and blamed her for insisting that we move to Fernlea. Then Mom accused Ethan of being egotistic and ungrateful. It was getting pretty ugly between them, so Mom left. I wish Ethan would control his temper around her. I don't know if I ever told you. Mom helped us get the mortgage on this place."

I pretended I didn't know. "Oh."

She leaned against the counter. "She's been so good to us. It's not as if she ever asked for anything in return. Well... We did agree to her suggestion that we name the resort Jessica's Lodge. It was a small request. No big deal—considering how much she helped us. The least we can do is let her spend as much time as she wants with her granddaughter, who adores her by the way."

"You have a perfect arrangement, Jessica. What's the problem?"

"Ethan is the problem." She raised her hands in annoyance. "He looks at everything in a negative way. He feels as if Mom is taking Amy away from him. Every time they're in the same room, an argument starts up between them. Ethan says she never lets him forget that this place is called Jessica's Lodge."

I put myself in Ethan's shoes. "It's possible he feels out of place. I'm sure he wants to feel connected to the family—especially to Amy. He worked long hours at the office and missed doing things that parents normally do with their kids. Now that he's taken some time off, maybe things will change."

"I don't know about that. His mood swings have become so unpredictable. With all that's been happening lately, I think Mom's home provides a less stressful atmosphere for Amy."

I couldn't argue with that. A fire that destroyed their shed and new freezer, the discovery of a corpse, two threatening letters, and erratic mood swings would add stress to any household.

Jessica digressed to another subject. "Oh... Remember that newscast we watched the other day? The one where Ted appealed to the public to help find his father?"

The vision of Vincent's body at the bottom of the pool sprung to mind. "Uh...."

She misinterpreted my reply. "Vincent, the middle-aged, heavyset man who made a delivery here from the meat shop. You remember him, don't you?"

"Yes, yes."

"We heard on the news that the poor man was found dead in his swimming pool last night." Sadness filtered through her voice. "He seemed so happy and easygoing. How do these horrible things happen?"

"Well—"

There was a knock at the back door. It was Detective Cole.

Jessica invited him in. After she asked Ethan and Michael to come upstairs, we all gathered in the living room.

Jessica handed the detective the two plastic sleeves. "Ethan and I are the only ones who touched these letters."

He gave them a cursory glance, then slipped them into his portfolio. "We'll run the usual forensics tests on them."

"How long before you get the results?" Ethan asked.

Detective Cole pulled out a pen and notepad. "Not any time soon. Having to drive out here so often isn't helping any."

Ethan glared at him. "You make it sound as if it's our fault someone sent us these letters. You know, Detective, I live in constant fear that something horrible is going to happen to my wife, my child, or me." He turned to Jessica. "We should sell the property and leave this damned town."

The detective kept his cool. "I understand you're under a lot of pressure these days. Let's study the situation rationally and not do anything rash. Okay?"

Jessica reached for Ethan's hand, and he relaxed somewhat.

The detective asked the usual who, when, and where questions regarding the retrieval of the letters from the mailbox. Then he ventured into another area. "Can either of you think of anyone at work that might want to harm you?"

"No," Jessica said. "The employees at the public records office where I work part-time are the friendliest people."

"I wish I could say the same," Ethan said. "There's the usual employee rivalry where I work. You know, jealousy, the race up the corporate ladder... Stuff like that."

The detective eyed him. "So there's tension between you and the other co-workers?"

"Some."

"Physical tension?"

Everyone went silent.

Jessica nudged Ethan. "Tell him."

Ethan complied. "There was an incident—a scuffle—at work with another employee. He was bad-mouthing me. The company put me on stress leave."

The detective took notes. "How about this place? Any guests who might be holding a grudge against either of you for one reason or another?"

"We've had no complaints or problems," Jessica said. "Our guests love the resort."

The detective scribbled another note. "How about neighbors? Other residents?"

"We haven't met any of the neighbors, except for Burt Garner," Jessica said.

Detective Cole put away his notepad and pen. "I don't know of another family in this town who's had as many problems as you folks. I have to say that the events of this last week have been the most puzzling I've ever encountered."

Ethan stuck out his chin. "How many outsiders actually tough it out after the community rejects them?"

The detective stiffened. "Well, I—"

"Detective," Jessica cut him off, perhaps to prevent another outburst from Ethan, "do you know anything more about how Burt Garner's body ended up in our shed?"

"As you already know, we considered the possibility that delivery people from Freeze-It or Build-a-Floor could have been involved in transporting the corpse. Our forensics team proved otherwise. They found no trace of Burt Garner's DNA in the trucks that arrived here. In fact, they tested the entire fleet of vehicles belonging to those two companies and found nothing."

Oh, hell. Forensics had tested *all* the trucks at Build-a-Floor. It meant Chuck was off the hook.

"This wraps it up for now." Detective Cole pushed himself out of the armchair. "I'll get back to you as soon as I have these two letters processed by forensics."

Michael stood up. "Detective, can Megan and I have a word with you in private about another matter?"

He gave us a nod. "Let's take it outside."

We followed him to the cruiser parked behind the house.

He dropped his portfolio in the front seat, then asked us, "What's up?"

"I'm working on a cold case file at my news desk in Montreal," Michael said. "It involves a major robbery in that city in the 1990s. Rusty Homer was the mastermind behind it. His two partners escaped with millions in gold bullion and cash and were never caught. Their identities were unknown."

The detective retrieved his notebook and pen. "Rusty...Homer." He scribbled a note. "The name is familiar."

"Ted Bouchard gave us a copy of his father's letter. He told us you have a copy too. His father mentions Rusty Homer in the letter."

The detective raised his pen. "Yes, I remember now. My team is following up on the information contained in it."

Michael continued. "In the letter, Vincent Bouchard refers to Dizzy, his young friend and partner in crime. We believe Dizzy was Burt Garner."

Interest registered on the detective's face. "You're implying that Burt Garner and Vincent Bouchard were the getaway partners in that 1990s robbery?"

"Yes, it all fits. Rusty Homer spent twenty-five years in jail for shooting a police officer at the scene of the robbery and was released months ago. Word is that he's in the area and seeking revenge against his partners. He's also searching for the stolen loot."

The detective studied him, silent for a moment. "Where are you leading with this?"

"Sources imply that Burt Garner and Vincent Bouchard spent time behind bars for minor offenses when they were teenagers," Michael said. "Can the OPP verify if they were in jail at the same time? It would prove they knew each other from way back."

"Where's the jail?"

"In Montreal."

The detective took down the information. "You said they were juveniles at the time?"

"Yes."

"It might be a problem." His forehead creased. "The RCMP expunges minor crime records after a certain number of years if the perpetrators haven't committed any other crimes as adults. Even if it turns out that the records are still on file, you wouldn't be privy to the information."

"I understand, but it's worth the long shot," Michael said. "If the two men knew each other and were partners in the 1990s robbery, it's a step forward in proving that they were murdered by Rusty Homer. Or one of his minions, like Chuck at Build-a-Floor."

"You got this information from your sources too?"

"Not exactly, but they confirmed that Chuck was in jail at the same time as Rusty Homer. The two men could have met. Call it a coincidence, but the fact we saw Chuck with Vincent before he died is suspicious in itself."

I waited for a reaction from the detective, but his expression remained poker-faced as he took more notes. "If Rusty Homer is in the area, he'll stand out like a thorn among the good folks. I'll look him up in the database."

"He's had facial surgery," I said. "He might not resemble his mug shot at all."

"I'll give it a try anyway." The detective put his notepad away. "We follow every lead we get—even if it sounds far-fetched. I'll get back to you."

21

———

Jessica clutched the phone in one hand and gestured wildly with the other. "What do you mean, you can't find her?"

Ethan stood staring at her, arms folded. He addressed Michael and me as we walked back inside after our discussion with Detective Cole. "My mother-in-law can't find Amy. Who the hell loses a kid?" He passed a hand over his face in frustration.

"Okay, Mom. I'll do that." Jessica ended the call. She looked at Ethan, her expression strained. "Mom said she didn't leave Amy alone for more than a minute. Can you stay here while I go over there?"

"Can I help?" I asked her.

"Yes, please," she said. "Michael, do you mind staying here?"

"I don't need a babysitter." Ethan clenched his jaw.

Jessica softened her approach. "One of us should stay here in case Amy wandered down the road toward home."

"Fine," Ethan said, still livid. "It beats going over there."

Would Amy have simply walked away from Mrs. Holt's home? Unlikely, but kids can be unpredictable. I didn't want to increase the friction in the room, so I held back from voicing my thoughts.

Michael tapped Ethan on the shoulder. "Come on. Let's go check outside in case."

"Jessica, we should help them search before we drive to your mother's house," I said.

"Okay," she said. "Let's split up. It'll go faster."

Jessica searched the house.

Ethan and Michael scanned the river's edge.

I knocked on the occupied guest cabins. Since Jessica had locked up the empty cabins, I wouldn't have to bother with them.

Foster opened the door to his cabin. He held a phone to his ear and immediately put the caller on hold. "This is a nice surprise, Megan. I just got back."

I had no time for niceties. "Amy is missing. Have you seen her?"

"Amy?"

"Jessica's little girl."

"Oh, my, that's troubling." His forehead puckered. "No, I haven't seen her. Has she wandered off in this direction?" He stuck his head out and surveyed the area.

"No. She went missing from her grandmother's house down the road."

"Children are curious by nature. Maybe she trotted off and fell asleep somewhere."

"Maybe." Behind him, the tabletop was covered in papers. "Sorry to have bothered you, Foster."

Sam's cabin was next. I knocked.

He opened the door at once but didn't seem surprised to see me. "Hi, Megan. I saw you heading this way."

"We're searching for Amy, the Bryants' little girl," I said. "She went missing from her grandmother's house not far from here."

"Oh. It sounds serious."

"Have you seen her?"

"No, I haven't. I've been inside the cabin all morning. Catching up on some reading material I picked up in town." He waved toward a pile of books on the table behind him, then turned back to me. "What can I do to help?"

"If you see Amy, please notify the family."

"I certainly will." As an afterthought, Sam added, "If you need help, let me know. I have experience in such matters."

"Experience?"

"In tracking down people."

Oh, I'm sure you do.

I crossed the lawn and ventured into Burt's backyard. If Amy had come this far, she might have grown disoriented or tired and fallen asleep on the porch.

"Hi, there." Jeremy appeared out of nowhere.

I jumped. "Oh... Hi, Jeremy."

He took a few steps toward me. "I heard about the old man who died in his swimming pool in Ostfield."

My pulse increased at the memory of the gruesome discovery the other night. "You mean Vincent Bouchard."

"Yeah. Jessica told me how nice he was and how much she'd miss him." He kicked a stone. "The cops said they don't know how he died. My dad was right. It's dangerous these days. We have to be careful. We have to protect the ones we love."

"Those are pretty deep thoughts."

"My dad is smart. He reads a lot. Me, not so much. I like to work with my hands."

"You've done an amazing job with Jessica's property. She told us she was happy with your work."

Jeremy smiled. "She told me that too." He hesitated. "Well, I'd better go." He started to walk away.

"Wait," I called after him. "We're looking for Amy. Have you seen her?"

"Amy?" Confusion washed over his face.

"She's missing."

Jeremy looked down. "No. She's not missing."

My heart picked up speed. "Do you know where she is?"

"Amy is..." He hesitated, kicked a stone across the lawn. "She's with her grandma."

My hopes were dashed. "No, Amy went missing from her grandma's home."

"Oh."

"Will you help us search for her?"

He grew flustered. "I—I can't. I gotta go. I got a job to do." He slipped into the woods behind Burt's property.

Jeremy's behavior was beyond weird. For someone who was so

protective of Amy, I'd expected he would have gone berserk to find out she was missing.

And what was he doing in the woods behind Burt's old house anyway?

I was tempted to follow him, but I couldn't abandon Jessica for a probable wild goose chase. After I checked Burt's porch and saw no sign of Amy, I cut through the row of trees and headed back to Jessica's house.

The others soon joined me. Their disheartened appearance told me they hadn't found Amy either.

"We'll take the SUV," Jessica said to me, clutching her keys. "Amy is probably playing hide-and-seek at my Mom's somewhere. She loves that game. See you guys later."

Jessica was putting on a brave front for Ethan. She'd often done the same for me whenever I experienced a personal setback or had a bad day at work.

She didn't say a word on the drive to her mother's house. She didn't have to. The anxiety that she exuded now betrayed the hopefulness she'd mimicked moments earlier.

She drove the SUV up the road in record time. All the while, I kept watch for Amy on the off chance that she might have wandered from her grandmother's house.

But there was no sign of the little girl.

Jessica had just parked the SUV in front of Mrs. Holt's home when the woman rushed out, tears streaming down her ashen face. "Oh, Jessica. I still haven't found Amy."

Jessica scrambled out. "Mom, tell me what happened."

Mrs. Holt dabbed at her eyes with a tissue. "We were putting together the pieces of a puzzle on the kitchen table. You know, the one with the penguins in the snow." She took a deep breath. "Amy seemed to be quite busy with it, so I went to the laundry room to check on a batch of clothes and—"

"Mom, get to the point."

Mrs. Holt placed a hand on her chest and took another deep breath. "Not more than a minute passed before I returned to the kitchen. Amy wasn't there. I called out her name. There was no answer. I looked in the bathroom, but she wasn't there either. I thought she might have gone outside, even though I know Amy isn't strong enough to open the doors from the inside."

Jessica turned to me. "Mom's right. Amy can't open the front and back doors in this house. I've seen her try. She's not strong enough to pull the lever down."

"Do you keep your doors locked?" I asked Mrs. Holt.

"Locked?" she repeated. "Never. Except for the other day when Jessica called me. I locked the front door. It's still locked. No one locks their doors around here anyway. It's safe."

"Let's search the house before we call the police," Jessica said.

We split up, each of us taking a floor. After we'd searched inside every closet, under every bed, and inside every storage bin in Mrs. Holt's four-bedroom home, we extended our search outdoors.

Jessica began to tremble when she found Amy's favorite teddy bear on the back porch. "Amy never goes anywhere without Pokey."

The brown bear was dirty and spindly and probably earned its name from the fact that it had only one eye—a black button that had been sewed on.

"This bear goes to bed with Amy every night and comes along on every car trip," Jessica said. "She always has it with her. I have to call the police before it's too late."

Detective Cole's arrival at Mrs. Holt's home seemed like a replay of episodes in which we'd recently taken part. The main difference this time was that the subject of the tragedy hit much closer to home and tore into our hearts.

After the detective had taken our statements, he asked Mrs. Holt, "Did you have any visitors here today? Any service people?"

Mrs. Holt balled up a tissue in her hand. "No. Nobody." She blinked. "Yes. Jeremy came over to fix part of the fence around my property."

"What time did he leave?"

"I'm not sure. I went out on the back porch right after Amy—" Her words caught in her throat. "Jeremy usually sits under the large oak tree behind my property when he takes a break or has lunch, but he wasn't there ."

"I saw Jeremy on Burt Garner's property before we drove here," I said.

Detective Cole didn't spare the irony. "That boy sure gets around fast. How does he travel? By jet?"

"By canoe," Jessica said. "He paddles across the lake."

The detective asked Mrs. Holt, "Have you checked to see if his canoe is docked at your property? He could have paddled back here."

"I'll go see." Jessica ran out the back door.

I followed her out onto the porch.

She surveyed the lake. "I don't see a canoe. I'll run over there to make sure…" Her words drifted away as she put space between us and dashed toward the water's edge.

Mrs. Holt and Detective Cole joined me on the porch.

Jessica's mother hadn't stopped crying since the moment we arrived. "It's all my fault. I shouldn't have left Amy alone. If anything ever happened to her—"

"Now, Fiona, don't do this to yourself." The detective placed a hand on Mrs. Holt's arm and spoke softly. "I've known you since we were in high school together. You'd never let anything happen to that child. Maybe she wandered off and fell asleep somewhere nearby."

Their close relationship came as a total surprise to me. Because of it, I was all the more surprised that the detective would suspect Jessica's involvement in the fire. Or was it Ethan that he actually mistrusted?

I shifted my view to the lake.

Jessica stood on a strip of pebbled shore. She scanned the water's edge in both directions. Then she turned around and trudged back, her shoulders drooping with despair.

As she came up to us, she said, "Detective, I've been thinking about the threatening letters we received. What if Amy was kidnapped? If someone took her, we're wasting our time here."

Mrs. Holt's voice trembled. "Lionel, as sure as I'm standing here, an intruder came into my house by the back door and kidnapped my granddaughter. She could be in grave danger. I want you to do something about it right now."

The detective calmly replied, "I'll get the OPP to issue an Amber Alert. We'll distribute the information to the media across the region." He turned to Jessica. "I'll need personal items that belong to your daughter for our search and rescue dogs."

Jessica handed him the teddy bear. "Amy never goes anywhere without Pokey. It's her favorite toy." She spotted a stained cotton jersey on the back of a chair and held it out to him. "This is the jersey she wore this morning."

"She spilled orange juice on it," Mrs. Holt said. "I changed her outfit."

Detective Cole tucked the item under his arm, then pulled out a pen and notepad. "Tell me what the child was wearing when she disappeared."

Mrs. Holt gave him a description.

Jessica motioned toward the items the detective was holding. "Are those enough? Do you need more?"

"These are fine," he said. "One more thing. Would you have a recent photo of Amy? Digital is okay."

"I took some photos of her the other day." Jessica reached for her phone.

"Email them to me." The detective handed her his business card. "I'll send an officer to dust the back door for fingerprints. In the meantime, let's all go inside. Nobody touch the door."

We followed the detective inside. He remained by the back door and shut it with his elbow after we'd entered. "If any of you need to leave the house, use the front door. Fiona, you should stay here in case your granddaughter returns. I'll be in touch shortly." As he let himself out the front door, the tinkling of wind chimes filtered into the house.

The wind chimes. So much for keeping bad luck away.

Mrs. Holt and I watched as Jessica scanned the photos on her phone and chose two that had been taken at close range. "Done. The photos are delivered. I'd better call Ethan and let him know what's happening."

~

An OPP officer arrived at Mrs. Holt's home shortly before noon to dust the back door for prints. He didn't say a word until he'd completed his task. "It's okay to use the door now." He gave us a polite nod, then left.

When Mrs. Holt suggested she make us sandwiches, I couldn't even begin to think about food.

Jessica said she'd lost her appetite too but prepared a pot of tea anyway. As soon as we'd sat down at the table, her phone rang. It was Ethan.

"No, we haven't found her yet." Jessica struggled to keep her voice steady. "I'll be staying here a while longer... Okay. Bye." She rubbed the nape of her neck. "Ethan seems to have calmed down. Michael is a good influence on him. He knows how to keep him from going crazy. I hope they find Amy soon."

Mrs. Holt touched her daughter's arm. "I'm so sorry, Jessica. Please don't hate me."

"I don't hate you, Mom. The reality is that Amy doesn't wander off without her teddy bear. She couldn't possibly have opened the door to go outside either. I think what you said is true. Somebody must have come into the house and taken her. Oh, my poor baby!" She sobbed.

Mrs. Holt's eyes welled up. "Who would have the nerve to come into my house in the middle of the day and take Amy? Not any of my neighbors. I can vouch for that. I've known these people for years. We know each other's children and grandchildren by name."

"It has to be someone who knew you were taking care of Amy today," I said.

Mrs. Holt put a hand on her chest. "My goodness. You think someone's been following me?"

"Not necessarily. Maybe someone mentioned that you were minding Amy, and word got around."

Mrs. Holt gazed downward. "Well..."

Jessica stared at her. "Mom, all your friends know you babysit Amy, right?"

"They're my friends. They've known about it for months. We often talk about our grandchildren."

Jessica rolled her eyes. "I'll never hear the end of this from Ethan."

I stepped in to prevent a potential mother-daughter feud. "Mrs. Holt, if any of your friends wanted to kidnap Amy, they would have had lots of opportunities to have done it sooner."

"You're right." Mrs. Holt reached over and patted my hand. "Thank you, Megan."

"Then it has to be a stranger," Jessica said. "Who else did you talk to, Mom? Anyone in town?"

"No, I haven't gone shopping in a while." Mrs. Holt grew silent, thinking. "I did speak with some of your guests the night of the fire, though. I told the ladies how much I enjoyed babysitting Amy. In fact, they saw me leave with Amy at breakfast one morning."

Jessica shook her head. "It can't be any of my guests. They were too busy shopping, fishing, or visiting the sites in town. It had to be someone else."

"Who else is there?" Mrs. Holt gaped at her. "The only other person who knows that I babysit Amy is Jeremy. Do you think he took her?"

"No, not Jeremy. Everyone is always blaming that boy for something."

My phone rang. I stood up. "Excuse me. I'll take this outside." I slipped out the back door. "Hi, Michael."

"How's everyone holding up over there?" His voice sounded tinny.

"As best as can be expected. Where are you? You sound as if you're standing in an echo chamber."

Michael chuckled. "I'm in Ethan's man cave in the basement. I guess the reception is bad here."

"Where's Ethan?" I moved from the porch to the lawn and started walking toward the lake for no particular reason.

"He's outside talking to Detective Cole."

"Any news on Amy?"

"Not yet. The detective came by with another officer. They searched the house and the grounds. They questioned Foster and Sam. Both men were in their cabins all morning and didn't see Amy."

"That's not surprising. She couldn't have walked back home from Mrs. Holt's house in such a short time anyway."

"I know, but the cops have to cover all the bases," Michael said.

"True," I said. "Anything else?"

"Ethan asked the detective if he'd questioned Jeremy. The boy happened to be working here."

"And?"

"Cole is bringing him to the station for interrogation."

I drew in a quick breath. "What? Wait until Jessica finds out. She'll be furious."

"I figured that much."

I'd reached the strip of pebbled shore. For no reason, I glanced down at the multicolored stones.

What the—?

A white feather stuck out between two pebbles. I picked it up, my pulse accelerating. "Oh, hell."

"What's wrong?" Michael asked.

I tried to reason it away. Birds often lose feathers, and birds were as common as the pebbles on this shore. But there were no other feathers around as far as I could see. Then again, I'd be crazy to believe the predictions of an old woman who—

Michael raised his voiced. "Megan! Are you there?"

"Yes, I—"

A woman called out my name. I turned to see Jessica frantically waving me back to the house.

"I have to go, Michael. I'll call you later." I dropped the feather and ran to Jessica.

She was trembling, clutching a sheet of paper in her hand. "Megan, you won't believe this. I went to Mom's mailbox by the road-side and found another letter."

The cutout lettering had the same tilted pattern, but the message was different. It read: "Get out of town now—or else!"

22

____

Jessica called Detective Cole immediately. He promised to drive over as soon as possible.

She was distressed that he couldn't come over right away, but it was my guess that the detective was interrogating Jeremy. I made a mental note to follow up with the teen later.

While Jessica waited for the detective to arrive, she called Ethan. Mrs. Holt and I sat in the kitchen, listening to her side of the conversation. Her emotions were raw with fear, but she tried to remain composed for Ethan's sake. She talked about the recent measures Detective Cole was taking and how confident she was that the police would find Amy soon. Her efforts to keep her voice steady failed, and she held the phone away from her ear as Ethan cried uncontrollably at the other end of the line.

The truth had been revealed through a series of anonymous letters. The same monster who had threatened the Bryants had now kidnapped their little girl. There seemed to be no end to the devastation one person could inflict on this young family—a family who happened to be my dear friends, a family with no ties to crimes of the past.

I rubbed my cold hands, then tucked them under my thighs, pledging to do everything in my power to help catch this beast.

Jessica was crying now, sniffing away her tears while she continued to soothe Ethan, telling him things would be back to normal soon and everything would be okay.

I couldn't begin to put myself in her shoes. I'd never been a mother, but I understood how fear could make any mother imagine the worst. I'd also seen enough newscasts about missing children to know that many kids turn up dead within the first two days, while others are never found. I didn't want to go there.

Detective Cole arrived an hour later. Wearing vinyl gloves, he made speedy work of the latest piece of evidence that Jessica had retrieved from her mother's mailbox. He scanned it and sent it to the OPP headquarters where a special team had been assembled to analyze the letters. Then he placed the latest letter in a clear plastic envelope.

"What's going to happen next?" Jessica asked him, her eyes red from crying.

The detective carefully placed the envelope in his portfolio. "We're releasing a photo and physical description of Amy to media channels this afternoon to notify the public about her suspected abduction. It'll officially launch the Amber Alert. I suggest you print and distribute posters with Amy's photo around town. People might come forward with tips."

"What about Jeremy?" Mrs. Holt asked him.

"We questioned the boy, but he knows nothing. We had to let him go."

I breathed an inner sigh of relief.

The detective turned to Jessica. "You said you found this letter in your mother's mailbox?"

"That's right."

"Hmm..." He pursed his lips.

"What?"

"You found the other two letters in your mailbox, Jessica. I'm wondering why the change in the drop-off point."

"Do you think someone followed Mom and Amy here?"

"I don't know." His forehead creased. "One more thing. There was no ransom request in this last letter either."

"Ransom request?"

"It might be too early yet."

I knew that ransom notes were usually received during the first twenty-four hours after a kidnapping. Fulfilling the demands of the ransom—normally through a monetary payment—often led to a successful outcome.

Sudden awareness spread across Jessica's face. She shrieked, "What if we don't get a ransom note? Will the kidnapper kill Amy?"

Mrs. Holt raised a hand. "I've heard enough talk, Lionel. What are you doing to find my granddaughter?"

Detective Cole gave her a measured look. "Since a child is implicated, we're taking the threatening letters seriously. Our police team is making the necessary preparations to launch an official search. We'll appeal to local associations and the public for volunteers as well."

"Ethan and I will be there," Jessica said, resolve replacing fear in her voice.

"You can count on Michael and me," I said.

"I'll call my friends, and I've got lots of them." Mrs. Holt raised her chin. "Many of them are neighboring land owners. They know the area extremely well."

"Good." The detective's gaze encompassed the three of us. "That wraps things up for now. I'll contact you later." He left.

Jessica fought back tears as she explained to the print shop owner in town what had happened. Without hesitation, he dropped his current work and offered to print her posters and flyers and anything else she needed at no charge.

His eyes brimmed with tears as he handed her the printed materials. When Jessica turned to leave, holding back a sob, his eyes found mine. He nodded sadly. I nodded back. It was all one could do.

We distributed the posters around town, keeping the flyers for handouts to members of the search party assembling in a few hours. We affixed posters to lampposts and poles and handed them out to local churches, shop vendors, and restaurants.

Residents, noticing the fair-haired child's photo, stopped to chat with us. Their compassion knew no bounds, and Jessica thanked them for their prayers and good wishes.

At Il Tavolino, Teresa listened as Jessica briefed her on Amy's disappearance. "Give me a bunch of flyers," she said. "I'll hand them out to my clients. Many of them live on the outskirts of town. You never know."

Our circuit of the town was almost over. After we'd put up the last of the posters, we went back to the SUV.

Jessica hunched over the wheel. "Amy's alive. I know she is. I have to have faith that we'll get her back okay. But it's so damn hard." She burst into tears.

I hugged her as she sobbed. "Things seem hopeless right now. But I promise you, Jessica, we'll look everywhere for Amy. We won't give up until we find her."

I thought about the white feather I'd seen earlier at the shore by Mrs. Holt's property. Damn that Madame Ora!

Jessica pulled away and wiped her eyes with a tissue. "Enough of this crying. I have to be strong. I have to find my baby girl."

"Do you want me to drive?"

"No, no. I'm okay. It'll help me concentrate on what I need to do." She swung out of the parking space. "I'm going back home. I want to see Ethan."

I was surprised. "Won't your mother be expecting us to go back to her place?"

She waved the idea away. "I'll call her later. She can contact her friends for moral support. Ethan only has me."

Jessica was hurting inside, yet here she was, holding on and trying to prioritize her time for whoever needed her more. She was determined to be strong and wouldn't give in to futile feelings of despair until Amy was found.

No matter what.

23

———————

Michael stood with his arms folded and Ethan with his fists clenched as they faced the path leading to Jessica's Lodge. Jessica and I noticed their confrontational stance as soon as we drove up and wondered what had happened here in the interim.

"Good thing you're not reporters." Ethan relaxed somewhat. "We got rid of the last bunch minutes ago. You should have seen this place. You'd have thought the circus had come to town."

"The Amber Alert must have driven them here." I walked up to Michael.

He immediately put his arm around me and kissed me on the forehead. "How did it go in town?"

"We put up dozens of posters of Amy."

Jessica took Ethan's hand in hers and summoned enthusiasm in her voice. "The police are confident they'll produce leads."

Ethan snarled, "They'd better produce leads."

"Any news from Detective Cole?" Jessica asked him.

"No." Ethan tensed up. "How could this have happened, Jess? How could your mother let her guard down? This is our daughter we're talking about."

Jessica pulled away from him. "Let's not argue, okay? Things are bad enough."

Ethan was relentless. "It's not like your mother had anything else to do. She shouldn't have brought Amy to her house in the first place. Damn!" He stormed toward the house.

Jessica followed on his heels. "Ethan, wait up."

As they entered the house, I whispered to Michael, "So much for that. How did you manage to calm him down earlier?"

"He talked and I listened." He kept his voice low. "It's clear he has issues with his mother-in-law."

"I've been thinking about what Mrs. Holt told us. It must have been a blow to Ethan's self-esteem when she signed as guarantor on the mortgage to this property."

"It was the only way they could have purchased this place. But the problem is more personal than that."

"How?"

"Ethan told me he gets frustrated because he doesn't have time to help Jessica with the business the way he wants to. He sees the close bond between Jessica, her mother, and Amy and feels like an outsider. In a way, I understand where he's coming from."

"Because of your father," I said.

"Right," Michael said. "He made me feel inept when I told him I was going into journalism. The offer of a job at his high-tech company wasn't for me. I followed my heart instead. You'd think my parents would have accepted my career choice by now. Maybe time will smooth things out between us." He looked away.

I seldom probed him about it, suspecting that communication with his parents was sporadic at best. And yet, I had to know. "Have you talked to them lately?"

He stalled so long that I didn't think he'd answer. "Not in a while. I'll give them a call when we get back home."

I changed the subject. "Speaking of parents, Jessica is trying to hold it together for both of them."

"Tell me about it. I was sitting in the living room with Ethan when he was on the phone with her. It's hitting him hard."

"After what they're going through with Amy, I'm glad we don't have kids."

Michael gave me a quizzical look. "What? That's not fair. Not every kid gets kidnapped."

"When I see what's happening here, I'd be too afraid to take that risk."

"Are you saying you'd never want to have children?"

"That's exactly what I'm saying."

"What if I want children?"

I caught the intensity in his blue eyes. "Are you serious? You never mentioned it before."

"You never asked."

Michael's phone rang. He answered and hit the speakerphone button.

Detective Cole's voice came through. "I won't mention names. This is about the two people we discussed earlier. I can confirm they did know each other from their brief stay in Montreal years back. For your ears only. Understood?"

"Understood. Thank you." Michael hung up. "That's what we needed to hear. Proof that Burt Garner and Vincent Bouchard knew each other from their time in jail when they were teens."

"That's good news," I said. "So their prison records hadn't been deleted all this time?"

"Right. I doubt neither Burt nor Vincent wanted to draw suspicion to their files by asking that they be expunged—even years later."

"What's important is that Detective Cole is aware of the connection between them."

"You bet. Now we have one more player in our corner. If the detective can link Rusty Homer to these two deaths, he can start looking for him."

"And take unwarranted pressure off Ethan," I added.

"Let's hope so," Michael said.

"The detective didn't mention if he'd obtained a mug shot of Rusty Homer."

"Probably not, or he would have said so. We can ask him about it next time."

Something else came to mind. "This new information about Burt and Vincent might lead the police to the stolen gold bullion. I hadn't thought of it before, but do you think there's a reward out for its return?"

"Let me check." He accessed the Internet on his phone and

scrolled through files. Moments later, he laughed. "How does a hundred thousand dollars sound?"

"Incredible! I wonder if our resident historian knows about this." I glanced at his cabin. Foster's car wasn't parked there.

There was movement behind us.

"Hi." Jeremy popped out of nowhere as usual.

"Hi," Michael said. "Finished working for the day?"

"Yeah, I finished later today." Jeremy fidgeted, put his hands in his pockets. "I had to go to the police station. I rode in a cruiser."

"Your first time in a cruiser?"

"Sort of." He kicked a stone. "Detective Cole said Amy was missing. He asked me questions. I didn't know what to say. I was scared."

"Why were you scared?" I asked.

Jeremy's shoulders sagged. "Because Burt and Vincent died. I was afraid Amy would die too."

From the hollowed sadness in his eyes, it was obvious that the boy's attachment to the little girl ran deep. I tried to reassure him. "Don't worry, a lot of people will be helping to look for Amy. Her parents want her back as much as you do."

"Bad people do bad things. It's not safe here for Amy."

"We'll catch the bad guys," Michael said. "You can bet on it."

The teen's face lit up with enthusiasm. "Can I help?"

"Keep your eyes and ears open. If you notice strangers or anything weird happening around here, let me know."

"Cool. Gotta get home now." Jeremy ran off toward the dock.

"Poor kid," I said.

Michael's attention was fixed on a point in the distance. "Something's off," he said.

"With Jeremy?"

"No, with the letter dropped in Mrs. Holt's mailbox. Why would the perp change his routine and drop off the third letter in a different mailbox?"

"It's possible that someone followed Mrs. Holt and Amy from here to her house," I said.

Michael continued to stare into the distance, thinking.

"If anything, the timing of the letters is interesting. It might be a coincidence, but Jessica received the first threatening letter days before Burt Garner's body was discovered in the fire. The second letter came after we found Vincent Bouchard's body in his pool. The third, after Amy went missing. If Rusty Homer's connection to the two deaths is anything to go by, we have to assume he sent the letters. If so, does it mean he has Amy?"

He hesitated, then said, "I'm not buying it."

"Why not?"

"In the first place, we're talking about a cold-blooded killer. How does kidnapping Amy fit into his MO?"

"His MO? What do you mean?"

"Rusty Homer has a specific *modus operandi*—a particular way of performing a crime. If he killed a cop and two buddies, he's not going to turn around and start kidnapping little kids."

He had a good point, yet Rusty Homer could have had help. "What about Chuck? We suspect he's linked to Burt's death and Vincent's too. Maybe he has Amy." The idea made my stomach queasy.

Michael stood firm. "Like I said, I'm not buying it."

As my mind searched for clues, it replayed the contents of the letters. "The message in each anonymous letter is the same. Each one threatens Jessica and Ethan if they don't leave town. Someone is trying very hard to scare them off their property."

"The question is: Why?"

"In the last letter, the kidnapper didn't even hint at a ransom for Amy. It's obvious this isn't about the money."

A grin crept up on his face. "Not Jessica and Ethan's money."

The puzzle pieces were slowly taking shape. Rusty Homer. The gold bullion robbery. The death of his two accomplices. Jessica's purchase of land from Burt Garner...

"The kidnapper didn't ask for ransom because he has a much better alternative." Michael's eyes sparkled. "He knows where the stolen loot is hidden."

My breath caught in my throat. "It's somewhere on Jessica's property!"

~

Given the angst of the situation, Detective Cole had thought it best that family members not be available while the press conference took place on Mrs. Holt's property. He suggested that Jessica invite her mother to stay over at her house. When Mrs. Holt protested, the detective insisted that she would be a familiar face to Amy should the toddler find her way back home. Mrs. Holt conceded and packed an overnight bag.

We gathered in Jessica's living room to watch the press conference on TV. Crews from media vans had staked their claim to positions near Mrs. Holt's front door. The camera zoomed in on Detective Cole who stood behind a cluster of microphones. He stated it was too soon to determine if foul play was involved in Amy's disappearance. He indicated that investigators remained hopeful, since only a few hours had elapsed since the child had first been reported missing.

The detective described Amy and what the eighteen-month-old girl was wearing when she disappeared. "She has blue eyes and is fair-haired. She measures about two and a half feet tall and weighs twenty-two pounds. She was wearing a yellow and white striped top and matching shorts, and white sandals." He urged anyone with information to call the police hotline number. Another officer proceeded to distribute the flyers that Jessica had had printed in town.

The moment Detective Cole opened the session to reporters, they bombarded him with questions:

Where are Amy's parents?

Will they be taking part in the search?

Can we interview the grandmother?

There have been two unexplained deaths in the area. Residents are speculating that they were murdered. Do the police suspect a serial killer is on the loose?

Are you holding out hope that Amy will be found alive?

When will the OPP hold the next press conference?

The TV coverage had Jessica, Ethan, and Mrs. Holt in tears. Michael and I stepped outdoors to give them time to overcome their emotions. We would be driving over to Mrs. Holt's place soon to join other volunteers in another organized search for Amy.

Except for Mrs. Holt, the four of us had driven there earlier this afternoon to take part in the first sweep. Jessica had been visibly moved to see that hundreds of residents from Fernlea and Ostfield had shown up to help search for Amy. No longer able to fight back the tears, she'd let them run down her cheeks until they became permanent streaks. Ethan often wiped his tears with the back of his hand. The encouraging show of support from strangers more than compensated for the resentment they'd experienced when they first moved to Fernlea. Words of encouragement from strangers boosted hopes that the toddler would soon be found safe and sound.

Michael parked the car behind two police cruisers on the road adjacent to Mrs. Holt's property. Most of the camera crews had gone, leaving a skeleton staff on standby.

With Jessica and Ethan in the back seat, we watched from the roadside as the police search team combed the countryside this evening, their fluorescent vests and searchlights visible in dusk's fading light. Their wood sticks fanned the tall grass, leaving nothing untouched.

It was the second sweep of the same area in the last twenty-four hours—the farmland bordering Mrs. Holt's property where Amy was last seen. Firefighters, officers with police dogs from multiple districts, and additional volunteers had joined this search. They walked in groups of ten, side-by-side, and kept the same pace as their team members. With heads bowed, they scanned the ground for a telltale sign that might indicate Amy had wandered into this area.

I sensed a chill, despite the warm temperature.

We would be joining a third wave of police, firefighters, and other volunteers in fifteen minutes. This time, we'd be searching along the water's edge.

It was going to be a long night.

24

Stars peeked from behind clouds that drifted like ghostly figures across the sky. The stillness permeated the car as Michael drove back to Jessica's house, leaving each one of us to our own thoughts.

Like the preceding searches for Amy, the third sweep had ended in disappointment. Police officers and volunteers had dispersed once the search had ended, their faces haggard after hours of combing farmland and forests. With darkness setting in, Detective Cole had called off additional searches until morning.

Michael parked at the side of the house to drop off Jessica and Ethan.

"It's eleven o'clock," Jessica said. "Ethan and I are too worried to sleep. Would you like to come inside? I'll make coffee."

An affirmative nod from Michael told me that, like the rest of us, he wouldn't be able to sleep either.

"Okay," I said.

We followed Jessica to the back door. I was relieved to see, as she pulled out her keys, that the door was locked. With a killer on the loose, one could never be too safe. She turned on the lights in the kitchen.

"I'll go check on Mom." She headed for the hallway.

"You guys must be famished." Ethan opened the pantry door. "There should be some leftover muffins around here somewhere."

His casual demeanor disconcerted me. It almost refuted the fact his daughter was missing. Then again, it was an improvement over punching a wall when confronted with a stressful situation.

Jessica entered the kitchen. "Mom fell asleep on the living room couch."

"Good thing some of us can sleep whenever we feel like it," Ethan mumbled under his breath. "Jess, where are those muffins you baked yesterday?"

"On the top shelf."

"I don't see them. How many were left?"

"At least six." Jessica scanned the pantry shelves. She moved jars and containers around. "That's strange. I'll ask Mom."

"Ask me what?" Mrs. Holt walked in, rubbing her neck.

"I had a container of muffins in the pantry," Jessica said. "Any idea what happened to them?"

"Not a clue."

She kept her eyes on her mother. "Did you have any friends over here tonight?"

Mrs. Holt stiffened. "I did no such thing. Do you think for one moment that I'm in the mood for entertaining friends when Amy is still missing?"

I froze. Was her comment meant for Michael and me?

"Forget it." Jessica grabbed a bag of chocolate chip cookies from the back of a shelf. She placed the cookies on a platter while Ethan prepared the coffee.

No one spoke in the interim. We were each lost in our own thoughts about Amy—thoughts that swung between hope and despair.

We had settled around the table when there was a knock at the back door. Ethan opened it.

Detective Cole stepped inside, trying to catch his breath. "I have new information. I thought I'd stop by and bring you up to date."

Jessica started to tremble, put a hand to her mouth. "Oh, my God! Have they found Amy?"

Mrs. Holt echoed, "Well, have they?"

Michael reached over and held my hand. Like the rest of us, he sensed anticipation in the detective's demeanor.

"We haven't found Amy yet, but we might have a break." The detective pulled up a chair, calming down to a normal breathing pattern. "We received a call from a neighbor who owns property across the lake from here. He was one of the volunteers who took part in the sweep tonight. He told me there was activity on the lake not long ago. It was pitch black on the water, but he thought he heard a little girl crying. Her sobs echoed across the lake, but he couldn't tell what direction they were coming from."

"Was he certain it was a child crying?" Skepticism swept over Ethan's face. "Some wild animals sound the same."

"I asked him the same question. What he told me convinced me the child was most likely your little Amy."

"Oh!" Mrs. Holt's hand flew to her chest.

Jessica drew a quick breath. "What did he say?"

"He couldn't make out every word," the detective said, "though he was certain the little girl said Granny and Pokey a few times."

The detective's revelation had given us newfound optimism. We were all the more eager to resume the search for Amy as we met up with Jessica and Ethan outside their home early the next morning.

Jessica gazed at the sandbox by the house. "That's strange. I remember putting Amy's plastic shovels in her pail and setting them in a corner of the sandbox. Now they're gone."

"When was this?" I asked her.

"The day Mom came by to pick her up." She blinked, as if she couldn't recall what day it was. "You know, the day Amy disappeared."

Ethan hurried out the back door. "Everyone's here? Good. I'll drive."

Jessica pointed at the sandbox. "Do you know what happened to Amy's plastic pail and shovels?"

Ethan glanced at the empty sandbox. "No. Maybe your mother took them."

"She didn't."

"Did you ask her?"

"I don't have to. Mom would have mentioned it if she took them." She shook her head. "No, I distinctly remember putting everything in the pail and tucking it in that far corner."

"Why don't you go ask your mother anyway?" Ethan suggested.

"Fine." Jessica ran indoors, only to return moments later. "No, Mom said she didn't take the toys."

"This might be a connection to the kidnapper," I said to her. "I think you should tell Detective Cole about it."

"Megan's right," Michael said. "It could be a lead."

Jessica pulled out her phone and sent the detective an urgent message, then moved toward the car. "Okay. Let's go find Amy."

Detective Cole had mapped out a different route for the search on Saturday morning. The area stretched along both sides of the lake and entailed volunteers knocking on doors. The detective had targeted this area based on the tip he'd received from a resident who lived across the lake from Jessica's Lodge.

Jessica and I handed out flyers to new volunteers who were taking part in this latest search. Among them were dozens of familiar faces—the same people who had taken part in yesterday's sweep. We made a point of thanking each one for giving their time to our cause.

Jessica and I were part of a group of five participants assigned to scan the pebbled shore bordering Jessica's Lodge. Stretching several acres, Burt's property took up a sizable length of the shore. I was finally going to see what was on the other side of the thick and gnarly forest beyond his backyard.

Michael and Ethan were tasked with going door-to-door and handing out flyers to people who lived across the lake from the lodge. The possibility that they might be knocking on the home belonging to Jeremy's father came to mind.

The thought vanished in the next second when Jessica said, "Isn't that Jeremy's canoe?"

Sure enough, a canoe was tied to a dilapidated dock. The dock had obstructed it from view until we'd neared it. The canoe had a familiar blue stripe along its side.

"Yes, it is," I said.

Jessica put her hands on her hips. "What is he doing all the way out here? Let's go see."

She didn't have to ask twice. To the other three members of our team, I said, "You go on ahead. Jessica and I are going to take a look over here."

They called out in agreement and carried on with their search along the lake.

Jessica had already crossed the pebbled patch of land and disappeared through the bushes on Burt's property. Her backpack was the last I saw of her.

I caught up to her, and we plodded along a narrow path. "Do you know how large this piece of land is, Jessica? We'll never cover it all."

She was insistent. "This path was hacked with a machete. If Jeremy is here, I want to know why."

"Maybe he's mowing Burt's lawn."

"He wouldn't come this way. It's too far. He always ties his canoe to my dock and cuts across the lawn to Burt's place." She turned to face me. "In any case, he mowed Burt's lawn not long ago. I doubt he'd be wasting his time mowing it again."

"Okay. Point taken."

We continued our journey.

"This path must lead somewhere," Jessica said.

I had another idea. "We should tell the guys where we are."

"Why? We're not lost."

True.

We must have walked—no, dashed—for about ten minutes.

I was out of breath and clearly out of shape. "Hold on, Jessica. Can we stop for a minute, please?"

"Okay. It is getting warm, isn't it?" She slipped the backpack off her shoulders. "You want some water?"

"Sure."

She dug out a bottle and handed it to me, then opened one for herself.

I took a few sips. The spring water felt cool going down my throat.

I hadn't realized how warm the sun's rays were until now. I drank more water, then tucked the bottle in my waist pack.

We both heard the tiny voice at the same time and froze.

There it was again.

Jessica mouthed the word *mama*.

We pushed forward along the constricted path, at times running into protruding branches that scratched our faces and arms before we could avoid it.

The child's additional cries for her mother propelled us all the more.

Jessica came to a sudden halt, causing me to collide into her.

I regained my balance and followed her line of sight.

A small structure built with mismatched pieces of plywood stood in the clearing. Instead of glass windows, square openings were covered with pieces of fabric nailed to the wood boards. The oversized doll's house gave the impression it had been built by a carpenter trying to learn the trade.

Shrubbery surrounding it had been cleared by several feet to allow for easy passage. Amy's pail and shovels sat in the earth to the left of the structure.

Jessica dashed to the front door and yanked it open. "Amy!"

"Mama!" The child leapt into her mother's arms.

25

———

Was Jeremy a murderer and a kidnapper?

The question reverberated through my mind like an echo in the Grand Canyon.

While Jessica held Amy and had her drink some bottled water, I called Detective Cole. He didn't answer, so I called 911 and left an urgent message.

Then I called Michael. I gave him the good news and told him our location. He said Detective Cole was nearby and that they'd borrow a neighbor's canoe to paddle over.

In the meantime I peeked inside the pint-sized house and spotted layers of blankets, a battery-operated heater, empty bottles of fruit juice, and a couple of muffins inside a container. Pokey lay on the wood floor. I picked up the one-eyed teddy bear and gave it to Amy. She took it and held it tightly.

My eyes took in the entangled forest around us. "Where could Jeremy be?"

"He can't be too far," Jessica said. "He'd never leave Amy."

"Jerm'y!" Amy called out, smiling.

I turned to see the teen standing several feet away.

"What are you doing here?" Jeremy raged. "You're not supposed to be here. This is a safe place for Amy."

Jessica put Amy down but held her hand. "This is *my* daughter. *My* child." She pounded her chest to accentuate her words. "You had no right to take her. Do you know how much trouble you're in, Jeremy? The police and hundreds of volunteers are out there right now looking for Amy."

Jeremy's lips quivered. He seemed to be struggling with what to say. "Amy is like my little sister. I can take care of her."

Jessica waved a finger at him. "What you did wasn't right, Jeremy. The police will be here soon. They'll have questions for you."

He began to cry. "I did nothing wrong. Please, Jessica, don't let them take me to jail. My dad will be real mad."

Jessica wasn't fazed. "If you cared about Amy so much, why did you send those threatening letters to Ethan and me?"

Confusion spread across Jeremy's face. "What letters?"

"The letters demanding that we leave town or else."

He took a step back. "I don't know nothing about those letters. It wasn't me."

Jessica was about to buckle in frustration, but I reached out and touched her arm. "Maybe he's telling the truth."

She softened her approach. "Okay, Jeremy. Maybe you sent those letters, maybe you didn't. Either way, you have to leave."

His face collapsed. I had never seen a young man look more like a small child.

Jessica swallowed. "You've broken my trust in you. You're no longer welcome on our property. The same goes for my mother's property."

"I need the money," Jeremy said, sniffling. "My dad will be real mad at me if I don't work."

"You should have thought about that before you took Amy. You kidnapped her. That's what you did."

Jeremy sobbed. "I—I didn't kidnap her. I was protecting her."

"From what?"

"From bad people."

"Who?"

"I don't know. Michael said he'd find them."

Branches snapped behind us. Detective Cole, Michael, and Ethan stepped into the clearing. They were followed by a police officer in uniform that I didn't recognize.

Ethan lunged at Jeremy and grabbed him by the neck. "You creep!" He raised his fist, but Michael intervened and blocked his punch.

The uniformed officer clutched Ethan and pulled him back.

"For your daughter's sake, get a hold of yourself," Detective Cole barked at Ethan. He turned to Jeremy. "Son, you go with this officer. If you take him across the lake in your canoe, he'll give you a ride in the cruiser to the station. Okay?"

Jeremy hung his head. "Okay." He took a few steps, then stopped. He waved at Amy and she waved back. The teen didn't say another word before the officer led him away.

"Papa!" Amy smiled up at him.

Ethan picked her up. He held her in his arms and sobbed.

Jessica hugged them, releasing a new flood of tears.

Witnessing the emotional family reunion, I fought to keep back the tears but lost. I hastily wiped my eyes with the back of my hand.

It was too late. Michael had noticed. He put his arm around me and kissed me on the cheek.

Detective Cole led us back through the forest to the pebbled shore where Jessica and I gave him a recount of the events that led us to finding Amy. We included Jeremy's admission that he'd taken the little girl because he felt he needed to protect her.

"Please go easy on Jeremy," Jessica said, surprising me. "I'm sure he had no intention of harming Amy. He's a kind soul who wouldn't hurt anyone."

"I'll take your opinion under consideration when we question him later," the detective said, wrapping up the interview. "In the meantime, I'll have to notify Jeremy's father that we'll be bringing his boy to the station again." He got into the borrowed canoe and paddled back across the river.

Our party of five sauntered back to Jessica's Lodge, our journey lighter this time, our expressions of joy and bursts of laughter reverberating over the water.

Mrs. Holt bolted out of her chair as we entered the kitchen. "Oh, my Lord! Amy, come see Granny!" She hugged and kissed the child. "Thank goodness this terrible ordeal is over."

She sat Amy on her lap while the child had a bowl of cereal and milk. When Jessica announced it was time for the toddler's nap, Mrs. Holt wouldn't let go of Amy. She insisted she was quite capable of taking the child upstairs and tucking her in bed herself.

Michael and I wanted to give the family some time alone, so we left. We'd catch up with them later.

As we crossed the lawn to our cabin, Michael grew pensive. "We have some loose ends to tie up before we leave here."

He could only mean one person. "Rusty Homer, right?"

"You bet. The guy's as elusive as the wind."

"What's the plan?"

"Let's go have a chat with the detective."

We waited outside Detective Cole's office while he concluded a phone call. The OPP station in Ostfield wasn't much larger than the cabin we'd rented at Jessica's Lodge. The detective's office took up half of it. Two desks and filing cabinets took up the rest.

"Detective, there's a matter of unresolved issues," Michael said after he'd invited us into his office.

"We've got lots of those. Anything in particular?" The detective closed the door and sat down at his desk.

"The threatening letters sent to the Bryants. Especially the last one."

"What about it?"

"I doubt Jeremy put it in Mrs. Holt's mailbox. No offense to the boy, but I think his ability to work with his hands far outweighs his capacity to dream up such intricate schemes."

"I have to agree with you there. We've interviewed him and concluded that he meant no harm. He understands the pain he caused Amy's family and shows remorse. His father came by to pick him up earlier. He quoted him passages from the Bible on the way out the door and probably all the way home. To me, that's punishment enough." He closed the topic. "What were you saying about the third letter?"

"If the same person sent all three letters—"

"Incidentally, it's been confirmed that all three letters did come from the same source."

Michael went on. "My question is, how did the sender know that Jeremy had taken Amy?"

The detective pulled out his notebook and a pen. "Very good question. Any idea who's pulling the strings?"

"It's someone who knows Jeremy or was following him. They got a lucky break when he took Amy and used it to their benefit."

I offered my opinion. "This person has probably been spying on ongoing activities at Jessica's Lodge. They knew the family's daily agenda. Like Michael said, they knew that Jeremy had taken Amy to his so-called safe place. The timing of the third letter is too coincidental."

"I agree," the detective said.

Michael jumped in. "The same circumstances were in place the day the fire happened. Hardly anyone was at the resort when Burt Garner's body was deposited in the shed. Yet someone must have known that the coast was clear so the body could be dropped off without any questions asked."

Detective Cole rubbed his chin. "If I recall correctly, those young newlyweds were in their cabin when the trucks arrived." He flipped through his notes. "Ah, here it is. They reported they saw one white truck, maybe two." He flipped to the next page. "Foster Wade saw one truck arrive with the freezer. Sam Norton saw no trucks. Conflicting information. Not much help there." He closed his notebook.

Michael wasn't discouraged. "We should be looking for Rusty Homer. He has valid connections to the two deceased men."

"Oh...you reminded me." The detective reached for a folder in his in-box and opened it. "They sent me a photo of Rusty Homer taken about five years back. I warn you. It's a gruesome shot." He placed it on the desk.

The photo was of a middle-aged man with white hair that fell below his ears. He had a visible red scar that ran down one cheek. The rest of his face had cuts and bruises and looked as if it had been used as a punching bag. His nose was crooked—or maybe broken. Out of a disfigured face, dark eyes stared at the camera lens with defiance, as if he were about to pounce on the photographer.

"The warden told me inmates had beaten up Rusty Homer on several occasions before they took that photo," the detective said. "They never did find out which convicts were involved."

"We learned he had reconstructive surgery since then," I said. "We'd have a hard time identifying him based on this photo."

"Yes, Rusty Homer is one sly dog." The detective picked up the photo and slid it back in the file.

"You confirmed that Burt Garner and Vincent Bouchard were jail buddies decades ago," Michael said. "If they were Rusty Homer's partners in the Montreal robbery, it's possible he hunted them down and killed them. If not, he got one of his minions to do the job for him. We suspect that Chuck Dorey works for Rusty Homer."

The detective raised an eyebrow. "You got proof?"

"Not yet." Michael changed the subject. "You mentioned you did a clean sweep of all the company trucks at Build-a-Floor and found nothing."

"That's right."

Michael hesitated, pondering his next words. His reference to Chuck...to the company trucks... He probably wanted to point out that Vincent also owned a white truck, but he didn't want to reveal that we'd seen it in Vincent's garage when we broke into his home. We couldn't mention we'd seen a freezer in Vincent's basement either —a freezer large enough to hold a dead body. It might not have been a crime scene when we first entered, but it was now.

I gave it a shot. "Detective, I was at Jessica's home one day when Vincent Bouchard made a delivery for the meat shop in a white truck. The truck didn't have the shop's logo on the side panel, so I'm guessing it belonged to Vincent personally. Vincent's letter to his son states that he did Rusty Homer one last favor. He could have used his own truck to help transport Burt's body to the shed."

Michael gave me an appreciative glance.

To my surprise, the detective's expression remained blank. "As part of our investigation, we ordered a sweep of Vincent's truck and his home. We're waiting for DNA results." He opened another file on his desk. "This is for your ears only. The preliminary autopsy reports on Burt Garner and Vincent Bouchard indicated they died from heart failure. However, slightly elevated levels of certain chemicals in their bodies led to further analysis. It's believed that the two men had taken the same drug—heroin."

"They could have been forcibly drugged," Michael said.

"Maybe." The detective pursed his lips. "We've labeled the deaths as suspicious and won't release details to the family or the media until we get a solid lead."

"Which brings us back to the reason behind the threatening letters sent to the Bryants. Rusty Homer is trying to scare them off the property. He's played all his cards now. He's desperate to get his hands on the stolen loot."

The detective didn't hide his astonishment. "You think that's where the gold bullion is hidden?"

"It's possible. Burt Garner's mother sold that piece of land years ago, but Burt didn't know about it. He could have buried the loot in that patch of land decades earlier."

"We might have proof that it's buried." I briefed the detective about our visit with Burt's mother at the retirement home. I described how upset she'd become when she simulated digging movements. "Maybe she watched her son bury the gold bullion in the ground. The sad part is that she can't remember anything else about it."

The detective closed the file. "Aside from getting hold of a gold detector and asking the Bryants for permission to dig up their property, I don't see how anyone is going to find the bullion."

"I have an idea," Michael said.

The detective sat back. "I'm listening."

"Let's catch Rusty Homer in his own web of deceit."

26

Detective Cole refrained from sharing Jeremy's involvement in Amy's kidnapping with the media. His reasons were twofold.

First, the Bryants didn't press charges against Jeremy, who they believed had acted out of concern for Amy's safety. They didn't want to damage the boy's reputation or diminish his opportunities to find work in the community. However, they insisted that they no longer wanted him to be on their property. Mrs. Holt requested that her property be off limits to the teen as well.

Second, the detective agreed to proceed with Michael's plan to lure Rusty Homer out of hiding. The OPP required access to the Bryants' property to do so and, consequently, had to discourage the media from lurking around.

So the detective issued a media statement to announce that the search team had found Amy asleep under a rug on a neighbor's porch. He confirmed the little girl was in good health and had not suffered any harm. He asked that the media honor the family's request for privacy at this time.

The Bryants put up a large "For Sale" sign on their property the next morning that was easily visible from the road. It was the first step in a strategic plan to draw out Rusty Homer.

Michael and I stopped by Foster's cabin after breakfast to return the book he'd lent me. "Thanks for the opportunity to read your book, Foster. Good luck with the next one." I handed it to him.

"Thank you." He tucked it under his arm. "I finished packing and will be leaving soon. It's time to collect the fruits of my labor here and move on." He chuckled.

"Too bad we couldn't find out more about Rusty Homer's two partners in the Montreal robbery," Michael said. "We got sidetracked with other stuff."

Michael's evasiveness was deliberate. We'd come to the point where we couldn't share what we'd discovered about the two local deaths with anyone.

"I'm sure you both had more interesting things to do." Foster grinned. "By the way, I couldn't help noticing that your friends put the property up for sale." He motioned in the general direction of the main road.

"They gave the business a try," I said, feigning disappointment. "It didn't work out for them."

"How unfortunate. Since Sam and I are the only guests here, business can't be that good. I suppose the fire didn't help things either. Do your friends have other plans?"

"They'll be closing up the place and driving back to Ottawa today. A moving company will pack up their furniture and the rest of their belongings next week."

Foster shifted his posture. "So their decision is final."

"The fire was the determining factor. And the corpse."

Foster blinked. "Yes. Well, I'd better get going. Oh... I almost forgot. I'm giving a speech on local historic events at the Fernlea Antique Shop this afternoon. I won't be selling any books. They don't allow competition, seeing as the town bookstore already carries my books." He winked. "If you like, you can drop by and offer your support."

"Sorry, we have other plans," Michael said.

Foster nodded. "Of course. Well, nice to have met you both. Who knows, maybe our paths will cross again one day."

On the way back to our cabin, we noticed Sam Norton walking toward his car, a suitcase in one hand and a couple of shopping bags in the other. The fishing poles were still in the back seat.

"Good morning," he said. "You guys checking out today too?"

"Yeah, soon," Michael said.

"Not that we have much choice." Sam placed the suitcase and bags inside the trunk. "The Bryants told me this place was up for sale."

"They're closing up this morning and driving back to Ottawa," I said.

"Sorry to hear it. I didn't have the chance to explore the area as much as I would have liked. I hope they'll find a buyer soon so I can come back here with my grandchildren." He hesitated. "So... Where are you headed now?"

"Back home to Montreal," Michael said. "And you?"

"Ottawa," Sam said. "I own a small business there."

"What kind of business?"

Sam hesitated. "Information sharing."

A door slammed, diverting our attention.

Foster hurried out of his cabin, threw his suitcase and an overnight bag into the trunk of his car, and sped off. He waved without even glancing our way.

"I guess this is goodbye for me too." Sam slid into the driver's seat and drove off.

"Information sharing," Michael said. "That's a good one. He probably works in computer systems."

"The way they drove out of here, anyone would think they're still playing their cat-and-mouse game," I said.

"That's Foster's problem." He put his arm around my shoulder. "Come on. Let's go activate the next step of our plan."

We packed our bags and placed them in the trunk of our car. How events unfolded the rest of the day would determine where we'd be sleeping tonight—if at all. We walked over to the house and helped Jessica and Ethan carry their luggage to the SUV.

The Bryants made a display of leaving town, hoping that Rusty Homer or his minion had them in their sights. As arranged, they would take the highway to Ottawa and spend the next day or two at an undisclosed location until further notice.

～

Michael and I met with Detective Cole at the OPP headquarters in Ostfield later that afternoon. Aside from us, only three other OPP officers knew about the sting to snare Rusty Homer.

The sky was overcast, but rain wasn't in the forecast. We were counting on the pleasant weather to continue into the evening, not to mention a measure of luck in luring our intended target. If all went according to plan, Rusty Homer would soon see the inside of a jail cell again.

From what I gathered as I listened to their tactical discussion, OPP officers planned to put their focus on Jessica's Lodge. A plain-clothes officer in a canoe would pretend to fish nearby in case Rusty Homer chose that venue for his arrival. To appear less conspicuous, the officer would paddle to a different location from time to time, all the while keeping an eye on traffic on the lake.

A second undercover officer would hide behind one of the log cabins. He'd have a direct line of sight of any suspicious activity on the grounds.

A third officer would be stationed on Burt Garner's property within steps of Jessica's Lodge. Michael would assist this officer by providing an extra pair of eyes.

My hopes were shattered when Detective Cole made it clear that I couldn't take part in the surveillance aspect of the sting. He was also reluctant to accept Michael at first but eventually agreed to his partic-ipation, if only because Michael had attended similar operations during the course of his crime investigations.

I had a hard time accepting the detective's decision. "Give me one good reason why I can't participate."

Big mistake.

The detective's voice was gruff. "You can stay with Mrs. Holt until things settle down." He reached for his phone.

I turned to Michael to plead my case, but he shot me a subtle warning glance. I took the cue. Detective Cole might ban Michael from the team if I pushed the matter too hard.

"There, it's all settled," the detective said to me after he'd hung up. "You can go over to Fiona's—Mrs. Holt's—any time you want."

He sounded as if he were giving me permission to go visit a friend.

The detective pointed a forefinger at me. "Don't forget. You've been sworn to secrecy about what you've heard here."

"Of course." I turned to Michael. "See you later." I grabbed my handbag and left.

Self-pity flowed through me after Detective Cole's rejection. I needed to do something to raise my spirits. I'd have lots of time to chat with Mrs. Holt later, so I decided to go shopping. I didn't want to leave Fernlea without visiting the local bookstore, and it might be my last chance to do so. I'd missed the opportunity on my first visit into town with Jessica.

Traffic was light on the drive back to Fernlea, which was why I noticed the white van in my rearview mirror. It had been tailing me for a few minutes. The windshield was tinted, so I couldn't see who was driving.

As I entered the town and turned right on Main Street, the van drove past. I exhaled. I needed no additional proof that I was getting paranoid about white vans.

I found a parking space on a side street. The Main Street Bookstore was only half a block away, so it was a quick walk there.

I pushed open the door to the quaint shop. A familiar scent drifted my way—the aroma of new books hinting of plastic covers and purified crispness of pages. I could spend the better part of a day in a bookstore reading the blurbs on the back covers of new books, but today I was more interested in old books.

After browsing through the shelves in the nonfiction section and not finding what I was looking for, I approached a middle-aged clerk. *Hazel,* read her name tag. "Would you have any of Foster Wade's books on historical sites in Canada?"

"Foster Wade," Hazel repeated, adjusting her bifocals. "Now there's a name I haven't heard in a long while. I'm quite the history aficionado, you know." She smiled. "Give me a minute. I'll go check our surplus inventory."

She strolled to the back of the floor, the wood boards creaking under the weight of her ample frame. I hoped she would return with a copy—any copy—of Foster Wade's books. I'd visit him afterward at the antique shop where he was giving a speech. Adding his autograph to the book would be the perfect touch.

Hazel ambled back moments later, dusting off a thick book. "You are one lucky lady. I found this book in a collection that's been sitting in the back for years. I'm pretty sure the book has been out of print for decades." She placed it on the counter.

I took in the musty scent of Foster Wade's *My Journey in La Belle Province*. The yellowing edges were a testament to its authenticity. I flipped open the book to the title page in case it had already been autographed. No, it hadn't.

I was thrilled and handed Hazel my credit card. "The author was actually staying at the same resort as me this week. I'll be meeting him later to ask him to autograph this book."

Hazel peered at me. "Are you sure about that?"

"About what?"

She opened the book and flipped to the copyright page. "Hmm... it doesn't say. I'll check the Internet."

"What are you looking for?"

"Hold on. I'll get to it soon enough." She hit a few keys on the computer, then pivoted the screen so I could see it. "Foster Wade, the historian, is dead. I don't know if the man staying at your resort has the same name, but he certainly isn't who you think he is."

The title on the screen read *Famous Canadian Historians* and was posted on a national library website. The short biography under Foster Wade's name included a list of his published books. The photo of the author was the same as the one on the book he'd lent me. The clincher was in the last line: Foster Wade had died five years ago.

I gasped. Hazel was right.

"Do you still want to buy this book?"

I could barely speak. "Huh...no...thank you." I retrieved my credit card and rushed out.

I was confused and didn't know what to believe.

How could Foster Wade—at least the one I'd met—know so much about the history of the small towns he was visiting? He'd even claimed to be busy researching historic facts in and around town and meeting with like-minded groups.

And yet, the information about the "deceased" Foster Wade had been posted on a reputable website. He was dead. There was no doubt about it.

Then again, not everything posted online was accurate.

I regretted that I hadn't flipped through the front pages of the book Foster had lent me. The author's bibliographic information might have been listed there. It would have raised the alarm about him.

If the information on the website that Hazel showed me was correct, then who on earth was the Foster Wade I'd met at Jessica's Lodge?

Who was the man who'd shared intimate facts with Michael and me about his jail interview with Rusty Homer?

Was he a wannabe journalist looking for a scoop?

An ex-con buddy of Rusty Homer who was on an expedition to find the stolen loot?

I had to know.

I scanned the street in search of the antique shop that Foster was visiting. I spotted it about five doors down. Surely he'd set the record straight.

I froze before I reached the front steps. A "Closed for the weekend" sign hung on the inside of the door.

Shivers ran up and down my spine.

I pulled out my phone to warn Michael.

27

He didn't answer his phone.

I didn't want to leave a message.

I tried again. "Come on, Michael."

No answer.

It stood to reason that he was working with the surveillance team and had turned off his phone. I reluctantly left a message.

I scrolled my list of contacts for the phone number I'd entered from Detective Cole's business card.

A recorded voice message came on. "Detective Sergeant Cole is unavailable. Please leave your name, phone number, and a brief message."

I left a message and hung up.

Faced with no other choice, I'd have to contact Michael or the detective in person.

I hurried back to my car, but when I tried to start the engine, nothing happened.

I tried again.

Still nothing.

Damn!

I reached for my phone and searched the Internet for a local towing service. I found one in Ostfield, but when I called, I got an automated answering service. I hung up.

My ultimatum was to call the only other person who could help me. "Mrs. Holt? It's Megan. I'm having car trouble. I wonder if you could come and get me." I gave her my location.

"I have a friend visiting right now," she said. "I can leave in about fifteen minutes."

"Okay. Thank you." I checked the time. It was six o'clock. Mrs. Holt would be here by six-thirty.

I sat back and took in the view. The interior of most of the shops on the street were dim. "Closed" signs had gone up on many of the doors.

I tried to contact Michael and Detective Cole again, but to no avail. It was all so infuriating!

Relax, I told myself. After all, Michael was in good hands. The undercover police officers had experience in covert operations. If Rusty Homer popped up, they'd be more than equipped to take him down.

A shadow had fallen upon the town. Storm clouds were blowing across the sky, and raindrops began to patter on the windshield. Oh, terrific! Exactly what Michael and the OPP team had hoped wouldn't happen.

Breathe. Big boys can take care of themselves.

I closed my eyes and slowed down my breathing. The more I relaxed, the more the stress ebbed away. I envisioned a happy place where Michael and I strolled hand in hand along a sunny beach...the water lapping against the shore...

A loud tap startled me and I jerked. I had dozed off. I turned to see a woman gaping at me through the driver's window, her frizzy white hair defined by an overhead streetlight, her face blurred by the raindrops on the window.

It wasn't until Mrs. Holt put space between us that I recognized her. I grabbed my rain jacket from the back seat, tucked my phone in a pocket, and stepped out of the car.

"I'm sorry I'm late," she said, sharing an umbrella with me as I slipped into my jacket. "My friend is a bit of a chatterbox. I had a hard time getting her out the door."

I checked the time. It was eight o'clock. "Oh, no! Mrs. Holt, we have to hurry. Can you drop me off on the road by Jessica's Lodge?"

"Jessica's Lodge? Why? No one's there."

"I'll explain on the way."

Not satisfied with the sparse details I'd shared with her about the secret operation, Mrs. Holt pumped me with more questions. I was convinced she'd missed her calling and should have been a talk show host.

"You mean you don't know the name of the person they have under surveillance?" Mrs. Holt asked me for the second time.

"Like I said, the OPP requested Michael's help regarding the threatening letters Jessica and Ethan received. Right now they're doing surveillance work in the area of Jessica's Lodge. I don't know anything else."

"Does Jessica know about this?"

"No." To make sure she wouldn't contact her daughter, I said, "Mrs. Holt, what I told you is confidential. Please don't tell anyone— not even Jessica."

I hated misleading her about the police operation, but sometimes a dangerous situation called for a small but necessary evil.

Rain pellets hit the car and filled the silence between us. Mrs. Holt had finally put an end to her questions, though she was no doubt as curious about what was happening at Jessica's Lodge as I was.

The wind suddenly picked up, sending sheets of rain crashing against the windshield. The trees became a blur of dark green against charcoal skies, with the intermittent clap of thunder predicting a bolt of lightning across the sky.

A soggy smell seeped into the car, blending with the odor of our wet clothes. A button on the dashboard confirmed the heater was on, yet no warmth flowed through the air vents. Shivering, I stuck my cold hands inside the pockets of my rain jacket.

Mrs. Holt eased her foot on the gas pedal and thumbed a button on her steering wheel to increase the speed of the windshield wipers. "The weather people were wrong. No one forecast a storm like this." She turned on the radio.

A song finished playing and the local news came on. After a brief recap of the storm and its anticipated stay into late evening, the broadcaster announced that a major accident had occurred on a section of the highway not far from Fernlea:

> "A truck hauling propane gas has overturned, causing a twenty-car collision. Two people have died and more casualties are expected. The OPP has pulled in every available officer to assist with the emergency. Firefighters and hazardous materials teams are also on site. The highway has been closed in both directions, and authorities are asking the public to stay away from the area. An update will be provided shortly."

"Isn't that terrible?" Mrs. Holt shook her head in disbelief. "These tragic accidents always seem to happen when it rains, don't they?"

"Huh...yes, they do." My mind had digressed to another facet of the radio announcement. Extra law enforcement resources had been called in to deal with the accident. If Detective Cole and his team had left to assist with the multi-car pileup, it could explain why he hadn't answered his phone.

It could also mean that any police officers posted at the stakeout area for Rusty Homer had left.

If my assumptions were correct, Michael was alone, unarmed, and waiting for a ruthless killer to make his appearance at Jessica's Lodge.

I hoped I wasn't too late.

28

Mrs. Holt didn't object too loudly when I asked her to drop me off on the road by Jessica's Lodge. Nor did she insist on driving onto the property. Something told me she was eager to get home to defy my request and call Jessica.

All the better. The last thing I wanted was Mrs. Holt infringing upon the scene of a police stakeout.

"Take my umbrella." She offered it to me. "You'll catch your death of cold."

"No, thank you." It would make me an easy target for anyone who was trigger-happy. "I'll be fine." I flipped the hood of my rain jacket over my head and stepped out.

The rain was coming down in torrents as Mrs. Holt drove off. After her car disappeared down the road, I turned onto the gravel path leading to Burt's property.

It was hard to avoid the puddles in the dank darkness. My wet running shoes emitted a weird gurgling noise with each step I took, a sign that their life span would soon run out. The cotton sweater under my jacket didn't provide much insulation against the blustery wind either.

Undeterred, I plodded on, eager to see Michael and discuss what I'd recently discovered about Foster Wade's impersonator.

I thought about using the small flashlight I'd tucked in my pocket, then changed my mind. If the members of the OPP were still on site, I didn't want to confuse them into thinking I was their target. Nor did I want to warn Rusty Homer about my approach, should he be lurking in the neighborhood.

As I neared the edge of Burt's backyard, however, the heavy rain made it impossible to differentiate the shadows from the trees. I was about to pull out my flashlight when lightning flashed across the sky and lit up the backyard.

Michael wasn't there. Neither was the OPP officer. Maybe they'd changed location and were stationed on Jessica's property. Or maybe they'd called off the operation.

I squeezed through the familiar opening in the trees and stopped. Something was out of place.

Lightning flashed, revealing a vehicle parked on the turnoff to Jessica's property. The trees separating the properties had hidden it from view earlier.

I recognized the car. It belonged to Foster Wade's imposter!

The motor wasn't running, and I couldn't tell if someone was inside the car or not. Undaunted, I moved slowly toward it and aimed my flashlight inside. No one. I put away my flashlight.

A strong gust of wind blew a stream of rain into my face, and I gasped for air.

Where was everyone?

I started my trek across the lawn to the cabins. As a precaution, I raised my voice as well as my hands. "Hello, I'm Megan Scott. I'm unarmed. Don't shoot."

I cautiously crossed the saturated grounds to cabin five—the one where Michael and I had stayed. I hesitated, thinking twice about sneaking up on an armed police officer who might be positioned behind the cabin. "Hello?"

There was no reply.

"Michael?"

No answer.

I tiptoed to the back and peeked around the corner.

No one.

I dug out my flashlight. Shielding my eyes from the rain, I aimed the flashlight at the rear of the other cabins.

There weren't any OPP officers in sight. It made sense. If they'd been here, they would have acknowledged me by now. Maybe they'd made subsequent arrangements to hide inside one or more of the cabins.

I moved on to cabin four—the fake Foster Wade's cabin—and peeked through the back window. Lightning flashed and revealed something black and rectangular on the kitchen table.

A notebook? Did it belong to Foster Wade—or rather, the man who had professed to be Foster Wade? Had he forgotten it here?

I advanced to the other cabins and repeated the process.

My suspicions were confirmed. The OPP officers had received orders to leave the stakeout, probably to assist with the propane truck collision on the highway.

But where was Michael? Why hadn't he called me?

No lights were turned on in Jessica's house, but it didn't mean no one was inside.

I trudged back across the lawn and looked through the kitchen window. The place was spotless. No dirty dishes in the sink, no plates on the table...

I tried the door. It was locked and didn't appear as if anyone had tampered with it either.

I sprinted over to the car, my shoes squishing water between my toes, my jeans heavy with water and clinging to my legs. The rain hit me from every direction and was already leaking down my neck. I hoped the car doors were open so I could get away from the downpour.

No such luck. Each door was locked.

My phone rang. I retrieved it with wet fingers and almost dropped it. I stared at the screen and let out a sigh of relief. "Michael, where are you?"

"This isn't Michael," a raspy voice said. "It's Foster Wade."

I froze but recovered in the next moment. Okay, I'll play his crazy game. "Where's Michael?"

"He's hurt. He wanted me to call you, but I called 911 first because he needs an ambulance."

"What happened to him?"

"He was shot."

"Shot? Who shot him?"

"Rusty Homer."

"Put Michael on the phone," I insisted. "I want to talk to him."

There was a rustling movement at the other end of the line. "I checked on him again. He's slipping in and out of consciousness. Get here as fast as you can. You can ride in the ambulance with him when it gets here."

"Where are you?"

"Next door to Jessica's Lodge."

I spun around, even though I couldn't see the neighboring houses from where I stood. "Burt Garner's old house?"

"Yes, I broke into the place when I found Michael crawling in Burt's backyard. He was all alone and calling out for help. He's not doing too well. You'd better hurry."

Did I dare belief an impostor?

Since he had Michael's phone, it was feasible that he was with him. So why hadn't Michael called for help himself? Then again, if Rusty Homer had shot him, maybe Michael had been physically unable to do so.

I had to make sure Foster was telling the truth. "Why did you come back to Jessica's Lodge?"

"What?"

"You heard me."

"I'd driven halfway home when I realized I'd forgotten my notebook in the cabin. Hurry, Megan. You're wasting precious time."

"One more question. How did your speech go at the antique shop?"

"It was cancelled. The owner wasn't feeling well and closed up the shop for the weekend. For Pete's sake, hurry up!"

"I'll be right over."

I made one last quick call, then raced to Burt's house. I didn't know what to expect, but seeing Michael again was the most important thing in my life right now.

29

The back door to Burt's house was open. No surprise there.

I stepped into the kitchen.

A low-wattage light over the stove diffused a soft glow.

"Hello?" I called out.

"We're in the first bedroom," Foster's raspy voice reached me.

I crossed the floor to the unlit hallway. I flicked the wall switch to turn on the overhead light, but it didn't work.

I groped my way in the dark and stopped at the entrance to the bedroom. A lamp on the dresser cast more shadows than light, yet succeeded in revealing enough to send a shock wave through me.

Michael was stretched out on the bed, his face pale, his body still. Foster stood by his side, looking down at him.

"Michael!" I rushed to his side.

He was unresponsive, his eyes vacant.

I checked him from head to foot. "I don't see any blood. Where was he shot?"

"He wasn't." Foster smiled at me—a crazed smile that had my radar swinging wildly into the danger zone.

My heart pounded. "What happened to him?"

"You'll find out soon enough. You and Michael... You were too curious for your own good. You should have left well enough alone." His dark eyes bore into me.

"What are you talking about?" I pretended not to notice he'd dropped his English accent.

"Don't play dumb, Megan. You know exactly what I'm talking about. Rusty Homer's success story."

I didn't answer. In his twisted mind, he was already planning the next chapter in his life. I had to stall him and buy more time.

He raised his voice. "Did you hear what I said?"

My instincts told me to run away from him as fast as I could, but I refused to leave Michael, so I played along. "I don't care about Rusty Homer. I'm worried about Michael. I want him to be okay. You told me an ambulance was coming."

He shrugged. "I lied. About everything." He glared at me for a long moment. "Why are you still pretending you don't know who I am?" His voice sounded throatier as anger mounted inside him.

I had to keep him talking. He loved to chat about Foster Wade's escapades. "I stopped by the bookstore in town earlier. The clerk is familiar with your work. She's a huge history fan."

"Megan, Megan." He wagged a bony finger at me. "I'm losing patience with you. You don't want to see the angry side of me."

His deep-set eyes flashed with ferocity. They were the same dark eyes that had stared out from the mug shot Detective Cole had shown Michael and me. His surgeon had done wonders—filling out the cheeks to change the shape of his face, hiding the deep scar, fixing his nose to match the historian's.

My heart hammered in my chest. Sweat gathered along my forehead. I was standing in the same room as an egocentric killer. He'd paid for his crimes as a professional thief and murderer, having spent twenty-five years in jail. His evasive, unscrupulous ways indicated that he'd do anything to avoid going back behind bars.

I couldn't bluff my way out of this predicament any longer. It was time to reveal my hand, but I had to stroke his ego at the same time. He had chosen anonymity in the persona of Foster Wade, yet he would welcome the opportunity to flaunt his dark deeds under a spotlight at a moment's notice.

"Yes, I know who you are, Rusty." I struggled to keep the fear out of my voice. "You certainly had me fooled. How did you manage to deceive everyone? You even conned the police."

"I developed an ingenious plan." He raised his chin. "I had to reinvent myself before I left prison, so I searched online for the perfect identity. After several months, I hit gold." He laughed. "I read Foster Wade's books to learn more about him. Imagine my delight to discover that the historian was a recluse. It played in my favor. My surgeon did the rest. It worked like a charm, didn't it?"

"Until now."

His expression soured. "Indulge me. How did you manage to find me out?"

"Foster Wade's year of death is posted on the Internet."

Rusty scoffed, "You can't believe everything you read online."

"Except it's true in this case." I searched for topics to keep him engaged. "It all fell into place once Michael and I realized you were behind the two local murders."

"Oh?"

"Stealing millions of dollars in gold bullion wasn't enough. You had to kill Burt Garner and Vincent Bouchard."

"Their deaths were unfortunate, but I'll get over it. However, unlike those two losers, your sidekick wasn't an easy prey." Rusty gave a nod of his head toward Michael. "He put up quite a fight. The OPP should never have left him alone, but as you can see, it ended well. He toppled after I introduced him to Molly."

Ecstasy! He'd stabbed Michael with an injection of ecstasy. Damn him!

"Michael and I did nothing to you!" I shouted. "You used us to find the money that was stolen from the Montreal robbery."

"You're wrong. I knew who had it in their possession all these years. I didn't need your help or anyone else's. I simply needed to get rid of a few people who were in my way."

"Burt Garner and Vincent Bouchard were innocent pawns in the game you were playing. Like Jessica and Ethan were. Your goal all along was to get my friends off their property so you could find the buried treasure."

Rusty grinned. "You're one smart cookie. I can see you've done your homework. I was hoping you'd help Michael write his scoop about the infamous thief who got away when you got back home. But no. You had to interfere with my plans. Now I have to get rid of two more bodies."

I slipped a hand in my pocket and gripped my flashlight.

Rusty moved to the dresser and opened the top drawer. He took out a syringe and advanced toward me. "Now it's your turn to find out what it's like to spend time with Molly."

I flung my flashlight at him.

It hit him in the face, momentarily startling him. I turned and sprinted down the hallway, but he grabbed me from behind and pulled me toward him.

I tried to break his hold, but he was too strong. I twisted wildly, hoping that if I kept on squirming he wouldn't be able to stab me with the syringe.

Thunder crashed outdoors. Lightning flashed.

I wasn't sure, but I thought I heard the back door slam shut.

Rusty heard it too. He released his grasp on me. "You're not worth the energy. I'll ask Chuck to give me a hand."

Chuck?

Oh, no! I was as good as dead!

I pivoted and ran down the hallway in the opposite direction, toward the front of the house.

Rusty called out behind me, "You're wasting your time, Megan. We'll catch you and—"

Thump!

I turned around.

Rusty dropped to the floor, groaning, the syringe flying from his hand.

A man stood in the shadows, clutching a long object. "Don't move or I'll hit you again!" he yelled at Rusty.

I recognized his voice!

"Jeremy! What are you doing here?" I hurried up to him.

His hair and clothing were soaked, and he blinked away droplets of water leaking down his face. "I was in my canoe and it started to rain hard." His voice trembled. "I didn't feel like going back home. My dad and me, we argue a lot. So I came here." He let the stick of wood he'd used as a weapon fall to the floor.

"To Burt's house?"

"Yes. I still have the key he gave me. That's when I saw Foster Wade's car. I knew Jessica's family was gone. I saw them leave. Then I heard people fighting in Burt's backyard. I was scared, so I hid behind the trees."

"Fighting?"

"Yeah. Like throwing punches and stuff. I didn't know who they were until lightning flashed. That's when I saw Foster drag Michael's body into the house."

"He's not Foster Wade," I said. "His real name is Rusty Homer. He's an ex-con and a killer. The police are looking for him."

Jeremy gawked at me. "An ex-con? My dad will never believe this."

"So you've been here all this time?" I resisted the urge to shout at him. "Why didn't you show yourself earlier? Or at least tell me what had happened to Michael?"

"I—I was scared. I didn't know what to do. I saw you go next door and look inside the cabins...check the car... When you went into Burt's house, I knew you were in big trouble. I decided I had to come here to help." He pulled out a piece of rope from his pocket and dropped to his knees to tie Rusty's hands and feet. "Michael will be happy I helped him catch the bad guy, didn't I?"

"You certainly did." I pulled out my phone and dialed 911. There would be time for rejoicing later.

Before I could tell the operator why I was calling, the back door slammed shut.

A deep voice bellowed, "Hey, Rusty, where the hell are you? I've got the engine running." Heavy steps pounded across the kitchen floor.

A broad-shouldered man appeared at the entrance to the hallway. The snake tattoos on his arms were perceptible even in the dim light.

Chuck!

He noticed Rusty on the floor. "What the hell do you think you're doing?" He lunged at us.

Jeremy was the first line of defense. He grabbed the stick of wood and jumped to his feet. He swung as hard as he could, but Chuck obstructed the blow with his forearm.

Chuck seized Jeremy by the throat with one hand and landed a punch with the other.

Blood flowed from Jeremy's nose. While Chuck pinned him against the wall, Jeremy fought to break free, but he was no match for his beefy opponent.

I only had one chance...

I dropped my phone and snatched the syringe from the floor. Leaping forward, I plunged it into Chuck's thigh as he raised his fist to strike Jeremy again.

"What the hell—" Chuck's face registered annoyance and confusion, and he let go of Jeremy. He grabbed my neck, squeezing it.

I tried to pry his fingers off me, but his grasp was too tight.

I kicked his shin. It had no effect.

I couldn't breathe. I gasped for air. I was blacking out. I'd soon be unconscious—or dead.

Chuck's eyes suddenly glazed over. He wobbled, then released his grip on my throat.

A piece of wood flew through the air and hit Chuck hard on the back of the head. He fell to the floor with a thud.

Jeremy had struck the final blow.

30

____

Everything had happened so fast that I hadn't had the time to take it all in. All I knew was that we were out of danger.

Rusty Homer, also known as Foster Wade, had collapsed in the hallway and remained unconscious. Chuck Dorey was orbiting another universe, thanks to the syringe I'd stabbed in his leg.

My head was spinning from a lack of oxygen after Chuck's strangling hold on my neck, but I would be okay. I leaned against the kitchen counter and inhaled a few deep breaths. I repeated the process until I could stand up without tipping over.

Jeremy reached my side, his face bloody. "Megan, are you okay? I'm sorry I couldn't stop Chuck before he hurt you."

I took a gulp of air. "You did...fine, Jeremy. You saved...my life. Thank you."

Jeremy bent over Chuck. "He's out cold. Two bad guys down." He grabbed a dishtowel, tore it in strips, and tightly bound Chuck's hands and feet. He used the rest of the dishtowel to wipe the blood from his own face, then threw the rag in the sink.

My breathing back to normal, I searched for my phone and found it on the floor close to Rusty Homer's feet. The soles of his running shoes reflected bright green in the darkened hallway. The grooved pattern included tiny triangles.

I put the phone to my ear and was surprised to discover the 911 operator was still on the line. I briefed her about what had transpired. She assured me the police and an ambulance were on the way.

I dashed to the bedroom and checked Michael's pulse. It was faint. His eyes were still glassy.

Gathering the blanket on all sides, I covered him to keep him warm. "Michael, if you can hear me, hang on. You're going to be fine. An ambulance will be here soon." I squeezed his hand. He squeezed back.

Tears welled in my eyes. I was relieved the ordeal was over, yet furious about finding Michael in this condition. Damn that Rusty Homer!

From the doorway, Jeremy softly asked, "Is Michael going to be okay?"

Not wanting to cause him more worry, I said, "I think so."

"Cool. I want to tell him we got the bad guys."

"I'm sure he'd love to hear all about it when he gets better."

Jeremy shifted from one foot to the other. "They didn't find the treasure."

He was probably referring to the gold bullion bars. "I think we surprised them. They didn't have the time to dig holes in Jessica's property."

"Dig holes? They didn't have to dig no holes."

"How do you know that?"

Jeremy looked down. "It's a secret between Burt and me." He stole a peek at me, as if gauging my response. "If I tell you, promise not to tell?"

"I promise," I said.

"Burt said the treasure is in the house."

"Jessica's house?"

"No, this one."

"Where?"

He shook his head. "I don't know. I couldn't find the letter."

"What letter?"

"Burt told me if anything happened to him, I should look in his house for a letter about the buried treasure."

My heart beat faster.

So many theories bombarded my mind, and I grappled to interpret them.

Had Burt confided a decades-old secret to Jeremy?

Did that secret entail handing over ten million dollars in gold bullion to a teenage boy whom he'd known only for a short time?

Had Burt developed a form of dementia like his mother had?

"Jeremy, where—and when—did you search for the letter?"

"Weeks ago. In the basement, in the drawers, under the carpet... I couldn't find it. I didn't mess anything up in case Burt came back."

So the mysterious intruder who had ransacked the boxes in the basement was Rusty Homer after all.

"With the bad guys out of the picture," I said, "you'll have more time to search for it now."

"That's what Burt kept saying when I asked him where I should look. Time will tell, he said."

Time will tell. Words that an adult might use to calm any overzealous adolescent.

I tried another tactic. "Burt could have been referring to the other house he owned."

Jeremy was adamant. "No, it was *this* house. I'm sure. Even the bad guys came here looking for the treasure. Just like Burt said they would."

"Did Burt say anything else about the letter or the treasure?"

"No. He said the letter would tell me what to do. Time will tell."

The cuckoo clock sounded its hourly chime in the kitchen.

Time will tell.

"That's it!" I rushed past Jeremy to the kitchen.

He followed on my heels. "What are you doing, Megan?"

"The cuckoo clock." I picked up the wood chair and placed it under the clock. I climbed up and gently removed the clock from a nail in the wall. "If I'm right, we might find what you've been looking for." I stepped down.

Taped to the back of the cuckoo clock was a folded envelope with Jeremy's name written on it. I handed it to him.

"Cool!" He ripped it open and unfolded a handwritten letter. He read it out loud:

"Dear Jeremy,

When you find this letter, call the police right away and ask them to come to this house. Wait for them to arrive and show them this letter. They need to tear up the hardwood floor in the kitchen to find the treasure that I hid from the bad men. The treasure belongs to someone else and must be returned to the rightful owner.

I tried to be a good person most of my life to make up for the bad that I'd done in my younger days. Jeremy, thank you for taking care of my property and for being such a good friend to me.

—Burt."

The wail of sirens sounded in the distance.

31

———

Detective Cole released a statement to the media confirming that the OPP had arrested individuals linked to the demise of Burt Garner and Vincent Bouchard, former residents whose deaths were now officially labeled as homicides.

In another press release, the detective announced that the OPP had solved a decades-old case when they discovered millions of dollars in gold bullion stolen during a Montreal heist. For privacy reasons, the exact location of the find would remain undisclosed to the public.

The private investment company and target of the theft had offered a reward of one hundred thousand dollars for the return of the gold bars. The reward had been claimed, but the name of the beneficiary was being withheld. Again, for privacy reasons.

Word spread among local residents faster than you could say *buried treasure*. Although the OPP hadn't mentioned Fernlea or Jessica's Lodge in their statements, the media perceived them as the only possible sites of recent unusual events, and therefore, the location of the OPP takedown.

News crews swarmed the resort to get more details about how it had all played out. Ethan had to ask for help from the OPP to banish media from the premises.

However, there was an upside. Due to the publicity, our friends were busy booking cabins until fall.

Back in our Montreal condo, Michael and I reminisced about our stay at Jessica's Lodge.

"That trip was one for the books." Michael placed his cup of coffee on the corner table beside the sofa.

"Are you referring to our trip to the lodge or the one you took on ecstasy?" I teased him.

"A bit of both, actually." He smiled. "To think that I missed all the action…"

"What?" I stared at him. "Look at that shiner. You'll be the envy of the newsroom staff when you go back to work next week."

Michael laughed—a deep laugh that came from a sincere and caring place. Yet I sensed that something had been bothering him ever since we left Fernlea days ago. He hadn't shared much about how the horrid experience had affected him. Maybe talking about it would help.

"Michael, you never did tell me why the OPP left you alone and went to assist with the highway accident."

"What a nightmare that turned out to be." He rubbed his brow. "Detective Cole insisted that I leave the premises, but I refused. A gut feeling told me Rusty Homer would show up. I hid at the far end of the trees in Burt's backyard and waited. Then it got dark and the rain poured down in torrents. I couldn't even see three feet in front of me. You were there. You know what it was like."

"Yes, I do. Was that when Rusty drove up?"

"A car turned onto Jessica's property, but I couldn't see who was driving or the make of the car. Since Ethan had put up a "For Sale" sign on the property, I thought the driver might be a real estate agent. Who else would go out in that weather?"

"Rusty Homer," I said with sarcasm.

"That scumbag crept up on me by surprise."

I intertwined my arm in his and leaned against his shoulder. "I know."

"I'm telling you, Megan, I didn't see him coming. He jumped on me from behind and punched the air out of me. I couldn't believe how strong he was. He must have been high on drugs."

My hand automatically went to my neck. Chuck's fingerprints had left bruises—proof of my confrontation with him—that would take weeks to heal. The emotional healing would take longer, but I'd get through it. I always did.

Michael went on. "Rusty Homer had me going for the longest time. He even fooled Larry when he wore Burt's coat and had Chuck drop him off at Burt's home. Of course, Rusty had drugged and killed Burt by then, right after he'd had supper with him at Il Tavolino. When Rusty didn't find the loot in Burt's house, he walked away in the middle of the night."

"Rusty was a professional manipulator," I said. "And so elusive. Remember what Sam told us at the police station?"

"He lost track of Rusty on the highway after they left Jessica's Lodge that day. Too bad. It could have changed things."

"Sam had no idea our wannabe historian was heading back to Fernlea. Everyone thought the Bryants had closed the place down. No one knew about the police sting operation either."

"Good private investigators follow their instincts. In Sam's case, he was duped too. I wish he would have told us Vincent Bouchard had hired him to tail Rusty Homer—or Foster Wade, as we knew him."

"Sam regretted he never got the chance to warn Vincent until it was too late," I said. "He couldn't prove Rusty was involved in anything, yet he continued to follow him around. He said he wanted to catch him in the act of digging up the gold bullion."

A smile spread across Michael's face. "Burt was miles ahead. He hid the bullion from everyone—including his worst nemesis."

An image of the white feather popped into my mind. Madame Ora had been right about a third victim. Foster Wade, brought back to life by Rusty Homer, was now officially dead.

Michael gently ran a finger along my cheek. "If I didn't say it before, I'll say it now. I'm so sorry I got you into this mess. But if you hadn't come along, I'd be dead by now."

The appreciation in his eyes melted my heart. "I'm the one who should be apologizing. I wanted to go to Fernlea to visit my friends. My decision almost got us killed."

He grew quiet. "What we went through... I was afraid."

"That's normal. I was afraid too."

"No. What I meant to say was... I was afraid of losing you. You mean the world to me, Megan."

I kissed him on the lips. "You can't get rid of me that easily. Besides, you're my hero. You helped capture an infamous thief. Not to mention a couple of murderers."

"Right." Michael's expression brightened. "Rusty Homer and Chuck Dorey will probably spend their last days in jail."

"We went through a horrible ordeal, but good things came from it. Like sharing the reward money from the recovered bullion with Jeremy. I'll never forget how happy he looked when he said he was going to buy a motorboat for his father." I laughed. "Let's not forget that new landscaping job Jeremy got too."

"Thanks to Larry. It sure pays to have friends in the right places."

"Speaking of friends," I said. "Jessica sent me an email this morning. Construction of the additional log cabins starts in a few months."

"That's fantastic news. The section of neighboring land they offered to purchase from Burt's trustee will help to move things forward."

"Now that Ethan quit his job, he'll be working with Jessica at the lodge every day. They'll make an excellent team, don't you think?"

"Just like us, right?" He held me closer.

I snuggled in his embrace. "Just like us."

ACKNOWLEDGMENTS

It took the efforts of an incredible team to bring this book to fruition. In particular, I'd like to thank my cover designer, editor, and proof-readers for their creative and technical input. I also want to thank everyone who gave me moral support along the way—especially my family and close friends.

A special thanks to my readers who make it all happen.

ABOUT THE AUTHOR

Sandra Nikolai is the author of the Megan Scott/Michael Elliott Mystery series. In addition to her novels, Sandra has published a string of short crime stories, garnering awards along the way.

A graduate of McGill University in Montreal, Sandra held jobs in sales, finance, and high tech before leaving the corporate world to pursue a career in writing. She likes to think that plotting a whodunit reveals the lighter—yet more mysterious—side of her persona.

Visit Sandra's website at sandranikolai.com to sign up for her quarterly newsletter to receive her latest book news and exclusive offers. Your email address will never be shared and you can unsubscribe at any time. Become a fan on Goodreads or Facebook, or follow Sandra on Twitter @SandraNikolai

Broken Trust
Book #5
Megan Scott/Michael Elliott Mystery series

Hotel rooms often come with perks. A corpse isn't one of them.

Ghostwriter Megan Scott and investigative reporter Michael Elliott are stunned to discover the body of a young woman in their hotel room. She's wearing a black lace teddy. A carafe of red wine and two glasses sit on a table. Her purse contains thousands of dollars, three business cards, and a supply of pills — opioids. With Michael researching the recent opioid crisis for the media, this revelation hits close to home.

Who is this woman and how did she get into their hotel room?

As Megan and Michael dig deeper, elusive conspirators up the stakes and threaten to block their efforts at any cost.

Is their trust in each other enough to save them on a perilous quest for a cold-blooded killer?

BOOKS BY SANDRA NIKOLAI

Megan Scott/Michael Elliott Mystery series:

False Impressions

Fatal Whispers

Icy Silence

Dark Deeds

Broken Trust

Cold Revenge

www.ingramcontent.com/pod-product-compliance
Lightning Source LLC
Chambersburg PA
CBHW070450120726
47910CB00003B/996